I0667230

A Despicable Profession

**Book Two of the
American Spy Trilogy
by**

John Knoerle

This is a work of fiction.

Published By **Blue Steel Press**
Chicago, IL
bluesteelpress@aol.com
www.bluesteelpress.com

First edition – first printing 2010
Copyright ©2010 by John Knoerle.
All rights reserved.

Cover art and design by Katherine Bennett.

ISBN 978-0-9820903-0-5
Library of Congress 2010908640
Printed in the United States.

Also by John Knoerle:

"A Pure Double Cross,
Book One of the American Spy Trilogy"

"Crystal Meth Cowboys"

"The Violin Player"

The author would like to thank the following for their help and support:

Duff Kennedy
Professor Richard Münchmeier
Jane Knoerle
Mark A. Ward
Richard Procter
Jeanne Jenkins
Waldemar and Gabriele Unkel
Joe and Anne Schram
Wolfgang and Ulrike Wagner
and Mr. Helmut Lang

for JJ

"You talk of honor, but you are far away."
-- Prince Paul of Yugoslavia, 1942

I'm back on my well-polished barstool at The Harbor Inn. It's July, 1946.

I've been dubbed the 'Little Deutsch Boy' by the Cleveland Press. Is that dumb or what? So called because I kept my finger in the dike against the rising tide of Soviet Communism. The rising tide hasn't receded. The Russians control everything east of "Stettin in the Baltic to Trieste in the Adriatic" as Churchill said earlier this year.

But they haven't crossed the Elbe.

The local newshounds say I deserve much of the credit for that but I know different. I never met the man who was primarily responsible for stemming the tide and keeping Western Europe safe for democracy. I couldn't tell you his name to this day.

They say that history is written by great men but that's not strictly true in my opinion. Sometimes a little man, in the wrong place at the right time, can make all the difference.

Chapter One

Being a hero is a rotten job. Yeah you get a lot of free drinks and claps on the back but once John Q. Public has paid and clapped he just sits there and looks at you. And looks some more, waiting for you to rescue a kitten from a tree or bend I-beams into pretzels.

I'm not looking for a big payday any longer. Never was, though I didn't know it at the time. What I was really after was some recognition for what I'd done. Got that now, in a backass way. Got my picture in the paper for shooting a bank robber, a bank robber in a bank robbery I willingly took part in. I felt lousy about that.

The paper also mentioned my behind-the-lines work for the OSS during the war. I felt good about that, till those stares started boring in.

Americans love their heroes, in more ways than one. The only thing they love more than seeing a hero ascend to greatness is to watch him take a header off the pedestal. I didn't intend to give them that satisfaction. And I wanted to atone for my sins. How I intended to do that by drinking beer with my pal Wally at The Harbor Inn I couldn't tell you.

Wally's the mail boy at FBIHQ and he keeps me up on all the scuttlebutt since the feebs and I parted company three months ago. He was making chin music about nothing and everything one Thursday in May when I noticed the flat beer. Guy next to me hadn't touched it, which made me nervous. He was a burly man with a shiny dome, wearing a brown suit and a blue tie. Could be one of the dear departed Schooler's armbreakers or one of Jimmy Street's playpals likewise, but I didn't think so. No self-respecting mob goon wears a brown suit.

I grabbed a shaker. "Throw some salt in there, it'll kick the head up. Nothing worse than a flat beer."

The man took the salt shaker with his gun hand, the hand his beer stein handle was turned toward. That was good.

"I'm Hal, this is Wally. What's your name?"

"Herbert."

This set Wally to giggling for some reason. "D'you ever hear that radio piece? When the announcer says the President of the United States?"

Herbert said he had not.

"He says - the announcer - he says, in his big radio voice, 'Ladies and gentlemen, the President of the United States, *Hoobert Heever.*'"

Wally collapsed into a puddle of beery mirth. I joined him. We were three sheets to the wind and if old Herbie wanted to talk to me, as I suspected, he would just have to wait till we came to our senses.

It took awhile. Herbert salted his beer and didn't drink it. He waited until Wally peglegged off to the john to say his piece, quick and quiet like.

"Mr. Schroeder I work for Hendricks and Lee Construction. We're an international concern based in New York City."

"What brings you to Cleveland?"

"You do."

"Me?"

"Yes sir."

"Well, I'm not much good with a hammer."

Herbert's smile was brief. He wanted to get this said. And I wanted to hear it. It wasn't every day that portly gentlemen from New York came calling.

"Our company has major construction projects underway throughout most of the cities of Europe, with one exception. Berlin."

"And Berlin, I'm guessing, is chock full of major construction opportunities."

"Yes sir."

Again with the *sir*. I'm 25 years old fer Chrissakes! Wally stumped out of the whizzatorium about then. He's got a short leg from polio. Herbert picked up the pace.

"You served in Germany, you speak Deutsch. You're a hero, people know your name..."

"Not in Berlin they don't."

"They will," said Herbert. He said it with a cool certainty.

Wally heaved himself onto his barstool with a sigh and said, as always, "You don't buy beer, you rent it." Then he laughed. As always.

"So you want a front man for your construction company. A glad-hander to open some doors."

Herbert winced at my crudity, but nodded.

"Why so hush-hush?"

Herbert leaned in. "We face a great deal of competition."

Wally and I looked right. We looked left. We saw only late afternoon sad sacks shelling peanuts and sounding out words in the early edition of the *Press*. Wally's lower lip quivered. He was ready to bust a gut provided I provided a punch line.

I declined to do so. I was getting barstool calluses on my keester. Not to mention my bank balance was lower than a snake in snowshoes. Herbert's proposal sounded pretty ridiculous but how does that old joke go? An out-of-work jester is nobody's fool.

I needed to be somebody's fool. I said I was interested. Herbert looked pleased, Wally did not.

"And now a bottoms up toast to seal the deal." Herbert stared forlornly at his salty beer. Sweet Rita served up two more Carlings. We poured. Wally raised his brimming stein.

"A faithful friend is the medicine of life."

"Where'd you get that from?"

"It's in the Bible, dumbass."

We clanked and chugged. Herbert raised his mug but did not partake. I shook Wally's hand and promised to drop a postcard.

Herbert poured me into a taxi. I told the hackie to drive up the block to Mrs. Brennan's rooming house and sobered up quick. I was about to travel to New York with a guy I'd known for ten minutes. "You got a business card Herbert?"

Herbert did, with raised gold lettering. *Herbert W. Merckle, Vice-President of Sales, Hendricks and Lee Construction, New York, NY.*

"What are some of your construction projects in Europe?"

He rattled off a few. They sounded plausible.

"How did you hear about me?" I knew I hadn't made the New York papers. I'd checked at the library.

"We subscribe to a news clipping service."

"Who am I supposed to meet with in New York?"

"The President of the company and the Executive VP of sales."

Guy had answer for everything but I was still on edge. What kind of salesman doesn't like beer?

"You didn't join us in our toast Herbert."

Herbert patted his ample gut. "Ulcers." Yeah, beer and ulcers, the salesman's friends.

Mrs. Brennan would be sad to see me go, ditto assorted bartenders in the greater metropolitan area. And Jeannie, I supposed, though I hadn't seen her since she whelped her pup. A baby girl, Margaret Ann Pappas. She called to tell me. Mother and daughter were doing fine. I asked her how it felt to be a mom.

Overwhelming was her reply. I asked if there was anything she needed. She paused a long time before she said a sad, crisp no. I wished her all the best and hung up the phone. It was time for Hal Schroeder to move on.

At the rooming house I dumped the contents of my dresser into my beat up suitcase. I took my Walther P-38 and my folding knife from the nightstand, grabbed my penlight and my lock picks, threw 'em in my dop kit and locked up my suitcase. I shrugged into my topcoat and clumped back down the stairs to Mrs. Brennan's kitchen.

She wasn't around. I left her a month's rent and a note that said *Gone fishin'*. I was now, officially, flat broke.

Herbert was waiting in the cab. I tossed my grip into the back seat between us and closed the door. We drove down Winslow at sunset on the prettiest day I had ever seen in Cleveland, Ohio. Which is to say it was above forty and not raining. We turned south on West 25th and kept going.

"Cabbing it to New York are we?"

Herbert looked a question at me. I hooked my thumb at the Detroit-Superior Bridge on our left. "The train station's thataway."

Mr. Merckle folded his hands atop his belly. "We're headed to Municipal Airport."

I nodded as if I did this every day. Truth was I had never been to New York City. And I'd never flown on a commercial airliner. I looked forward to it. In wartime they expected you to yell Geronimo and jump out the joe hole halfway through the flight. This figured to be a big improvement.

Commercial airliners have seats, that's the first thing you notice. Upholstered seats with armrests and little trays that fold down. The second thing you notice are comely young women in uniforms with cute hats pinned to their perfumed hair. Actually they're the first thing you notice. I would have stood in line to hit the silk over hostile territory if the USAF had provided such pleasant flight companions. *Stewardesses* they call them. When a sweet-smelling blond leaned down to take my drink order I thought I'd died and gone to heaven.

Almost came true a moment later when the DC-3 shuddered through some rough air. The cabin lights went dark, people gasped and shuddered. Then the lights winked on as the big bird shrugged its shoulders and winged east at two hundred miles per. The stewardess - Cindy by her name tag - handed me my rye rocks and smiled most fetchingly. She hadn't spilled a drop.

Manhattan sneered at me as I sat in the backseat of a Yellow cab. *Hey there, hayseed, think you've seen a big city? Think the Terminal Tower is a tall building, do ya?*

I stuck my head out the window when we passed the Empire State Building on 5th Avenue.

"Fourteen months," said Herbert Merckle, "they put up that building up in fourteen months."

I didn't argue with him, though it hardly seemed possible. I liked the idea of joining the construction biz. Show me another trade where you can put your head down, work hard for fourteen months, step back, crane your neck and say God*damn*. As an OSS operative behind German lines I had conducted surveillance and co-ordinated bomb runs. I did it, it worked, we won. But it might be nice to return as a builder not a blower-up.

The hackie pulled to a stop. A doorman wearing more gold braid than an Italian general opened the door and greeted Herbert by name. He collected my suitcase and escorted us inside the hotel. *The Pierre* read gilt letters carved in stone.

It was a swanky joint. Beyond swanky. The lobby had white marble columns and white marble floors and black vases with sprays of flowers in them and was the quietest place you'd ever seen. Or heard. It looked like the room you waited in just before you met St. Peter at the Pearly Gates.

Herbert waved to the reception clerk and walked directly to the bank of elevators. No check in, Herbert already had a room. Good for him but I wasn't keen on spending the night in a twin bed listening to him snore. I was about to say so when Herbert said, "We have a three bedroom suite with a dining room. Breakfast's at nine."

Herbie didn't say anything more after that. He let The Pierre do the talking for him.

I woke up to sunshine through the curtains. Bright sunshine given the drawn curtains of damask or muslin or fine linen hand stitched by blind nuns in a Belgian cloister. I cleaned up quick and reported to the dining room.

It had three windows. One looked north up 5th Avenue, the other two overlooked Central Park. An elderly Negro in a starched white tunic refilled my coffee cup for the second time and asked again if I wouldn't like some nice fresh strawberries with cream. I said a polite no thanks and checked his wrist. He didn't wear a wristwatch either.

The three-bedroom suite had a crystal chandelier, antiques older than Abraham and overstuffed chairs that made you dozy just to look at them. What it didn't have was a damn clock. It had to be well past nine a.m.

I was about to ask the old gent if he carried a pocket watch when the front door opened and a gaggle of Ivy Leaguers spilled in. I don't know how I knew they were Ivy Leaguers exactly, their couldn't-care-less attire maybe. Oxford cloth shirts pocked with cigarette burns, navy blazers shiny with age, club ties loosely cinched.

They introduced themselves and shook my hand. But Herbert W. Merckle was not among them when we sat down to breakfast. I got those strawberries and cream, a glass of grapefruit juice and a soft-boiled egg. Slim pickin's for a growing boy.

We seemed to be waiting for someone. Presumably the President of Hendricks and Lee Construction.

A skinny guy in tortoise shell glasses held a leather-bound legal pad upright as he read some notes. The cover was embossed in gold letters. *Global Commerce Ltd.* The room got quiet when I asked him what Global Commerce was.

"Global Commerce?"

"Yes. Global Commerce."

"Well, it's…in point of fact I am not the person to answer that question."

Hmm. The Office of Strategic Services had Ivy League bloodlines. Director William Donovan and right hand man Allen Dulles were Wall Street attorneys who staffed OSS headquarters with members of their exclusive law firms. We low-level slugs called them yachtsmen. They were young men very much like the one's arrayed around this dining room table, sucking down coffee and soft-boiled eggs.

I hadn't been whisked across the country and installed in this high-priced mausoleum because of my international renown. I was a hick from the sticks to these guys. A hick from the sticks who wasn't afraid of getting his hands dirty.

So. Who were we waiting for?

Could've knocked me over with a feather when he strode in a minute later, Herbert trailing along behind. I shot to my feet, drawing a jaunty smile from the blue-eyed ruddy-faced man with a shock of white hair. The legendary commander of "The Fighting 69th" in WWI and the Office of Strategic Services in WWII. Major General Wild Bill Donovan himself.

He crossed to my side of the table, shook my hand and said my name like he knew me. Then he worked the table, mauling the Ivy Leaguers with his big mitts, pounding their backs as Herbert gave me a sheepish look that was half apology, half boast. By the time my rear end found my chair I was steamed.

The OSS had been disbanded right after the war despite Wild Bill's efforts to make it a permanent agency. President Truman thought that spying was un-American and Congress went along.

Dumb. Our espionage shortened the war and saved the lives of thousands of Allied soldiers. Our counter-espionage prevented the D-day invasion from becoming the bloodiest rout in military history. But the war was over. I had done my duty to God and country. It was somebody else's turn.

Bill Donovan walked to the head of the table and leaned his weight on his hands. "Mr. Schroeder, I understand you want to know about Global Commerce Limited." Wild Bill didn't wait for my reply. "We are an international trading company dealing in commodities - gums, spices, oils and such. Hendricks and Lee is one of our subsidiaries."

I just looked at him. Was I supposed to believe this? Bill Donovan, who made a handsome living as a Wall Street lawyer in between shaping world events, would waste his time trading gums and spices?

I guess I was. He hadn't winked or grinned when he said it. He did have a twinkle in his eye but he's Irish, he can't help it.

"Permission to speak freely sir."

"Granted," said Donovan with a wave.

Coffee cups returned to saucers, mouthfuls of strawberries were quickly swallowed, all eyes were mine. How the hell to say this? Hurry up numbskull, the Great Man is waiting.

"Sir, the OSS taught me one ironclad rule. A spy's first allegiance is not to career, colleagues, not even country. A spy's first allegiance is to the truth."

Bill Donovan nodded approvingly. I said the truth as I saw it.

"Sir, my OSS training and experience leads me to suspect that Global Commerce is a commercial front for espionage."

"Well, of course it is!" said Wild Bill, tripping an eruption of snooty merriment around the table.

Donovan went on to say that he was not one to pass up a punchline and that Global Commerce Limited was, of course, a viable business concern that merely employed a few former OSS operatives for their international connections and language skills and so on and so forth etcetera. He paused, then said the following:

"Mr. Schroeder is a distinguished alumnus of the Office of Strategic Services. He served with distinction behind German lines from late '43 to VE Day. Extremely dangerous duty." The Ivy Leaguers eyed me with new respect.

"Upon returning home he joined the FBI as an undercover agent." The Ivy Leaguers eyed me with new suspicion.

"Yes he worked for our friends at the Bureau. No shame in that. He foiled a big bank robbery as I understand it. But it was the way in which he foiled it that caught my attention."

Wild Bill grinned and twinkled for all to see. I struggled to find my tongue but he was on to other matters.

He asked for sales reports from around the table. The Ivy Leaguers read them off. Donovan made a few comments on the reports and said a hearty farewell. Herbert escorted him out of the room.

I had a head fulla bees, I did. What the hell did Donovan mean about the way I foiled the bank robbery? He liked it that I put one over on J. Edgar Hoover? Could be, guess so, beats me. I was clear about one thing. I wasn't shipping out for another miserable Atlantic crossing without a straight answer.

I got up and chased after Herbert and Bill Donovan. I caught up to them just as Herbert W. Merckle was closing the front door and General William J. Donovan was striding down the corridor. I followed.

"Sir," I said. "Sir!"

Donovan turned on his heel. He was not happy to see me. I approached anyway. "General, I am no longer interested in being a spy."

Donovan gave me a blue-eyed half-second before he said, "I'm not asking you to be a spy. I have no authority to ask you to be a spy."

With that he walked to the bank of elevators and pushed the call button. I stood and watched and tried to think of something to say. The bell sounded and the operator cranked open the door. The General looked my way and said, just before he stepped into the elevator car, "I'm just asking you to keep your eyes open."

Goddamn spooks, I'd forgotten how they were. Always the dance of the seven veils. I returned to the suite with Herbert Merckle and asked what was next. Wild Bill Donovan had piqued my interest.

The bastard.

Chapter Two

I didn't cross the Atlantic in the hold of a troopship this time, mate. It was a luxury liner, with a stateroom and a steward I could summon at the pull of a cord. Herbert Merckle had given me a month's pay in advance - 500 bucks! - and a detailed itinerary. Arrangements had been made for me to catch a hop on a C-45 from Antwerp to Berlin.

Military aircraft. I didn't ask. I had five hundred bucks in crisp twenties and nothing at home but an empty barstool. I would give it a shot. I would keep my eyes open. What I wouldn't do was put my neck in a noose.

When the liner docked at Antwerp I was met by a driver who took me to Chievres Air Base. It was a very long drive. I showed my passport at the gate. The guard waved me through.

I went to Hangar Two. A cocky little twin-tail C-45 was waiting on the macadam, props spinning, wringing water from the heavy air. We were airborne three minutes later.

The co-pilot bent my ear when we reached altitude. He said Templehof had been the busiest airport in Europe before the war and that Lufthansa had its last commercial flight from there just ten days before the fall of Berlin. A flight to Stockholm, a dozen passengers. A dozen very happy passengers.

We came in low over the central city. It was something to see. Row upon row of busted open buildings, roofs gone, inside chambers exposed. A great gray honeycomb is what it looked like.

We landed at Templehof at 1:20 p.m. by the cockpit clock. The C-45 taxied toward the enormous arc-shaped terminal. It had to be a mile from end to end. Hitler designed it himself, said the co-pilot. It was supposed to resemble an eagle in flight. The terminal looked to be in halfway decent shape, the runway smooth. I asked the co-pilot how that could be.

"Your tax dollars at work buddy boy."

I thanked the pilots for the ride and offered a tip. The pilots recoiled from the twenty. Had I violated some Air Force superstition? Or was it something more? The talkative co-pilot hadn't asked me the obvious question. What are you up to in Berlin? Hadn't asked me any questions, come to think. I was, apparently, off limits. My way had been cleared from Otto Moser's to Templehof Airport. I was Wild Bill Donovan's fair haired boy.

I carried my suitcase to the terminal and looked around. Herbert said my employer would be there to greet me. He wasn't. I found a bench and watched construction workers climb the three story scaffolding like monkey bars in a schoolyard.

I waited. I got annoyed. You get used to the red carpet treatment real quick. I waited some more. I had no phone number to call, no address to go to. Somewhere along in there I noticed a pimpled dogface with pronated ears. He was studying me from a distance. I stood up as he approached.

"Are you Harold Schroeder?"

"No. I'm Dwight D. Eisenhower."

The kid looked me over for a long moment, decided I was pulling his leg, then jeeped me downtown.

'Germania, the capital of the world' as the Nazis styled it, had seen better days. It was almost a year since *Stunde Null*, hour zero, May 8th, 1945. A few streetcars were running, busses too along the main thoroughfares, flanked by ruin. I had never been to Berlin. My tour of duty was confined to southwest Germany. I told the jug-eared kid to give me the nickel tour. My employer had kept me waiting, I would return the favor. I was Bill Donovan's fair haired boy.

Hitler's steel-framed Chancellery Building on *Vossstraße* was still standing. Its courtyard, the 'Court of Honor' where heroes of the Reich were greeted with fanfare, was barely touched.

A few blocks north the Reichstag, site of a pitched battle with the Red Army, was a different story. The Reichstag was a magnificent wreck. Sandblasted and blowtorched, shell pocked and bomb cratered, blackened by smoke and speckled white where bullets gouged stone, the soaring glass cupola half gone, but the towers largely intact. Ditto the marble columns etched with the names of Russian soldiers.

Hitler had ballyhooed his Thousand Year Reich and if you didn't know better you might say he had made an accurate call. The Reichstag looked at least a thousand years old.

The Brandenburg Gate was next door, blackened and busted up but still on its feet. I'd seen pictures, who hadn't? It was Germany's Eiffel Tower. There'd been some famous statue of a wreathed goddess on a chariot atop the Gate that was gone now. In its place was a big red flag.

Fair enough. But where was the Stars and Stripes? The Union Jack? I had risked my neck for eighteen months behind enemy lines. I had moments when I wondered why, as the bombing runs I cleared rolled in and the civilian casualties mounted in the only war in recorded history where more civilians than soldiers died. Many, many more civilians. But the mission was clear. Destroy the enemy. So I did what I did and felt bad about it later. I felt bad about it a second time when I saw that Hammer and Sickle.

We drove on, past a large park with sawed-off stumps where trees used to be. I knew about the Reichstag and the Chancellery and the Brandenburg Gate from watching newsreels at the Bijou. But I knew nothing about this big swatch of green in the heart of the Berlin. I gave my driver a chance to show me up.

"What's that park called?"

"It's the Tiergarten, Mr. Schroeder, and I'm sorry, real sorry I picked you up late. I went to the wrong end of the terminal I guess but that's where they told me to go and then they sent me a whole 'nother way and then they sent me back again and, well, I hope I don't get gigged out of this and I'm sorry. *Real* sorry."

I assured the kid he wouldn't get gigged and told him to quit his blubbering, I wasn't worth it. I could see where this fair haired boy routine might get to be a pain.

We drove a block south of the Tiergarten. Several streets came together. A sign said *Potsdamer Platz*. From its location it figured to be the heart of the central city. From its appearance it could have been the Mongolian steppes. It was covered with grass and head-high nettles, and dotted with rabbit traps.

Another block south was a *Bierstube* on a corner. The blackened building looked as if it had been blown apart and put back together, brick by brick. My driver stopped at the front door. I went inside.

I had pictured my employer at Hendricks and Lee Construction as an older version of Herbert Merckle. A big-bellied guy with a bull neck and poor taste in clothes. But he wasn't like that. He was tall and well-dressed, with a high forehead and close cropped dark hair flecked with more gray than I remembered. He was Victor Jacobson, my Case Officer from the OSS.

Jacobson remained seated at the spy table - far wall, left hand corner. I stood just inside the door, profoundly confused.

I figured the job offer was something of a sham, a cover for gentlemanly snooping. But Victor Jacobson was a commissioned espionage officer who didn't like me one bit. Was this some sort of payback for my wartime failure to get myself killed? I didn't care. I wasn't going to work for this jerk again.

I pushed through the door and looked around for the jeep. No joy. I started to cross the street when the familiar voice said, "Schroeder, come inside. Let me buy you a beer."

I should've kept walking but I didn't have anywhere else to go and was so parched I would have drunk a Shirley Temple.

I went back inside and sat down. Jacobson let me take his seat, facing the door at an angle. A skinny young *Fräulein* plunked down two liter steins. I eyeballed the heady brew with lust in my heart but this was Victor Jacobson's tea party. If he expected me to clink and drink he would have to do some very smooth talking.

He knew this of course. Jacobson was both hell bent for leather and very smart. Much like The Schooler, without the charm and the human decency.

"I'm the reason you're here Schroeder. I asked for you personally." Jacobson let me chew on that for a moment. "You were the only wartime agent I ran who survived. That took a special kind of cunning. A kind of cunning I have come to respect."

Cripes almighty, respect from the high priest. I gripped my stein and, through a lifetime of the practice of mortification of the flesh, managed not to raise it to my lips.

"I'll drink up when I hear what you have to say."

Victor Jacobson wet his whistle. "Bill Donovan recruited me a few months after the OSS was dissolved. He saw what was coming, the gutting of US postwar intelligence capability. The current incarnation, the CIG - Central Intelligence Group - is understaffed and poorly funded. And toothless."

"How so?"

"The CIG is chartered for intelligence gathering only, debriefing refugees, clipping newspaper articles. They can open mail if it's truly dire. What they can't do is anything operational, anything covert. The Berlin Detachment is particularly weak. Not a single Russian-speaker on staff. It's December 6th, 1941 all over again. Poor intelligence and little to no co-ordination between State, FBI and the War Department at a time of great danger."

I didn't bite. If we were facing another Pearl Harbor Jacobson would have to say how before I got myself all hot and bothered. "What do you and Bill Donovan plan to do about it?"

"What little we can."

"How black, how wet? What are we talking about?"

Jacobson took another pull of beer. "We're talking about keeping the Red Army from rolling tank divisions across the Elbe and seizing all of Germany while we have our backs turned."

Huh? The papers were full of heartwarming stories about Yanks, Brits and Reds working together to rebuild Germany.

"You think our Russian allies are planning an *invasion?*"

"Some of our White Russian émigré friends think so" said Jacobson. "I only know one thing for certain."

"What's that?"

"If Stalin is planning to seize Germany he couldn't pick a better time."

This got my attention. A serious mission. I eyed my beer, it was going flat. Tough shit.

"Who does Global work for? Who's their customer?"

"POTUS."

"Who's that?"

"The President of the United States."

"Oh. Directly?"

"Donovan has a back channel."

"So CIG knows about Global."

"I have a relationship with the Chief of the Berlin Detachment if we need to co-ordinate."

"Sheesh, what a sideways setup."

"Ad hoc espionage. Best we can do."

"What's the chain of command?"

"You would report to me."

"And if I needed to take it upstairs?"

"You talk to Bill Donovan."

"And if I'm captured?"

"We never heard of you."

I grinned, or grimaced. Just like old times. "And my first assignment would be?"

Jacobson leaned in. "Track down Klaus Hilde."

"Who he?"

"A former *Abwehr* General with encyclopedic knowledge of Soviet orders of battle. He reached out to us before war's end. Word is he tried again recently but OMGUS screwed up."

"OMGUS?"

"Office of the Military Government of Germany, US."

"Where's Hilde now?"

"Headed south most likely, down the Rat Line to Lisbon and South America. Find him before the NKVD does. Take this."

My former Case Officer was acting like my future Case Officer. He handed me a small leather purse with a drawstring. It was heavy. "What's in it?"

"Gold sovereigns."

I fondled the purse. There had to be a dozen half-dollar-sized coins in there. A king's ransom.

"Okay, say I find this Hilde, what then? We turn him over to CIG?"

"No."

"Why not?"

"It's complicated."

"Try me."

"OMGUS wants us to work together with our Russian allies. They think gathering military intelligence on the Red Army would be provocative. Brigadeführer Hilde is a treasure trove of Soviet military intelligence."

"Okay."

"There's more. The Chief of the Berlin Detachment of the CIG describes his group as semi-covert."

"That's funny."

"Yes it is."

"Have they been penetrated?"

"I don't think so."

"Why?"

"Why bother?"

Jacobson had my motor running I will admit. A chance to be a hero, an opportunity to atone for my sins. And a bag of loot to pave the way.

"Why me?"

"I said why."

"Why really?"

"We're shorthanded. And you're a lifer."

Me? A *lifer*? No way, no how. I said so.

"Settled down in a cozy cottage with a doting wife are you?"

"Up yours!"

"And yours as well."

I giggled. I was dingy with travel and surprise and too much information. And so parched I was tempted to lick the beer rings off the table.

"Say I run this Nazi to ground, dangle these sovereigns under his nose and he still says no?"

"You're a very creative young man."

I was at that, good at one thing. Backing myself into a corner and then improvising my way out. And I liked the CO's proposal. It was the antithesis of the bureaucratic by-the-numbers FBI.

"Sir, my special kind of cunning is real simple," I said, leaning forward. "I was doing a decent job in Freiburg and Ulm and Karlsruhe logging troop movements and transmitting weather reports for bomber runs. I figured if I was dead my effectiveness might suffer. And why get croaked carrying out suicide missions dictated by some asshole Case Officer who was snug as a bug in Bern drinking Allen Dulles' wine cellar dry?"

"I wasn't," said Jacobson, "but please continue."

Please continue? They were shorthanded.

"I have only one job requirement sir. Survival."

"I'll keep that in mind," said Jacobson, drier than my swollen tongue.

My liter of beer had fizzed down to nothing. I pushed it away. Nothing worse than a flat brew. I flagged our skinny

Biermaid for another. It was quick in coming. I raised my stein. My old-new CO did likewise.

We clanked and drank.

Chapter Three

I was on the first leg of the Rat Line - the Berlin to Lisbon to Buenos Aires escape route favored by Nazi war criminals - watching the German countryside speed by from the comfort of a first class train compartment. The countryside reminded me of the Ohio Valley, rolling and green. Vegetable gardens were terraced against the hills, fields of barley held forth where the terrain smoothed out and every once in a while you got an eye-smacking acre of the bright yellow flowers they call *Raps*. They grind 'em up for cooking oil or something.

Krauts were still Krauts. We rattled past a partially flattened farmhouse, a burnt out barn and a freshly-plowed field with furrows so true they could've been drawn with a straight edge.

I was stretched out in splendid isolation in my compartment, my legs draped over my suitcase. I had the full kit. A drawstring purse full of gold sovereigns, travel documents proclaiming me a reporter for the American military newspaper Stars and Stripes, and three cartons of Lucky Strikes, the local currency at fifteen Reichmarks per. And that's not per carton, cousin, that's per cigarette.

I was already twenty cigs low from stops at Frankfurt and Mannheim. I was going to have to stop playing Santa Claus or my bag of goodies would be empty long before Lisbon. You would think that blocks of cheese or canned hams would be the currency of exchange in food-strapped Deutschland but it was cigarettes people wanted, coffee a close second.

Coffee and cigarettes, the building blocks of a better tomorrow.

My Luckies netted me nothing more than a series of head shakes at the photo of Klaus Hilde that the CO had given me.

I'm not a gumshoe but showing a five year old photo of a fugitive who had the means to completely remake his appearance is what we in the espionage game call *using your dick for a flashlight*.

It's a technical term. It means your question risks exposing more than the answer is worth. But I had to try. We didn't have any intelligence worth spit.

A conductor passed by. I asked him how long to Karlsruhe. He checked his pocket watch. One hour and thirty-eight minutes, give or take thirty seconds.

I mountain climbed my way to the dining car, hand to hand along the seat backs, dragging my loot-crammed suitcase behind me. Served me right. The train was wobbling over the rail bed our B-24 Liberators had spent two years pulverizing at my direction.

I had cleared bombing runs for Karlsruhe as well. I would soon get to see my handiwork close up.

The dining car was empty, save for an elderly waiter who grabbed up a menu and eyed me hopefully.

I smiled with my cheeks and found what I was looking for. A small semi-circular bar at the far end of the dining car. Two GIs sat in a cloud of blue smoke. I got there in time for the punchline.

"Parachutes? Ohh, we're using parachutes!"

The GIs were headed south to Marseille for a long boat home. They bought me a drink, I bought them a drink. And so on.

They had duffel bags full of black market swag that they just had to show me. Doug from Buffalo had a sterling silver serving platter engraved with two names and a date. A wedding present sold for cigarettes. His buddy had a topper. A bowling ball sized bronze bust of Herr Hitler. We set Adolph on the bar and drank to his health.

Doug and his buddy both had sweethearts back home and were itching to pop the question. Or were already engaged. Maybe one was already married, I forget.

I do remember one thing clearly. I remember thinking *Am I a lifer?* It wasn't a happy thought.

I looked out the windows streaked with rain. I recognized the distant outline of the Black Forest, low mountains covered in black firs. We were nearing Karlsruhe. I felt instantly sad, and stupid. How in the name of all that's holy had I managed to get myself back here again?

The train pulled into the station. I got up and wished my GI pals Godspeed. Though we had been deep in intimate conversation they waved a quick and cheery so long.

Soldier's wisdom. Here today, gone like that.

I climbed down from the railroad platform, grip in hand, to take in downtown Karlsruhe under a wet black sky.

The Fan City they call it because it's laid out in a semi-circle, the palace the hub that all the streets spoke out from. Behind the palace was a large greensward for ducal pheasant hunts and chasing maidens through the hedge maze and like that.

I hadn't set foot in the town but I knew the layout. Karlsruhe wasn't the Ruhr Valley but it had machinery-making plants and a harbor on the Rhine and had paid the price for that. And then some. The palace was a wreck.

I had plenty of pedestrian company on my stroll but saw no cars, trucks or busses. Just a couple of horse drawn carts and a determined young bicyclist on bare rims.

The locals looked more hale and hearty here. There were farms nearby. Milk and eggs for breakfast instead of rations of Zwieback and mock liver sausage made from breadcrumbs and beer yeast. I even saw a butcher shop with links of fat black *Schwarzwurstl* hanging in the window. Yum.

I was approached by two blue-black Africans in French uniforms suitable for a parade ground, wearing tall shako caps with the lacquered bills pulled low. They wanted to see my papers, best I could make out.

My onionskins passed muster and I walked on, wondering why in the hell African soldiers were patrolling Karlsruhe. I turned to watch them accost a doughty farmer and his two daughters.

I understood. We were in the French Zone of Control, the small sliver of southwest Germany that Charles de Gaulle had won from the Big Three at the postwar negotiating table. The Froggies had all kinds of colonies in Africa. Putting black troops in charge of the remnants of the Master Race sent an unmistakable message.

The light rain turned pinprick hard. And me with no lid. I ducked into a clothing shop and startled the owner by making a purchase. A dusty Tyrolean hat, good for yodeling in an Alpen gorge. It made me look ridiculous but I was used to that. Kept the rain off my neck.

I repaired to the local *Biergarten* to chat up the locals. They were sitting out back, at rough hewn picnic tables despite the plinking rain. Farmers, in straw hats and flat black skimmers like you see in Pennsylvania Dutch country. They were smoking Luckies and Camels under the tall trees and hoisting steins to beat the band.

This would be interesting. 'Hello, I'm an American reporter for Stars'n'Stripes, working on a story about fleeing war criminals.' 'Like who?' 'Well, like this gentleman in the photo for instance. Seen him around?'

That was the plan, designed to make my obvious manhunt a little less so. It was a stupid plan but so was sailing west to reach India and Columbus did okay. I drained a shot of schnapps at the bar to smooth out the wrinkles and waded in with my pad and pencil.

I didn't have any luck. The farmers were too busy enjoying their newfound prosperity to be bothered with anything about the war. The war was ginned up by halfwits half a world away so far as they were concerned. My tongue got tired from asking questions.

In this man's opinion the perennial cantankerousness of the *Deutschevolk* can be traced directly to their language. Take my pad of paper for instance. *Pad.* In English it takes a puff of air. In German, *Schreibeblock* requires exhausting facial calisthenics and a bucket of phlegm.

I gave up trying to explain myself, ordered a round of beer for the tables and passed around the photo of Herr Hilde. The photo made the circuit quickly, without comment.

I paid my tab with a twenty dollar bill and left the photo on the table. Nobody noticed. I asked for directions to a hotel, directions I didn't need, then hauled my suitcase to said hotel and booked a room.

The farmers had treated Hilde's photo as if it were radioactive. They knew I was a rich *Amerikaner*, they should at least have looked at the damn thing. A natural reluctance to get involved? Or a knowing ignorance born of fear? My gut said the latter. Which is why I asked for directions to a hotel. Someone would come knocking. Preferably not with the butt of a rifle.

The room had a private bath and a view of the ruined palace. There wasn't a showerhead so I took a bath in the huge clawfoot tub. What is it about soaking in hot water that makes you hungry? I got dressed and went downstairs to see about something to eat.

The hotel restaurant was under construction due to bomb damage. Served me right. I couldn't leave the premises so I dangled a pack of Luckies under the nose of the young desk clerk, said I was expecting a visitor and could he please go to the butcher shop and get me a couple of those fat black sausages that were hanging in the window? He was gone like a shot.

I took his place behind the counter and rifled the drawers out of habit. I found a French postcard, a gay *mademoiselle* with thumbprints on her bottom. I closed the drawer and listened to my stomach growl.

A middle-aged man in a homburg and a haggard black suit entered and approached the desk. He looked puzzled when he saw me. I must have Yank stamped on my forehead because he said "You are the American" before I could speak.

I nodded. He looked harmless enough, a *gut Bürger*, a banker or merchant fallen on hard times. But I slipped my hand into my gun pocket anyway.

"My name is Günter," said the man. His accent was thick.

"Sure it is. What's on your mind?"

Günter started to speak, stopped, looked around. He didn't like the set up. What was I doing behind the reception desk for instance. I didn't offer any explanation.

Günter had a brass pendant around his neck, some sort of a medal. He rubbed it between his fingers anxiously. "I know where is the man you are looking for."

"Really. Who's that?"

"Klaus Hilde."

I hadn't used Hilde's name at the beer garden. No point, he wouldn't be using it. Could be this Günter had something worth selling.

"How do you know where he is?"

Günter shook his head. Not here. I invited him up to my room for a private chat. My smoked sausage would have to wait.

No it wouldn't. I heard the desk clerk return when we were halfway up the stairs. I ran back down and grabbed the *Schwarzwurstl*.

My room had one chair, a high backed job with a cane seat. I offered it to Günter. He declined, preferring to stare out the window at the ruined palace. I flopped on the bed, unwrapped the butcher paper and attacked the fat black sausage with my folding knife. The aroma made me light-headed. I cut off a chunk for my guest. We chewed, happily.

"Let me guess, Günter. You were a successful man in town, knew everyone, knew how to get things done. Then you lost your livelihood during the war and looked around for another way to feed your family."

I paused to take another bite. How can something taste both sweet and bitter at the same time? I continued, mouth half full. "The war goes badly. Nazi officials need a place to hide. And a way to ship themselves, their families and their looted treasure to South America. A complicated undertaking, requiring a man of knowledge and influence." I swallowed the sausage and sliced more. "Any truth to that?"

Günter managed a sour smile. "I have no longer any family of which to feed. A wife only."

The way he said it made clear that his kids hadn't gone off to college. I asked how much for Herr Hilde's location. Günter shook his head.

"I am a man of principle. I will carry only your message ."

"A man of principle who helps war criminals to flee."

Günter's shoulders slumped. I felt bad for him, dug a gold sovereign from my leather purse. I shined it on my shirtsleeve. Günter's posture improved.

"Tell Hilde I have a message from Wild Bill Donovan."

"Who is that?"

"He'll know."

"What is this message?"

"I deliver it in person. Assure Hilde that I'll come alone."

"And with no weapons."

"Sure."

Günter fingered his brass pendant. It was copper bright in the center where he had rubbed it raw. I let the silence between us grow.

You're rusty, Schroeder. Rusty as a barn hinge. Flapping your gums about Bill Donovan to a complete stranger. A guy who had identified Klaus Hilde from a five year old photo. How?

I didn't ask. No point. Günter was all I had. I got up and placed the shiny gold sovereign in his palm. "You get two more if he shows up."

Günter looked at the half-dollar sized coin bearing the likeness of King George V and muttered something I couldn't make out. He tucked the coin in his vest watch pocket with great care and straightened his homburg.

"St. Bernhard's Church, three o'clock in this morning."

"Okay. But we, you and me, we meet outside beforehand. On the front steps."

Günter paused to consider this. Being my hostage going in.

He nodded and left the room.

Chapter Four

I am not the most devout Catholic that ever lived, but no baptized son of St. Peter wants to see a bombed out house of worship, much less one he might have had a hand in. So I was pleased to see that venerable St. Bernhard's was still in one piece. The church had a square four story bell tower that rose from its right front corner like an afterthought. The tower was the best recon spot for miles, best sniper's nest too. How was it still standing?

Bong. Bong. Bong.

Three o'clock in the morning, Harold Schroeder crouched behind a granite pedestal in the park across from the church, the pedestal's statue long gone, melted down for cannon balls. Three o'clock in the morning and no Günter on the front steps.

3:05. 3:10. 3:15. Or thereabouts. Time to blow or go.

I went. I crossed the street and climbed the stone steps, my eight shot Walther in hand. The endless plinking rain turned to hail about then, not that I noticed. I was a gun-wielding killer in a Tyrolean hat.

I put my ear to the gap in the great oaken doors and heard silence. I pushed open the door and jumped back. No gunfire commenced. I dug out my penlight and stepped into the vestibule.

Günter was waiting. He was seated on an armless straightback chair in his old black suit, sitting upright in the middle of the vestibule, eyes milky, dead as dead can be.

I kept all emotion at bay and concentrated on the task at hand. Figuring out how in hell a corpse was sitting rigidly upright in a straightback chair. I bored in with my torch beam. Günter was bound up with some kind of raggedy rope. Check that. The rope came from his blood-soaked abdomen and wound around and around. Günter was bound to the chair with his own intestines. The little ones, the ones lower down.

I told myself I had seen worse. I called up images of bloody horror from the war. Headless children, still-breathing soldiers with half a face. It didn't work.

I bent over and vomited beer and black sausage on the marble floor of the vestibule of historic St. Bernhard's Church.

Chapter Five

I had to untie Günter, that was the first order of business. No one else was going to see him like this. Some might say that Günter deserved to die for helping Nazi war criminals to flee. But he didn't deserve this.

I breathed through my nose, choked back bile and did what I had to do. I set the penlight on end and unwound Günter's bowels from the straightback chair in the spooky light. They were slippery and surprisingly taut, ropy. You know what they smelled like. I made a loop from my thumb to my elbow, wound them up like an electrical cord. Must've been ten yards long. Then I leaned down and used my knife to cut them loose from Günter's bowels. The blade was dull, it took a few tries.

Now what? They didn't cover this at spy school. How to properly dispose of a wagon wheel of human guts. I yanked open the great oaken door and held it ajar with my foot as I dug out my Walther in case the sick bastards who did this were waiting. Not likely. They were using Günter to send a message. *We're everywhere and we mean business.* Killing me, the messenger boy, didn't figure.

I stepped outside. No gunfire commenced.

I took the slick steps carefully, head swiveling, and saw a storm drain. I went there and shrugged Günter's guts off my arm with unspeakable relief. I fed them into the sewer. My stomach tried to heave but the tank was empty. I took out my knife and cut off the last link of Günter's lower intestines before it disappeared into the nether regions. It took some doing.

I put the piece of intestine in my handkerchief, folded it up carefully and placed it in my coat pocket. I went back to the vestibule and dragged poor bloody Günter into the nave, laid him out in the last pew. I dried my hands on my coat. I would have to burn my vicuna topcoat when this was done.

Holy water. There was a font of holy water by the door. I dipped my fingers and drizzled drops on Günter's forehead as I mumbled a quick prayer. I closed his eyelids and removed the brass pendant from around his neck.

Time to visit the French authorities.

It took me forever to find French Army HQ. St. Bernhard's bell tower had tolled four a long time ago. Black night paled, the hailstorm moved on. Lanterns were lit, a horse drawn carriage plocked by on a cobblestone street. Dawn is sobering. What the hell was I doing here?

I was furious that my contact had been murdered. I wanted justice. I would storm the Bastille and tell the French commander that I was a reporter from *Stars and Stripes* doing a story on fleeing fugitives. A local man had promised to let me talk to such a fugitive for a price. That local man was now dead, bound with his own guts. When the haughty French commander scoffed at me I would remove my handkerchief and unfold it on his desk.

Idiocy. I wasn't thinking like a spy. I shouldn't tell the French commander anything at all. I was the last person Günter visited. Did anyone know that? The hotel clerk hadn't seen Günter come up to my room but had likely seen him come down. And I was the rich *Amerikaner* trolling the beer gardens for fugitives. But so what?

Christ on a crutch, Schroeder, you gave Günter a gold sovereign then failed to search his vest pocket to see if it was still there. It's what they call *evidence*.

Every instinct told me to flee. The French authorities couldn't touch me outside their little slice of southwest Germany. I would be secure in Berlin.

Tough shit. I was no longer a lowly 'observation agent.' I was an emissary of Major General William Donovan who needed to clean up his mess. I double timed it back to St. Bernhard's Church. I arrived shortly after the tower chimed five. Was there a five a.m. Mass?

I brushed off my coat. The rain and hail had washed away most of the blood. I was reasonably presentable if you didn't look too hard or get too close. Oh yeah. My handkerchief. I returned to the storm drain and interred the last of Günter's lower intestines.

I climbed the stone steps and pushed open the oaken door. No pre-dawn Mass, though candles flickered on the altar, candles that hadn't been lit before. I hurried to the last pew. Günter was right where I left him, knees hiked up, head thrown back. Rigor mortis.

I wedged a finger into his watch pocket. The gold sovereign was still there. I took it back.

A door closed somewhere. I hooked my arms under Günter's armpits and dragged him up the side aisle, past the stained glass windows and the Stations of the Cross. I opened the door to the confessional, the priest's booth, sat the body on the padded stool and closed the door.

I heard a *thwunk*. The door popped open. Günter's legs protruded from the booth. He had fallen off the stool. I folded him up with great effort and stuffed him back inside. An unseen voice from the sacristy called out.

"*Hallo?*"

I looked down. My topcoat was slick with blood. I tore it off, transferred my Walther to my pants pocket and tossed the coat into the confessional booth with the corpse.

"Hello," I called back, moving quickly to intercept my inquisitor. With any luck he would be a half-blind old priest.

He wasn't. The good father who stood at the top of the altar steps in cassock and surplice was one of those muscular see-right-through-you SOB's we Youngstown ruffians loved and hated in equal measure. I stood at the communion rail and spoke in Deutsch.

"Father, as you can hear, I am an American. I cannot tell you my mission but it is sanctioned at the highest levels of my government. A murder has taken place, by the enemies of freedom. I have reason to believe the victim was a parishioner of St. Bernhard's. I would like to see that his wife receives some measure of compensation."

The priest surveyed my unkempt appearance and registered my lack of an overcoat in wet weather. I yanked my Tyrolean hat off my head.

"Who was murdered?"

I patted my pockets. Had I left Günter's brass pendant in my topcoat? Now would not be an auspicious time to retrieve it.

"He said his name was Günter. A middle aged man, wore a homburg, looked like he had been prosperous."

The priest considered for a moment then shook his head. I felt the chain of the brass pendant in my pocket. It was tangled up in my Walther. I had to remove my gun in order to extract the pendant.

Nice, Schroeder. Classy. Drawing down on the parish priest at the altar. I stuffed my Walther back in my pocket and handed him the brass pendant.

The priest recognized it, recognized the bright coppery spot that Günter had rubbed raw. He smiled at the recognition.

"Henrik won this medal in the Great War, at Verdun." He paused. "Do you wish to take confession?"

"No Father."

"You are certain?"

"Yes Father. I didn't kill him."

The priest stepped down the altar steps, opened the gate in the communion rail and stuck his face in mine. He only came up to my chin but he had the neck and shoulders of Bronco Nagurski. "What is your name?" he said in English.

"Harold Schroeder."

"I will take whatever alms you have to offer to the widow of Henrik Glunz, Mr. Schroeder. But she will refuse them."

"Why is that?"

"She will assume that they are covered in blood."

"I did not kill Henrik, Father."

"So you said."

What miserable sub-basement of hell do you get sent to for cold-cocking a priest?

It didn't seem right. Me, putting myself at risk to do the right thing and getting the third degree for my trouble. An altar boy peeped out from the sacristy. I met his gaze, he darted off.

A sudden wash of pink light indicated that an usher had opened the front doors for the six o'clock Mass. Time to do what well-heeled Americans do in postwar Germany. Make with the geet.

"I don't know who murdered Henrik, Father, even if I did I couldn't say."

I removed a gold sovereign from my leather purse. And another. I chunked them in my hand, musically.

"These are for Henrik's widow."

The good father's brow wrinkled ever so slightly. I dug out another. "And here's one for your church."

"Tell me what happened to Henrik,' he said. "I will convey to his wife only what she needs to know."

I ran down the grisly details. The priest took it more stoically than I gave it. It felt good to get the ugliness off my chest.

"And where is Henrik's body now?"

He would ask that. "He's in the confessional. In the priest's booth."

The good father's face cramp said he didn't believe me. Then he did. Then he didn't. The church was filling up with early morning worshippers. No time to check my outlandish claim. The priest gave me a damn-you-to-hell look and marched back to the sacristy.

I showed myself out.

Chapter Six

I stepped down the stone stairs of St. Bernhard's Church. The dawn was rain washed and almost warm. I set out to find the telegraph office, determined not to let the priest's burn-in-hell-you-bastard look get to me. That was their stock in trade. Guilt. I told myself it wasn't my fault that Henrik Glunz a.k.a. Günter had his guts yanked out. He came to me. I said it aloud.

"He came to me."

It didn't help.

I passed an open window a short minute later, heard a radio playing Benny Goodman's *Sing Sing Sing*, heard Gene Krupa pounding the tom toms.

I walked on, new spring in my step. The hell with guilt. We had something better to offer. Krauts had been marching in cut-time lockstep for far too long. We had something better to offer. A little syncopation, a different meter. A taste of freedom.

The telegraph office had racks of newspapers and magazines in the front, the dit-dah counter in back. Plus an old woman in a black shawl hawking homemade *Kuchen*. I bought a piece and ate it in two bites.

Time to deliver the bad news. I had the CO's designated address, had the cipher code inside my head. I took a blank telegram and set to work at a wobbly stand-up writing table.

And stopped. I was using a cipher based on the transposition of letters, A means K and so on. Dumb. I wasn't a lone wolf lugging a J-E transmitter around the hinterlands any longer. An operator would transmit this message. The NKVD was already in Karlsruhe. Telegraph operators would be high on their recruit list. I couldn't very well hand the operator a coded telegram.

Time to make shit up. I crumpled up my telegram and grabbed a blank. I thought and pondered, pondered and thought. I put pencil to paper.

Auntie Anne not here Stop Neighbors say she went away Stop Left no forwarding address

No. Not clear. It could mean Herr Hilde just disappeared down the Rat Line. How to say it without saying it? I scratched out the last line and added a new one.

Send mail to home address

Better. 'Home' meant 'home base' which meant Berlin which meant that Herr Hilde was headed back up the Rat Line which he would only do if he were caught and captured by the NKVD. The CO would figure it out.

But I didn't have a current code name and no self-respecting agent signs his own. I knew the CO enjoyed the classics. I would sign myself as a famous character in literature. Just as soon as I thought of one.

I wrote *Best regards, Ahab* and handed my telegram across the counter to a matronly woman whose left arm ended at her elbow. It felt strange to let someone else pound the brass. On the pretext of writing another telegram I hung around and listened to the transmission. It was slow, but accurate. Morse code, the universal language. Of the Roman alphabet anyway. What did the Russians use?

I turned to go. I hadn't checked the Reply Requested box because I had no intention of waiting for instructions. I knew what I had to do. Get my heine back to Berlin and get about finding Klaus Hilde before the NKVD shipped him off to Moscow. If they hadn't already done so.

I noticed a crudely printed newspaper on top of the rack of periodicals. The *Sued Kurrier,* a French propaganda rag by the headline: *de Gaulle Sprache!* My eyes registered the date, printed in bold above the headline.

May 8, 1946.

I scanned the front page for a story, looked out the window for a parade.

Could be there were Allied motorcades down the *Unter den Linden* and speeches under the Brandenburg Gate. But here in Karlsruhe the first anniversary of VE Day was a big dud.

Chapter Seven

Not all churches had been as fortunate as St. Bernhard's. The Kaiser Wilhelm Memorial Church stood just outside the Berlin train station. A black stone medieval structure, pink dawn peeping through its shattered stained glass, its bell tower burnt low like a guttered candle. I craned my neck to take it in. It got to me.

We had previously agreed to meet at the Potsdam Conference Memorial upon my return, Victor Jacobson and me. On *Charlottenburger Chausse*, the broad boulevard that bisected the Tiergarten. I hadn't indicated my arrival time on the telegram of course but I wagered that the CO could read a train schedule.

Die Trummerfrauen were already at work. Rubble women, hauling debris with wheelbarrows and bucket brigades, kerchiefs in place against the brick dust. I passed a young woman pushing a baby carriage. A pleasant sight, new life amid the ruins.

I stopped, set down my suitcase and doffed my Tyrolean hat. The woman was perspiring for some reason. I took a peek in her pram with a mind to cluck and coo. The baby carriage was filled with broken bricks.

I headed west toward the boulevard.

Potsdam is a suburb southwest of Berlin. The Potsdam Conference was held there in July of '45. It was the first Big Three post-war powwow. Why the Potsdam Memorial wasn't located in Potsdam I couldn't tell you but everyone stateside had seen it as a backdrop for their son's or husband's or brother's arms-around-their-dogface-buddies snapshots. It was impressive in real life. Large color portraits of Truman, Stalin and Churchill hung upon three marble pillars.

I got closer, read the names of the war dead inscribed on brass plaques above the portraits. I read them all.

Funny joke on Tony, Pete and Hymie, getting their pictures took in front of a monument to *Allied Co-operation in the Great Victory Against Fascism*. All the names of the war dead were Russian.

The Soviets took Berlin six weeks ahead of the U.S., though both armies had been poised to strike at the German capital in April of '45. Ike decided that the casualty estimates were not worth the capture of a mere 'prestige objective.' This made General Patton very unhappy. Churchill too. In any event it was plain that the Soviet Union had taken those six weeks to put their stamp on things.

I looked around. My Case Officer wasn't here. I tried acting like a spy for a change, walking down a side street, ducking down an alley, hiding behind an ash can and looking to see who followed. No one 'cept an alley cat, mewling for a handout.

I humped my beat-up suitcase back to the Memorial and sat on it and 360'd the plaza. No CO, no suspicious characters. My eyelids grew heavy. I stood up and stretched, did neck rolls and arms extensions. Then I sat down and fell asleep.

I woke up from a dark dream to see a tall figure towering over me, his hands vice gripping my right wrist, saying, "It's me, Schroeder, it's me!"

I released the grip on the Walther in my pants pocket and shook myself awake. I gave the CO a full report of my pursuit of Klaus Hilde and the grisly death of Henrik Glunz.

Jacobson listened without comment. When I was done he asked a question.

"Where did you get that ridiculous hat?"

We walked south down the boulevard. It was dotted with street vendors. Women selling flowers, shoe shine boys, a man and wife on accordion and violin, and one grizzled old coot renting the use of his bathroom scale. The price was one

American cigarette. I weighed in at 84 kilos, fighting trim. I think.

Victor Jacobson suffered this foolishness patiently, then detoured us through the treeless park.

"I'm not surprised at your report. We figured the Blue Caps had Hilde."

"Blue Caps?"

"People's Commissariat of Internal Affairs. The NKVD.

"Why do they call them Blue Caps?"

"Our only reliable sources are White Russian émigrés, with the occasional Ukrainian. Passionately anti-Communist, some worked with the Abwehr during the last year of the war. In hopes of keeping the Soviets out of Germany."

"Meaning they used to work with Klaus Hilde."

"Yes indeed," said Jacobson grimly. "Two of our White Russians have turned up in the last twelve hours. Killed in the most gruesome ways imaginable."

The CO stopped to observe a wild hare in a box trap. He studied the frantic animal for a long moment, as if it were a warning. Or a metaphor. We ankled on.

"There will be more killing. Our sources will scatter or go silent. And we'll be out of business. The émigrés are our eyes and ears out there," said Jacobson, gesturing toward the vast gray ruined city. "Without them we're the Helen Keller of spy agencies."

I laughed. Then repeated my stupid question. "Why do they call them Blue Caps?"

"Because that was part of their uniform. In the '30s."

"Blue caps?"

"Yes, Schroeder. Blue caps."

Like I said it was a stupid question. We walked on. A determined young woman, skinny as a matchstick, attacked a tree stump with a hatchet, harvesting chips of bark for kindling. Or soup.

"So you want me to track down Herr Hilde before the Blue Caps put the pipe to all our White Russians."

"Eventually," said the CO.

"I thought this was a crisis?"

"It is."

"Then why wait?"

"Because we have nothing to go on. Not yet. And you need a place to park that suitcase."

With that Victor Jacobson picked up the pace. Our meanderings had a destination. A sedan parked by a bridge that spanned the Spree. The car was sharp two tone job in dark green and light gray with a side-mounted spare. A Horch V-8 Cabriolet, I was quickly informed. Probably cost the old man ten cartons.

We got in. Jacobson was a lousy driver for a big deal intelligence officer. Hell, he was a lousy driver for a blind cripple. We clipped a couple curbs and just missed an old woman caning herself across the street. We drove a long time, detouring around steam shovels and narrow gauge train tracks laid down on top of the pavement, hopper cars filled with building remains hitched to little locomotives like you'd see at a kiddie park.

The CO turned the wrong way down a one way street, hitched a left down an alley, a quick right, then a left on *Hildegardstraße*. No one cared.

I spoke up. "You said 'not yet.' What's in the works?"

We do have one trick up our sleeve." Jacobson looked at me as he drove. I braced myself for a collision. "Our counterintelligence officer, Leonid Vitinov."

A CI officer. I was impressed. I knew enough about the game to recognize the importance of defensive intelligence in a nest of vipers like Berlin. The CI was in charge of security and spycatching. The in-house paranoid.

"Where'd you find him?"

"He's a Soviet Intelligence Officer."

"You mean a foreign agent run by the Soviets."

"No, he's a Soviet Intelligence Major."

"How in the name of Christ you recruit him?"

"He came to us."

Uh huh. Sure he did. Just wandered in off the street one day and leaned his elbows on the countertop. The OSS had had an entire section dedicated to that sort of thing. 'Talent scouts' they called them.

"Who did he come to sir? Global Commerce? The CIG? Bill Donovan? You?"

"None of your business," said the CO amiably.

"What sort of trade samples did he bring?"

Jacobson had settled into a more fluid rhythm at the wheel. We hadn't run over a pedestrian for blocks. I figured the CO was debating whether to tell me how he knew that the Soviet was the genuine article. He'd better. I wasn't working with this Leonid otherwise.

"He gave us half a dozen NKVD informers here in town. Including a clerk typist inside the Berlin Operating Base."

"That's it? A few two bit freelancers?"

"Two of them were Soviet Intelligence Officers."

"How do you know?"

"Leonid told us."

"Well," I said, "how convenient."

"They both swallowed L pills when collared by MPs."

I found it hard to argue with that. "And you think this Leonid guy can get us a line on Hilde?"

"He's working it. It's tricky. He's not need-to-know on Hilde's whereabouts."

We stopped at a traffic circle where a German policeman was directing traffic. He waved us on with a curt Prussian nod.

"Maybe you think it's nuts to have a Soviet inside and maybe it is," said Jacobson. "But we Yanks are lousy at counterintelligence, too gee whiz. The Brits are better, and the Russians, with their dark history, are better still."

Yeah, I thought, maybe a little too good. I asked Jacobson what Leonid's NKVD cover was.

"He works for Global Commerce as a translator."

"Doesn't the NKVD know that Global Commerce is headed by Bill Donovan?"

"Of course they do."

"And they believe we would hire a Russian?"

The CO shrugged, his eyes on the road. "They know we're shorthanded. And they think we're stupid."

"Let's hope they're wrong," I said as we passed two skinny young boys attempting to pry a battery from a parked car. They had gotten it unhooked from the cables but were too weak lift it out. A short minute later Jacobson ticked his head to the left.

"Heidelberg Platz."

A *Platz* is a square or plaza in my dictionary but this one was a shaggy green park studded with lean-tos and fire pits. Ragged kids played tag around a pale birch, which was the only surviving tree.

"Our CIG pals have commandeered Nazi villas out in Zehlendorf," said Jacobson. "Poor thinking. I got you something low profile."

Meaning it was a dump I supposed but that was jake. All I need is a roof and running water. Jacobson took a right turn onto a side street. A block of four story apartment buildings. He pulled to the curb.

"That's it, on the left."

It wasn't The Pierre but my four-story building was brick and glad of it, given the stucco disaster next door. An Allied bomb had found the gangway between the two. It had knocked a few teeth loose in the side of the brick building, but had sheared the facing wall of the stucco building clean off.

The CO handed me a key for unit #12, said, "Don't answer the door," gave me the time and place of our next meet and drove off.

Chapter Eight

I hauled my grip up three flights of the brick apartment building that teemed like an ant farm with toddlers and old folks and everything in between. I drew a lot of stares.

The fourth floor was better. No squalling brats, no sour cabbage smells. The penthouse. I keyed open #12 and understood why the CO told me not to answer the door. I found well-used pots and pans in the kitchen and an overlooked family photo above the stove. A young couple squinting at the camera, hands on the shoulders of their son and daughter. My living quarters had been requisitioned.

I settled in, hung my clothes in the empty closet, put my socks and underwear in the top dresser drawer and checked the larder for grub. Someone had provided a little taste of home, cans of Dinty Moore beef stew and Campbell's pea soup. There was even a can opener. And a box of kitchen matches on the stove. They had gas in this building? I fired a kitchen match and lit the range. Yes they did. Electricity too? I flipped a wall switch. Well, one out of two ain't bad.

I heated up a can of stew and searched the larder some more, came up with a pack of Zwieback. Would have to do, though a crusty heel of rye bread is the perfect complement to canned beef stew. Trust me, I'm an expert on canned grub.

I dug up a tin spoon and stirred the pot and remembered something I had said to the CO at the Bierstube. 'What a sideways setup.' A group of Russian émigrés as field agents, an NKVD Major as counterintelligence officer and our CIG liaisons cozily clipping newspaper articles 'out in Zehlendorf' wherever that was. Looked like Jacobson and I were all alone here in central Berlin, our Doctor Denton's unbuttoned and our fannies flapping in the breeze.

I crumbled the crackers into the pot and ate the stew standing up.

Gas. The building had gas. Meaning hot running water, if it had running water, meaning I could shave. I went to the dank bathroom and turned the spigot. Pipes groaned, coughing out brown water that got clear after a time. Clear but cold. I tried the tub. Same deal. Kitchen too. Puzzled, I opened a closet next to the stove and saw the tank of propane. The building didn't have gas, I did.

I gave the stew pot a quick wash, filled it with water, boiled it up and hauled it to the bathroom. I grabbed my blue blade and shave mug and made myself presentable for my noon meet. I washed up and gave myself the once over in the pitted mirror above the sink. Handsome as a hog, though I should've cleaned the pot better. My mush smelled of beef stew.

I no longer wear a wristwatch. My constant time checking got me into trouble in Cleveland, and helped The Schooler get dead. So I took the pledge. But this was no way to run a railroad. It felt well shy of noon but I changed my shirt, locked up, tripped down three flights and left by the back door.

The Berlin street grid was worse than Cleveland. Streets on the bias, dead end alleys, *Straßes* that bent one way and became *Allees* when they bent the other. I spent half an hour winding my way to *Konstanzerstraße*, a north-south thoroughfare. All of the building damage in this section of *Westen* Berlin had come from above. The facades of the buildings had been spared the Red Army tank rounds and machine gun fire visited on Ost Berlin.

The facades with their caved in roofs reminded me of something, reminded me of the expression of a baggy pants comic - goofy, grinning, wide eyed - in the split second after his partner smacks him on the head with a pig bladder.

I smiled at the image despite myself. Okay, I laughed. I laughed in the face of the tide of solemn silent pedestrians moving along the sidewalk as if every step were an effort, their eyes turned inward, or outward in the thousand yard stare. Anywhere but here and now.

Yeah, I know. I am a completely degenerate human being. When did I say different?

A bell tower tolled noon shortly before I did a quick 360 and pushed open the stout door of the Café Gestern, tinkling its entry bell. My eyes took a moment to adjust to the gas lit dim. I saw why they called it Café Yesterday. Hummel figurines along a ledge, lace curtains with tablecloths to match, sprays of edelweiss in crystal cruets. And a Victrola playing a scratchy recording of, for some reason, French songbird Edith Piaf.

I sought the spy table, far wall, left hand corner. No CO. But a small, very well dressed man acknowledged me with a glance. Leonid, the Soviet Major? The CO said we had a noon meet with our CI. We, as in you and me. Where was Jacobson?

The dapper little man did not stand up when I approached. Or did he? Hard to tell, guy was a midget. And almost pretty. Not what you'd expect a Soviet Major to look like. He nodded toward the chair facing him. I knew instantly that he thought me a rube, knew instantly that we would be adversaries. So I sat with my back to the front door, confirming his opinion.

"Victor will be along shortly," he said in lightly accented English.

"And you are…?"

"Leonid Vitinov."

"Hal Schroeder, pleased to meetcha."

I held out a paw. Leonid did likewise. I wiped my palm on my pants leg when we were done.

"I thought it best that we make each other's acquaintance, man to man," said Leonid, permitting himself a taut smile at the American idiom.

I nodded and said what young men say to older men when they want to polish the apple. And have a couple hours to spare. "I'm here to learn."

A waitress appeared, a stern *Grossmutter* with pulled back hair. She poured Leonid more black coffee, I ordered a beer.

"What is your experience?"

I told him I was good at hiding in hedgerows and counting truck convoys, not so up-to-speed on the polite skullduggery practiced at embassy cocktail parties. Leonid nodded his understanding, then spent time tutoring me in the fine art of espionage. Here are the highlights:

- The job description of a spy is contradictory - a person of impeccable integrity who is an accomplished liar.

- Do not use gadgets - dart guns, mini-cameras and such. If you are detained with them they cannot be explained.

- Never pry, let the conversation come to you. If a secret is revealed act dubious, and wait for more.

- Valuable information should be sliced very thin, and served sparingly.

I found this all very instructive. Especially the last part about info being sliced thin. Leonid didn't elaborate and I didn't ask but I took it to mean that...well, I'm not sure what I took it to mean but it sounded right.

His lecture concluded, Leonid leaned back and plucked a cigarette from a gold case. He offered me one. It was plump, oval. Turkish. Probably worth 100 marks on the black market. I declined. Leonid tapped his cigarette against the table, turned it over, tapped some more.

I had only one question. Why had Leonid Vitinov volunteered his services to the cause of freedom? I used his own words.

"So, Leonid, how did you become an accomplished liar?"

Leonid plucked a string of tobacco from his lip and examined it. I drained half my beer and suppressed a belch. No sense overdoing the rube routine. He kept one eye on me and one on the front door as he spoke. They were dark and liquid, his eyes. Deeply set with long lashes. Women would go for this guy.

"I am an only child, from a privileged Moscow family. We were what they call the White Russians though we never used those words. We were Russian, that is all. Russian. My father worked in the Ministry of Trade and we revered the Tsar. When the Bolsheviks took power we tried to flee to Germany. We were captured in Minsk. My father was taken away, he is long dead. My mother and I were permitted to return to our home, which now housed three families. Three families which hated us. We had to pretend happiness and contentment at the triumph of the proletariat. I was able to do this," said Leonid, his fat British cigarette sitting unsmoked between thumb and forefinger. "My mother was not."

"What happened to her?"

"Beria took her. To the Lubyanka. That is why he trusts me. If he thinks I am a traitor my mother will be executed."

"Then why are you? A traitor?"

Leonid's piercing stare softened, his eyes shone, his smooth voice roughened.

"Because she would want me to be."

I'll tell you one thing for certain. They should never recruit undercover agents from the Midwest. We're too damn trusting. Leonid Vitinov was an NKVD officer who was either a double agent for Bill Donovan and Global Commerce or a re-doubled agent who was playing us like a violin and yet here I was practically blubbering into my hankie.

"That's an amazing story."

Leonid looked up as the entry bell tinkled. Victor Jacobson entered the Café and didn't look at us. He ordered something at the bar and carried it to the rear of the building. Leonid lit his cigarette and paid the bill. He stood up.

Okay, he wasn't a midget. With stacked heels he might have cleared five foot. He patted my arm, pretending to make a congenial farewell as he instructed me to ask the barkeep for directions to the men's room, then enter the left-facing door at the end of the hall. He left by the front entrance.

I asked the big jolly bartender for directions and wondered why. Was this standard procedure, or had der sheisse haben der fannen gehitten? I stopped at the left-facing door and did a quick over the shoulder. All clear. I ducked in.

Leonid entered the small windowless room a minute later. The stern Grossmutter came in to take our drink orders, leaving the door open behind her. She left the same way. I got up and closed the door. Christ. This was poor tradecraft even by my standards. The CO read my mind.

"We need to change our routine. You two get along okay?" he said. To me.

"Yes sir. We're thick as thieves."

"That's good. Because, for the moment, we comprise the entire front line staff of Global Commerce, Berlin."

"Is there an office someplace?"

"One desk, one phone. In the Charlottenburg district."

And the CO said the CIG was undermanned. At least we had them beat in one department. We had a Russian-speaker on staff.

"What have you been able to determine?" said Jacobson to Leonid.

"I do not know Herr Hilde's location but he is held by the NKVD."

"How do you know?"

"Because they have not asked if he is held by us."

"Is he on his way to Moscow?"

"No. Our Berlin Bureau Chief is a rival to Beria. He would desire to hold Hilde close so long as possible. To strip him clean."

I elbowed my way into the conversation. "So they snatched Hilde in Karlsruhe?"

Leonid squared his well-tailored shoulders. "They did not, as you say, *snatch* Herr Hilde. They bought him."

"How do you know?"

Leonid relaxed his posture, smoothed the back of his neck, held up one finger. "The NKVD has the names of our White Russians. In one day. Torture takes time."

Jacobson and I looked to one another. What Leonid said made sense. It also made for very bad news. The most knowledgeable living member of the Nazi Abwehr was now in the employ of the Soviet Union. I asked the CO what he wanted me to do.

"Go find him!"

Well, it was hard to argue with that kind of thinking. I would. I would go find Brigadeführer Hilde. But I had done enough solo work for one lifetime, I wanted help. And I knew who I wanted that helper to be. A young man with a criminal past and no experience in espionage.

"This is a two-man job sir. I need a legman out front or a lookout in back. I can't do it myself."

I waited for the CO's response. He waited for me to stop waiting. Spit it out, Schroeder. You're Bill Donovan's fair-haired boy.

"Does Global Commerce have an office in Ireland?"

"Yes," said Jacobson. "Dublin."

"Is that in County Cork?"

"No, it's in County Dublin."

"What's the biggest town in County Cork?"

"Cork."

Of course. "Tell your Dublin office to send an agent on a pub crawl in Cork, looking for three brothers in their early twenties. They won't be hard to find. They're from the States, Cleveland, and they'll be spending a lot of greenbacks. It's the eldest I want. His name is Ambrose Mooney."

The CO appeared to consider this ridiculous suggestion. Expecting a long list of questions I got, "You swear by this guy?"

"I do."

"He'll be your responsibility."

"I understand."

Victor Jacobson nodded. Meeting adjourned.

Chapter Nine

Bill Donovan & Co. had Ambrose Mooney, wanted by the FBI for the robbery of the Cleveland Branch of the Federal Reserve, on the macadam at Templehof within 48 hours of my request. I knew this because Victor Jacobson interrupted my conversation with a reporter from Stars and Stripes to say he would be here soon.

Here was Dahlem, the CO's residence. A three story white brick mansion on a block untouched by war. The neighborhood was far enough south of the central city that the B-24s hadn't bothered it. And far enough west that it hadn't been shelled during the Russian advance. Step out onto the porch it might've been Shaker Heights. And me in a cold water flat.

We were attending a reception, with *Fräuleins* in peasant blouses serving trays of canapés and an elderly bartender in the kitchen pouring champagne with both hands. The CO was hosting members of the staff of Stars and Stripes for my benefit. My cover job was reporter for S'n'S, but the newshounds didn't know about my cover so we had to invent a cover so that I could ask them questions about being a reporter so that I could cover my cover. So to speak.

I had suggested that I could be part of an advance team for a congressional delegation. The CO nixed that, too high profile. So we settled on salesman for Global Commerce, specialty metals division. The reporters didn't ask any further.

I made the rounds and asked questions. What I learned was that being a journalist in post-war Berlin was difficult, monumentally difficult. I learned also that their paymaster could squeeze the beard off a buffalo nickel, that the barkeep gave a pour that was all bubbles and no blood and that they couldn't wait to go back home. I nodded and smiled and waited for Ambrose.

He arrived shortly. I don't know why I was so glad to see him. He didn't know the first thing about espionage and he'd be worthless undercover with his Irish brogue and Yankee ways. But my face split ear to ear when he sauntered in the front door, pigskin satchel in hand.

He had grown into himself, chest and neck thickened. Same widow's peak of copper hair biting his forehead. Sporting a brown tweed jacket and a green silk tie. He was going to be an Irish handful, he was.

His eyes found mine a moment later. I rubbed my nose lazily with my middle finger. Ambrose grinned. We were back in business.

We made our way around to each other eventually. He didn't ask why I had sent for him. I was prepared to introduce him as my associate at Global Commerce Specialty Metals Division but the staff of Stars and Stripes didn't ask. They were too busy draining glasses and scarfing grub.

We moved on to little Leonid and his skinny wife. Leonid had dressed down for the occasion, his brown suit and soup-stained tie indicating his station as a hireling. I introduced them to Ambrose.

"I am Leonid and my wife Anna."

I almost laughed. The way he said it sounded like he was both people.

Ambrose and I exchanged moist handshakes with Leonid. Anna regarded my outstretched hand as if it were another, cruder, appendage. I withdrew it. She stared at her shoes. Did Russian women not shake hands?

We made small talk with Leonid. Yes, it had indeed been a very rainy May. And so very cold! Anna followed our conversation from beneath long eyelashes. She was fair skinned, so fair-skinned you could count her veins. She opened her mouth to speak just as I felt a quick poke in the back and caught sight of the CO motoring past.

I asked Leonid if the gentleman's lounge wasn't thataway. He said that it was.

Ambrose gave me an eyebrow. I ran my hand over my head, back to front, indicating he should follow the CO. He spent a moment with Leonid and his wife before he ankled off. I went in the opposite direction. It was as silly exercise in stealth under the circumstances, the newshounds were spilling more than they were drinking. But I liked it that Ambrose understood without explanation.

I ducked into the hall, saw Ambrose climbing the stairs and followed. At the end of the second floor hall was the Communications Center. The CO was in the first room on the right. A room with a four poster featherbed and pale blue walls. I closed the door behind me.

Victor Jacobson looked grim. "The MPs found another one of our White Russians, what was left of him. Our émigrés don't sleep in the same bed twice. That they're being killed so quickly indicates that Klaus Hilde is moving among them, knows where they are at a given time."

I asked why the émigrés would trust Hilde.

"Well, they worked with him before war's end." Jacobson ran his hand across his mouth. "But that was a long time ago."

"We'll find Hilde sir, Ambrose and me. Just give us some idea where to start."

Jacobson grunted. He sat on the foot of the four poster and looked tired, looked like he wanted to flop backward and sleep for a week.

"Goebbels primed the pump for years. Russians were *Unter Menschen*, sub-humans bent on ravaging Aryan womanhood. Then the Red Army invaded and did just that, gang raped every female they could get their hands on," said the CO, his voice trailing off as he sank deeper into the featherbed.

We waited. Jacobson continued.

"Berliners hate their guts. The Soviets' greatest fear is that the White Russian and Ukrainian émigrés will link up with the locals and attempt to seize the Soviet Sector. They would need heavy weapons to do that," said Jacobson and yawned. And closed his eyes.

Ambrose and I swapped a look. The CO put his hands on his knees and stood up, refreshed after his five second nap. "We'll build you a light legend and send you in."

"As what?"

"International arms dealers. Don't worry, we'll provide sample wares, quality stuff."

I worried anyway. A light legend meant a half-assed cover story on top of our existing half-assed cover story and no backstopping if further inquiries were made.

"We have a contact," said Jacobson. "That is we know of one. A former Gestapo Captain who's procuring weapons. If you can do a small deal with him the word will spread quickly through the anti-Soviet underground. You'll be in demand. If you're lucky you can get a line on Hilde."

Ambrose posed a question. "What happens if we're not so lucky?"

The CO shrugged. "You'll be whisked off to a private meeting with Lavrenty Beria in the basement of the Lubyanka."

It was doubtful Ambrose knew what the CO was referring to but he got the gist. *The basement of the Lubyanka* has a certain ring to it.

"So we're bait," said Ambrose.

"Not at all," said the CO, wryly. "The proper term is 'throwaway lead.'"

Ambrose and I had a good laugh at our expense.

"We'll mock up an FBI Most Wanted poster," said Jacobson. "You're gun runners on the lam."

The CO opened a closet and grabbed a spiffy new camera with a flash attachment. "A Kine Exakta, cost me two cartons." Ambrose and I took turns posing against the back wall.

"Don't smile," said Ambrose. "It's a wanted poster for feck's sake." I gave the lens a curled lip scowl. "Now you look like George Raft. Relax." I relaxed. "Look bored." I looked bored. "Better."

Chapter Ten

I drove a big rumbling delivery truck east the following afternoon, toward the entry point to the Soviet Sector. Ambrose sat in the passenger's seat and took in the destroyed central city without comment. We weren't sure what we would find at the Soviet checkpoint though the CO had assured us we wouldn't have a problem.

We didn't. The checkpoint had a guardhouse and a wooden sign in four languages. 'You are now entering the Soviet Sector.' The guardhouse was unmanned.

I drove through. The delivery truck was the CO's idea. It made sense for our mission. Making a delivery to a grocery store.

The former Gestapo Captain's name was Horst Schultouer. He worked the loading dock of a grocery store, good cover for receiving black market munitions. The CO said Schultouer was desperate for quality product. We had a bit of that, in a crate in the back of the truck.

We found the narrow street and hunted the address. The late afternoon light was gray as dishwater. Papa Joe looked down upon us from a two story mural.

"Who's that?" said Ambrose.

He was kidding, he had to be. I drove on. Ambrose's blind trust in my judgment was starting to annoy me for some reason. You'd think a guy who got clonked unconscious with the butt of a shotgun and whose brother almost bled to death on our last operation would ask a few questions about this one.

"That's the market," said Ambrose as we passed a squat building made of cinder block. No display windows, no advertising banners, just a front door in a wall of concrete.

"You sure?"

"Saw a woman leaving with a grocery bag."

I nursed the delivery truck through two narrow right turns. The alley behind the store was littered with overflowing garbage bins and a couple old heaps on bare rims. The loading dock was puny, shielded by an overhang of corrugated tin. I pulled up alongside the concrete slab and tooted the horn like I had every right to be there.

There are two ways to work an undercover operation. Slow and cautious or fast and furious. Slow and cautious pays better odds over time. But we didn't have any clock to waste. And if you wanted slow and cautious why hire Hal Schroeder and Ambrose Mooney?

No one appeared on the loading dock. I leaned on the horn. A big-shouldered Kraut came stomping out, shouting *"Vas ist das?"* He fit the rough description the CO had given me, though he had grown a beard. I turned to ask Ambrose if he was ready to do this but he was already out the door.

Horst Schultouer demanded to know who we were as Ambrose rolled open the truck's back gate. I scooted across the cab to address the former Gestapo Captain through the passenger's side window.

I explained, in Deutsch, that we were the new kids in town, paying a courtesy call. That shut him up for the moment. I said we had a special one-time-only introductory offer for him and him alone. That brought a squint of interest.

Ambrose hoisted the crate onto the loading dock. I did a quick 360 and nodded. He crowbarred it open.

"Fresh pineapples," I said. "Right off the tree!"

Herr Schultouer looked down upon the gleaming lined-up bounty in the crate. Dozens of brand new American-made hand grenades. I removed two and stuffed them in his coat pockets.

"Free samples. We'll be back tomorrow morning after you test them," I said.

Ambrose re-sealed the crate. Schultouer wanted to know who sent us.

I handed him the freshly-minted FBI Most Wanted poster bearing the photos of Ambrose and myself. "J. Edgar Hoover." This was meant to establish our bona fides. Everyone in the Western World had heard of the all-powerful Director of the FBI. But even the old Bulldog himself would have been surprised at Horst Schultouer's reaction. His face paled and he reached into his coat pockets, as if to return the grenades.

"We have a no return policy on sample merchandise," I said in Deutsch.

Horst kept his hands in his pockets. I stepped forward, got close enough to smell his breath. Beer and braunschweiger.

"We don't care who you are or who you used to be. We're here to move some merchandise. We have everything from sidearms to howitzers. All new, all clean." Horst started to speak. I cut him off. "No, I'm not going to tell you how. All I'm going to tell you is how much. Interested?"

Herr Schultouer didn't answer right away. In fact he gave me a fearsome stare, which annoyed me no end.

"*Sind...Sie...interessiert?*" Are you interested?

Horst sneered and shuffled his bearded mug around. I did an over-the-shoulder to Ambrose but he wasn't there. When I turned back he had Schultouer down on one knee.

Ambrose yanked one of the samples from the man's coat pocket, pulled the pin and handed the live grenade to Schultouer, who clutched the suppressor handle with both hands.

"Go test the merchandise, Captain," said Ambrose with a friendly clap on the back. "We'll be back tomorrow at ten."

I translated his remarks as Ambrose put the crate in the back of the truck and climbed in the cab.

"What the hell you do that for?" I said when we pulled away from the loading dock. "He tosses that grenade under the truck and the whole crate goes up and us with it."

"He won't," said Ambrose.

I checked the side view mirror. Schultouer was climbing down from the loading dock, the grenade clutched to his chest. I watched him cross the alley with small quick steps. Ambrose stared straight ahead. He wasn't going to look.

"I don't know," I said and lugged into third, slowing our progress. I pretended to study the side view mirror. "Our Gestapo Captain is rearing back with that grenade like Bob Waterfield looking to go deep."

Ambrose stiffened ever so slightly. I downshifted and stalled out. Ambrose shot me a panicked look. I cranked the ignition without depressing the clutch.

"Push the feckin' pedal!"

I nodded dumbly and pushed the feckin' pedal. It would happen right…about…KA-BLAMMO!

Ambrose bent over and covered his head with his arms and kissed his ass goodbye. I engaged the clutch and drove on, whistling a little tune.

The Irishman's head popped up, he checked his side view. I watched what he watched. An abandoned Volkswagen spewing smoke and flame.

"Guess he changed his mind about where to toss that grenade."

"I owe you one arsehole," said Ambrose in reply.

Chapter Eleven

We returned to the Soviet checkpoint the following morning in the delivery truck. It was raining again. Hard. Sideways. And me with no coat. The windshield wiper on the driver's side didn't work so Ambrose was acting as my seeing eye dog. *Slow down. Turn here.* Like that.

We had the same crate of grenades in the truck bed. Also a few trade samples to further whet Schultouer's appetite. A Browning automatic rifle, light and heavy mortars, even a 3.5 inch armor-piercing bazooka. All boxed and crated. All new, all clean.

The guardhouse at the checkpoint wasn't empty this time. A sentry with a rifle slung over his shoulder stepped out as we pulled up. Not what I wanted to see. Ambrose rolled down his window.

"We're delivering groceries," he said and gave the address of the grocery store.

The sentry didn't understand. He did know one word of English however. "Passports!"

I breathed a sigh of relief. This wasn't an inspection it was a shakedown. Berlin was still an open city, governed by the four powers. We were not crossing an international border, a passport was not required. I slipped a five dollar bill into mine and handed it to Ambrose to hand to the sentry.

The sentry opened the passport, pocketed the five and handed it back. He wore three watches on his wrist. One bore the likeness of a popular cartoon mouse. I started to drive off. The sentry jumped on the running board and said something angry.

I stopped the truck. "Show him your passport Ambrose."

"Don't have one."

"Then how did you…never mind."

I tried using Deutsch to explain that my colleague had left his passport at home. I tried hand gestures. I tried another fin. Nothing doing.

"Passport!"

That we didn't need passports to enter was beside the point.

"Give him your wristwatch Ambrose."

"Bloody hell!"

"Give it to him."

"It's a family heirloom!"

"It's brand new."

"Cost me ten quid!"

"Give it to him."

Ambrose unpeeled the braided leather wristband furiously. It was a nice piece, rimmed in gold. He tossed it to the sidewalk in disgust. The sentry scrambled after it as we drove into the Soviet Sector in a sideways rain. Harold and Ambrose, the timeless twins.

Ambrose guide-dogged me down the narrow streets of the Soviet Sector, stewing about his watch, jaw muscles clenching.

"If you're thinkin' that this meet might be a good time to get me back for yesterday, think again," I said. "This is too important."

"Slow down and turn right. You just passed the market."

I turned right, and right again, down the cluttered alleyway. We passed the burnt out VW. The grocery store loading dock took shape beyond the rainy windshield. I pulled up and tooted the horn. No one appeared. I leaned on the horn. Likewise.

Had we cheesed off Herr Schultouer by handing him a live grenade as a going away present? You bet. Enough to keep the former Gestapo Captain from taking us up on our once-in-a-lifetime offer? Not likely.

I sounded the horn again and got a very prompt response. Two tarp-covered troop trucks flying Red Army flags approached from both ends of the alley.

"What now Chief?"

"Not sure."

The troop trucks closed in at a stately pace. Why not? We had no escape route. One question blurred across the rainy windshield. Why would Horst Schultouer, a Red-hating Nazi, rat us out?

I considered our options. They were two. Make a run for it through the back door of the grocery store that was doubtless locked and bolted or sit tight and attempt to explain to the Red Army why our grocery truck was carrying an armor-piercing bazooka.

Our options, more accurately, were zero. Poor Ambrose. He hadn't been properly introduced to the game. I had given him the basic lay but he wouldn't be prepared for this. He wouldn't understand why I had to shoot him in the head before I ate my gun.

My fault. My fault entirely.

The Red Army troop trucks stopped in front and in back of us, a hundred feet away. A man in full combat dress climbed out of the truck in front. He was a large man, it took him a while. Soldiers piled out of the trucks and stood behind him. Lots of soldiers. The big man strode forward in a deliberate manner. His troops followed.

I waited for inspiration to strike. I am well known for my ability to improvise a solution to a crisis at the last possible moment, famous even. So where the hell was it? The only sad shred of a plan I could glim was…I came to at the sound of a crowbar prying wood.

Ambrose jumped back into the cab a moment later with an armful of grenades. He dumped some in my lap, dumped more onto the floorboard in front of him and pulled the pins on the two in his hands.

"Hard to argue with a live grenade," he said with a grin.

Well. So much for Ambrose not being prepared. His suggestion wasn't the sadass plan I'd been mulling – take the big man hostage somehow, try to back out of the Soviet Sector. His suggestion was clear and clean. Go out, flags flying, in a blaze of glory.

"Who is this now?" said Ambrose.

I followed his look to see a big white fancy car, a Rolls Royce or a Bentley, honking its way up the alley, a Union Jack flying from its radio antenna. The big man and his soldiers turned to look.

Chapter Twelve

It was a Rolls not a Bentley, the big white car that squeezed past the troop truck in front of us. The Soviet soldiers raised their bolt-action carbines but their superior barked a command and they stood down. The Rolls Royce came to a stop.

The man at the wheel wore a chauffeur's cap. The rear deck of the land yacht had darkened windows. Time crawled to a standstill as we waited for its occupant to make an appearance. The chauffeur climbed out, opened an umbrella and opened the rear door. The rain slackened, right on cue.

A puff of smoke preceded him. A tall raffish pipe-smoking gent of middle years stood to his feet. He wore a brightly striped tie. He wore other clothes too – Navy blue blazer with an emblem on the pocket, pleated slacks – but the tie was what you noticed.

He looked at Ambrose and me and gave us a cheery wave. I waved back.

The tall Brit greeted the big Soviet commander like a long lost friend. They shared a laugh. The Brit whipped out a stack of tickets of some kind. Soldiers clustered around. The Brit held the ducats above his head against their outstretched arms like Father Christmas with a fistful of candy canes.

Ambrose and I turned to one another, and shrugged.

The tall Brit handed the stack of tickets to the big Russian and headed in our direction. I looked down at the grenades in my lap, the cluster on the floorboard and the two in the hands of Ambrose, pins pulled. Too late for housekeeping. We were at the mercy of this pipe-smoking Brit who chugged up to our delivery truck like an ore train, a puff of smoke at every step.

He leaned into the driver's side window and showed no reaction to the mess of pineapples strewn about.

"Colonel John Norwood, pleasure to make your acquaintance." He addressed Ambrose. "I'd shake hands but I see you're otherwise occupied." He took a puff of pipe tobacco. "Follow me out. Stay close."

Colonel Norwood returned to the Russian commander and held a brief intense conversation. The Russian looked stern, unconvinced. Ambrose and I held our collective breath. The Colonel leaned into the Russian with a whispered comment. The big Russian's face froze.

Norwood patted the commander on the shoulder, gave the troops a regal wave and resumed his hand-stitched leather seat in the only Rolls Royce I had ever seen outside the pages of *AutoCar*.

And then we drove away, Ambrose and I. Drove away from the puny grocery store loading dock in the Soviet Sector, site of our certain and gruesome demise. I can't say for certain that the clouds parted and the sun shone at that particular moment, but that's the way I remember it.

We followed the Rolls west toward the British Sector. The chauffeur took pity on us, driving slowly as I nursed the delivery truck along in fits and starts. The fuel gauge said half-full but it felt like we were cruising on fumes. We stopped at a red light at the intersection of *Spandauer* and *Unter den Linden*, the main drag. The beat down, blown up Berlin Cathedral was a block to our left.

"Throw it in neutral and floor it," said Ambrose.

"Why's that?"

"I smell gas. Could be a clogged fuel line. You need to blow it out."

I did as instructed. The truck revved and shuddered and farted a fat black cloud out the tailpipe, then settled back into a steady thrum. I pulled out at the green. We were about to cross the Spree and enter the British Sector when Ambrose, hefting the live grenades he held in either hand, asked a pertinent question.

"What should I do with these?"

I waited till we were on the bridge. The cab of the truck was a good vantage point. No pedestrians, no boats in the river.

"Toss 'em!"

Ambrose tossed the grenade in his right hand into the river where it exploded with a muffled *whomp*.

He glanced ahead. "Slow down, you'll rear end him!"

I braked and returned my eyes to the road. Braked too hard apparently because Ambrose pitched forward with a live grenade still in his left hand.

And then it wasn't.

It was rattling around on the floorboard amidst the nest of other grenades. *Jesus H. Christ on a crutch* I thought as I watched Ambrose frantically sorting through the pineapples that were about to blow us all to kingdom come, *a silly end to a stupid life!*

Ambrose finally dug out the live grenade and cocked his arm to pitch it out the window.

But he did not. He made a face and said, "Ow. My arm is sore."

The grenade he held had its pin in place.

Ha ha. Very funny. I floored the delivery truck to catch up to the disappearing Rolls. Ambrose had tossed the second grenade when I was tromping on the brakes.

"And now we're even. Arsehole."

Ambrose settled back with a smug smile. We followed the Rolls west, then north through the central city. We left the British Sector and entered the French. The neighborhood got gritty, industrial. I would have followed the Colonel to the Arctic Circle at this point but it seemed an odd way to go.

"Where the feck are we?" said Ambrose. "I figured this toff for a big mansion on a hill."

The Rolls signaled a right turn on *Ernststraße*, a brick street of machine shops on one side and modest homes on the other. We drove a quarter mile and then slowed before a two story chalet on a double lot with a high hedge in front. We followed the Rolls down a short gravel driveway with an ivy-covered arbor overhead. The lot was deep, with another two story building in back, sheltered by trees.

The Rolls Royce came to a stop. Colonel Norwood opened his own door. The chauffeur opened the door of the one-car garage. I put the truck in park.

"Come up, dear boys, come up," called the Colonel as he pounded up the steep wooden staircase at the rear of the chalet.

We did so. Leaving behind a delivery truck littered with enough weaponry to overthrow a Balkan republic.

Chapter Thirteen

Colonel Norwood's chalet was full to bursting. Oriental carpets topped with throw rugs, portraits of British royalty hung next to Arab tapestries, a cactus plant in an orange pot sitting on a cracked leather ottoman next to a jade Buddha atop a display cabinet that held a bullet-riddled cavalry canteen, a rusty bayonet, a yellowed *Citation of Merit*, a cut glass crystal bowl inscribed with the royal seal on a purple display pillow and, on the top shelf of the cabinet, a cedar humidor with a gold plate that bore the initials W.L.S.C. A lot of stuff to haul to a foreign posting. It looked like the Colonel planned to stay awhile.

"Recognize the initials?" said the Colonel off the humidor.

"No sir."

"Winston Leonard Spencer Churchill. A going away memento," said Norwood, seating himself on a chesterfield loosely covered with a hunk of Chinese silk. Brocade I think they call it, red and gold dragons. He smushed the silk cover into the corners of the couch and tapped out his pipe on a stray saucer on the coffee table.

"Where's your friend?"

I didn't know. Ambrose was behind me when we climbed the back stairs. I called his name. He appeared shortly, zipping up his trow.

"Here I am."

The Colonel filled his pipe from a leather pouch and didn't bother to turn his head. "Tell your friend to sit somewhere where I can keep an eye on him."

"The name's Ambrose sir," he said, perching on the arm of a wing chair that faced the couch.

I took the matching chair next to him. "And I'm Harold Schroeder."

"So I have been informed," said the Colonel pleasantly.

Huh? A British Colonel knew my name? And what was he a Colonel of anyway? MI6, had to be.

"Colonel, Ambrose and I would like to express our profound thanks for…"

"Hauling your chestnuts out of the fire?"

"Yes sir."

"Happy to be of service dear boy. Happy to be of service."

He loosened his brightly striped tie from Oxford or Cambridge or one of those. He lit his pipe with a gold Ronson and sat back and looked content. The chauffeur entered from the back door, hung his cap on a peg and lumbered off to the kitchen. It felt like a scene that had taken place a hundred times before.

"We need you cheeky Yanks, don't you see?" said the Colonel suddenly. "Britain is spent, defeated by victory, the French haven't been worth a fig since Waterloo. Only you cheeky Yanks, only you batboys can keep the Red Army from crossing the Elbe. Where *is* the bloody tea Sedgewick?"

Sedgewick let the whistling kettle answer for him. The Colonel puffed his pipe impatiently. I had heard this doomsday scenario before, from the CO. But he was a Gloomy Gus. That this jolly Brit thought likewise made it seem more real.

"I don't know much about the big picture sir, Ambrose and I are just pawns in the game…"

"Pawns in the game who would like to know, sir, how you knew to come to our rescue," said Ambrose, brashly.

The Colonel shrugged his considerable eyebrows and sat very still. Ambrose leaned forward on his perch.

There are few tasks in life more thankless than being a referee. I learned this while mediating disputes between my strict Catholic parents and my wild kid sister Beth. This was the like. A brazen Mick versus a Limey toff. Just what I didn't need.

"I don't believe I am under any obligation to tell you," said the Colonel.

"Of course not, sir," I said. "It's just…"

"But what's the harm?" grinned the Colonel. He had good teeth for an Englishman. "Horst Schultouer stopped by last evening, had a bit too much refreshment and confided to one of our ladies that he was meeting with some Yankee gunrunners the following day."

Ambrose pricked up his ears. "What ladies?"

"The ladies in the coach house," said the Colonel, craning his neck toward the kitchen.

"This is a whorehouse?" said Ambrose. Sedgewick approached with a wheeled cart draped in linen.

"This is my private residence," said Norwood crossly. "The building at the rear of the property is a whorehouse."

Sedgewick poured dark aromatic tea into china cups. The act, the ritual, seemed to relax Norwood. He placed his pipe in a gnarled wood receptacle designed for the purpose and said, "Though we prefer bordello. Darjeeling anyone? It's fresh off the boat."

Sedgewick served us steaming cups of tea, with cream. Real cream that clotted in the cup.

I took a sip and pondered. Norwood's disclosure explained how he knew of our meet with the Gestapo Captain. It didn't explain how the Soviets knew. Or how he knew they knew. I could hear Ambrose toting up the same sum. It was a question that needed asking, but not yet. I spoke up before Ambrose could queer the pitch. Or tried to.

"Colonel, you suggest that…"

"The Red Army is poised to cross the Elbe? Precisely! The Soviets are about to consolidate control of Poland and Romania and are laying the groundwork for Czechoslovakia. But Germany is the key. If they can seize the industrial heartland of the Ruhr the game is lost. Your President Truman seems not to know this. He gave a party in January to announce the formation of the CIG. Guests were given black cloaks and paper daggers, as if this were all some silly parlor game!"

"Colonel," I replied, preparing to reveal something I wasn't authorized to reveal but figuring if you can't trust a British colonel who had rescued you from certain death and had Churchill's cigar humidor in his cupboard who can you trust? "We are just trying to track down a fugitive."

"You never know what great good can come from a humble act," said Norwood. "The British SOE deposed the truckling Prince Paul of Yugoslavia in March of '41. We installed a Nazi resistance leader, Dusan Simovic, who promptly engaged the Wehrmacht. The results were murderous, 17,000 dead in Belgrade alone. But Simovic tied up Nazi air and armor for five weeks, delayed Hitler's eastern push for five precious weeks." The Colonel looked crossly at his empty tea cup. "And you know what became of that adventure."

Yes I did. German divisions got within ten miles of Moscow before they bogged downed under the assault of the Russian winter.

"So dear boys, pray tell me, I'm keen to know."

"The name of the fugitive we're after is a terrible big secret," said Ambrose. "If that's what you're askin'. And over here, on this side of the table, we might be wonderin' hows come two truckloads of Russian soldiers rolled up right after we did. Sir."

Ambrose's reply was accurate in every detail. That Ambrose said it in an exaggerated Brit-baiting County Cork brogue may have prompted the Colonel to snatch up his pipe and bite down on the stem so hard that the bowl jumped up and made him look, for a moment, like Popeye the Sailor Man.

"Ambrose, apologize to the Colonel for your demeanor."

"I was just…"

"Now."

Ambrose apologized, even managed to sound like he meant it. I turned to Norwood. "We owe you our lives sir, and we are allies in a noble cause. Allies with separate interests however."

The Colonel sat so far back on his silk-draped sofa that it teetered on its hind legs. He set his feet and leaned forward, blue eyes blazing, enjoying my performance. He extended his hand, palm up. The stage was mine.

"How did the Red Army know we were meeting Herr Schultouer?"

"I don't know."

"No idea?"

"I always have an idea," said the Colonel.

"And what would that be?"

"Our circle is a small one. And you had a secret rendezvous with a man who can't keep a secret."

"So the lady who told you about Schultouer meeting Yankee gunrunners also told the Red Army?"

"Absolutely not."

"Who did the telling then?"

"The man was drunk as a bosun's mate, he may have told any number of people, he may have been overheard."

"And that's how you knew to come to our rescue?"

"Call it an educated guess," said the Colonel, coldly.

Ambrose piped up. "Not to seem ungrateful Colonel, but why did you give a hang?"

"I believe I have explained this previously," he said, leaning forward, biting off his words.

Sedgewick crossed to the back door and held it open. We stood up and made for the exit.

"Stop by some evening," called the Colonel over his shoulder, suddenly cheery. "I set the best table in Berlin."

Chapter Fourteen

Ambrose and I returned to the delivery truck and policed up the loose grenades, repacked them in the crate. I backed down the gravel drive and drove back down *Ernststraße*, giving Ambrose the silent treatment. Not that he noticed.

"Helluva setup he's got there. Rolls Royce, snooty butler, and you should see the wine rack in the bedroom. Plus a bleedin' – what'd he call it? – bordello. A bleedin' bordello in the back yard! Man oh man, the feckin' Brit's got it knocked."

"Interesting to hear you say that. Because you didn't show him much respect."

Ambrose waved me off. "That's just part of the routine."

I stopped at the intersection with the main north-south thoroughfare. I turned south, towards Dahlem, with no clear idea how to get from here to there. The CO would be wondering what the hell happened to us. And our cache of weapons.

"What routine?"

"The nip and nack. My brothers and me used to run it. They'd nip, I'd nack."

"Ah. Well. Glad we cleared that up."

"Don't be a dope, you know what I mean."

I crawled down the thoroughfare. The sidewalk in this block was buried in rubble. We shared the road with one-legged men on crutches and old women pulling two-wheeled grocery carts. I did know what Ambrose meant. Cops and crooks do it all the time. The brash rookie grabs the suspect by the lapels, the grizzled vet calls him off. How I got stuck being the grizzled vet at the tender age of 25 I couldn't tell you.

"I wonder what those tickets were for?" said Ambrose. "The ones the Colonel gave out to the Russians."

I jammed the brake pedal to the floor in front of a bone skinny old man who had either lost his balance or was attempting suicide. The truck smoked to a stop just a foot shy of his prostrate figure. A passerby hauled him to his feet.

I turned to Ambrose and poked my right index finger in and out of the hole in my left fist.

"You think?" said Ambrose with a grin.

"Yeah," I said. "I think."

Ambrose's wide-eyed leer made his words redundant. "We need to get us a couple of those tickets."

I agreed with him. We drove south down the thoroughfare, two young men with sap in their veins and lead in their pencils, buzzed with the exhilaration that only dodging a fatal bullet can bring. I felt great for about five seconds. Then I remembered what we were hauling in the bed of the truck.

"Uncrate that Browning AR and jack in a magazine."

Ambrose climbed into the back of the truck without comment or question. I checked the mirrors and settled in for a long nervous drive.

The CO ticked off our failures on long blunt fingers. "Your cover is blown, you failed to do a deal with the Gestapo Captain, and you told the head of a rival agency that we're hunting Klaus Hilde."

Ambrose and I were standing in front of Victor Jacobson's desk in his windowless office at the white brick mansion in Dahlem. In back of the mansion actually. The garage. The long drive south had been uneventful. The delivery truck and its load of weapons was now parked in the driveway, secured by a single chain across the entrance. Henka, the foul-tempered Polish cook, would doubtless beat back any approaching teams of Soviet sappers with her soup ladle.

"We never identified the fugitive sir."

"Norwood will figure it out."

"Could be, but we didn't tell him. I told the Colonel that we were pursuing a fugitive as a professional courtesy, seeing as how he risked his neck to save us." That no one on our side was capable of doing likewise I left unsaid.

That was the crux of it. The Brits might be 'defeated by victory' but their MI6 put our OSS and CIG to shame. Always had. We were the country cousins come to the big city to see how it's done. That the Berlin Bureau Chief of MI6 had to rescue Victor Jacobson's raggedy-ass operatives was the reason the CO was clutching a pencil so hard his fist got white.

"Klaus Hilde is still at large, intelligence from our émigré informants is next to nothing. I don't..." Jacobson stopped and pinched the bridge of his nose. The walls squeezed in. The CO heaved a sigh. "You got any ideas?"

Only one thought occurred. One the CO wouldn't much like. "Well, if Colonel Norwood knows we're chasing Herr Hilde, why not join forces with him in pursuit?"

Jacobson paused to consider, then pressed an intercom button on his desk. "My office" is what he said.

Ambrose and I stood there like schoolboys called on the carpet while Jacobson made notes on a legal pad. Leonid appeared a short minute later, magically, in a puff of smoke. He stood to the side of the CO's desk and looked, blank-faced, at a garage wall that wasn't worth looking at unless you fancied plasterboard with hairline cracks in it.

The CO told him the story of our misadventure, concluding with the possibility of joining forces with Col. Norwood and MI6 to hunt Hilde. The way he said it made it sound like his idea, not mine.

Leonid shook his pretty little head. "Too vulnerable."

"How so?" said Jacobson.

"John Norwood is a decorated veteran of The Great War, a Cambridge graduate who speaks five languages, a casual acquaintance of Winston Churchill and is married to a noblewoman who has an estate in Norwich."

He stopped. We waited.

"He is also a flagrant homosexual."

No one said a word. The walls that had squeezed in seemed to back away. A homosexual. I guess I shouldn't have been slack-jawed with surprise at this revelation. But I was.

Chapter Fifteen

Ambrose and I unloaded the cache of weapons from the truck to the garage and drove home to our four story building near Heidelberg Platz. There were lights in the windows. Electric lights. It was a sight for sore eyes because the afternoon was gray and bleak and us with it.

The CO and Leonid had kicked around some half-hearted plans to get a line on Hilde. Send us into the DP camps, Stars and Stripes reporters doing a feature on the hard life of a displaced person. Or we could meet with our liaison to the émigré network, code named MANTIS, provided he wasn't dead. The CO finally shooed us off, saying only that he would be in touch.

We were not a group brimming with confidence and ready for action. The gung ho, Wild Bill, try anything attitude was breaking down.

Not on my watch it wasn't. I don't like queers any more than the next guy. Not sure I'd ever met one before, come to think. But it didn't matter what Col. Norwood was, MI6 trusted him. And he was playing the game at a higher level than we were.

During the war Allen Dulles, Bill Donovan's right hand man, had turned Bern Station into what the hoity toites call a salon. Though I spent some r&r time in Switzerland during my OSS service I was not invited to his posh digs staffed with servants and a Parisian chef. Plus a wine cellar that rivaled the Vatican's. I was low scrotum on the totem, what they call an 'observer agent.' Dulles wasn't interested in me. He was busy courting 'agents in place,' German officials and the like.

Word was Dulles did some good in his Bern salon. Looked like Col. Norwood had a poorer, craftier version here. The bordello in back was a stroke of genius.

I reported to Jacobson but I served at the pleasure of Wild Bill, who was six thousand miles away and busier than a one-armed paperhanger. It was a dumbass way to run an organization but it had its advantages. So long as I got results I could do as I damn well pleased. We were going to pay another visit to Col. Norwoood.

"Don't answer that," said Ambrose.

"Huh?"

"The knock at the door. Don't answer it."

I got up anyway. We were shivering on the musty couch in the parlor. The room had a radiator that clanked out heat at regular intervals – once every 24 hours. I intended to answer the door. If you don't answer a door how do you know what's on the other side of it? But I'm not a complete idiot. I said, "Who's there?" in a loud voice and put my hand in my gun pocket.

No answer. The knocking resumed. Pecking really. Tap tap tap tap tap. I fisted my Walther and yanked open the warped door with an angry "What?!"

A bald ten-year-old boy looked up at me with big brown eyes. I checked the hall behind him and put up my gun. Ambrose ankled over to see what was what. The kid stood there and looked grimy, looked familiar.

I took a buck from my billfold and told him to scram. He took it and didn't.

"*Unser Topf. Der gross eine.*"

He wanted his family's cooking pot. The big one. He was the son in the left-behind family photo that hung in the kitchen. I left Ambrose to watch him at the door and fetched the pot. The kid asked for the lid also. Ambrose chased him down the hall. When he returned Ambrose wagged a finger at me. "He'll be back."

"Why did they shave his skull?"

"You don't know much about bein' poor, do ya?"

I grew up in a row house in Youngstown, Ohio. Mom and Pop and Beth and me. One bathroom, two bedrooms, a kitchen and a parlor. My old man ran a corner candy store six days a week. But we had a two-door Ford, a big Philco radio and food on the table every night so, no, I didn't know much about being poor.

"Head lice," said Ambrose. "We planning on doin' anything anytime soon?"

"Yes we are."

"You gonna tell me or do I hafta beg?"

"Nothing wrong with begging, Ambrose. Many of the holiest saints in heaven..."

"Spill it, Schroeder, or I'll wipe the floor with ya."

"You and what army?"

We eyed one another. Was a time I could have put the headstrong Mick's nose in the dirt in five seconds flat. It would be a much longer fight now. I grinned, glad he was on my team.

"I propose that we return to Colonel Norwood's compound. This very evening. I suggest that you..."

But Ambrose was already in the bathroom, washing up.

The chalet on *Ernststraße* was necklaced with red and yellow Chinese lanterns, expensive automobiles were parked in the driveway and along the curb. We had to park the delivery truck a block away and walk back in a drizzling rain, slipping on wet bricks and gathering our courage to crash the party. Mine anyway. Ambrose was fully gathered.

"Seems an odd way to go but maybe it makes sense," he said. "He can stand back from it all. Like a priest tellin' married folks how to get along."

"What in the name of God are you talking about?"

"A fairy put in charge of a whorehouse."

I laughed. "You're just jealous."

"You're right. We got a plan?"

"I brought a photo of Klaus Hilde. When the time's right I'll show it to Norwood and say here's our fugitive."

"And if Norwood says 'That's Hilde' we know he's already on the case."

"Something like that."

We stopped at the foot of the driveway and looked at the Chinese lanterns and listened to the muffled music and bawdy laughter spilling from the second floor.

"Shouldda brought a bottle of something," said Ambrose. "If you don't bring a gift to a poof party the Colonel might figure you're it."

"Figure I'm what?"

"The gift," said Ambrose. "Me, I'm making a beeline for the back building, with your say so. I won't be any help up there."

He was right. Ambrose would clock the first guy who got close, queer or no. I told him to go to the brothel before he blew a gasket and I'd catch up later. I watched him hurry off, enviously. Being a responsible duty-bound adult ain't no way to live.

I walked to the front door of the chalet and pulled the bell knocker. The first floor windows were dark. I heard heavy footsteps on a creaky staircase as I shivered in my sports coat. If I didn't get a new topcoat soon I would croak from pneumonia. The front door opened in a blast of heat, noise and light. Sedgewick, in a black suit, boiled shirt and bowtie, eyed me without apparent recognition.

"Hal Schroeder here to see Colonel Norwood."

Sedgewick nodded and started to climb the steep staircase. I stayed put, wishing I had a snazzy card with my name on it. That's the way they did it in those drawing room movies. The butler answers the door and you put your card on his silver tray.

Sedgewick stopped halfway up the stairs, turned and beckoned with his arm.

"Please. The Colonel is expecting you."

Chapter Sixteen

"Come in dear boy, I was hoping you'd stop by," said Col. Norwood as I made my way across his crowded parlor. He wore a Hawaiian shirt, white duck trousers and canvas deck shoes and held a drink with a little umbrella in it. "We chanced upon a pineapple so we thought we'd go tiki this evening. Mai tai?"

"Sure."

The Colonel instructed Sedgewick to fetch me a drink, smiled broadly and lowered his voice. "What name, what job?"

"Hal is fine. Reporter for Stars and Stripes." Norwood shook his head. I saw why. One of the newshounds we hosted in Dahlem was stuffing his face at the banquet table. "Just say I'm a salesman."

The Colonel took me by the arm and introduced me around the room. There looked to be four distinct groups. Handsome lads in sweaters and saddle shoes, fierce bespectacled men with food in their beards, quiet thin-lipped men in cheap suits and loud men wearing gold tie bars, matching cufflinks and spit-shined brogans. Homosexuals, academics, government functionaries and black market profiteers'd be my guess. There wasn't a female to be seen.

Col. Norwood dragged me into a circle of the bearded gents, who were busy spewing spittle at one another. He listened a moment and said, to the accompaniment of Hawaiian guitar music on the Victrola, "I disagree. What we are trying to do here has never been done in human history. Not even Paris, 1814, was a successful joint operation by a coalition of victors."

I wasn't sure what happened in Paris in 1814 but I put in my two cents. "And from what I hear, we're unprepared. Just like December 6 of '41."

"Act-tu-ally," said the Colonel through a cloud of pipe smoke, "it's more like June, 1919. Germany lays in tatters, the Big Four dither at Versailles and the Bolsheviki swarm at the castle gates!"

This remark stirred fierce debate amongst the group of bearded men. Col. Norwood dragged me along to the next circle of conversation. I told him we needed to talk but he seemed not to hear. Cripes. If I was going to be the his prom date the least he could do was get me a corsage.

The animated conversation of the group of handsome lads subsided as the Colonel and I approached. I felt myself appraised from head to toe. The nods and elbow pokes said I passed muster. I took a certain satisfaction. How sick is that?

The Colonel surveyed their appetizer plates. "Three chunks of pineapple? Wesley, you glutton."

Laughs all around.

"We were reminiscing about the bad old days," said a young man who wasn't Wesley. "1937. Jurgen Fehling's famous production of Richard III."

"Ah yes, I have heard tell. The empty, cavernous stage mirroring Speer's anti-humanist architecture, the crippled Goebbels come to life as Richard of Gloucester, hobbling across the stage."

Norwood hunched over and stumped up and back, arms flailing.

"Why I, in this weak piping time of peace

Have no delight to pass away the time

Unless to spy my shadow in the sun

And descant on mine own deformity!"

The handsome lads found this terribly amusing. My timing was poor. The Colonel was already looking around for a new circle to conquer. I wasn't going to get him alone to display my Hilde photo. Not now.

I considered taking my fat billfold and my Hilde photo to the bordello in back. Who knows more about the netherworld than ladies of the night?

I know what you're thinking. Not true. I wasn't really envious of Ambrose. I'd had my fill of ladies of negotiable virtue. The big-eyed gals who'd approached me at Otto Moser's after I got my mug on the front page weren't much different than the working girls in the doorways of wartime Antwerp and Zurich and Mannheim. Worse in a way. They weren't starving.

When the Colonel went off to fill his pipe I slipped out the door to the back stairs.

The two-story building in back was sheltered by a stand of poplars. It faced the street north of *Ernststraße* and was well lit behind lacy curtains. A canopy-covered side door looked to be the main entrance. I put four crisp tens in my pants pocket, made the acquaintance of the door and invited myself in.

I entered a big wide open room supported by 4x4's where the walls had been removed. An empty bar to the left and table booths along the wall. Seated in the booths were older men in horsehair suits and silk cravats nuzzling florid buxom women who laughed, tittered and giggled on cue.

There was a staircase in the middle of the room and cocktail tables and a piano to the right.

Well, there's something you don't see every day. The piano player had only one hand. I watched his right mitt fly across the high keys and his feet pump the pedals as he bent down low to let his elbow stump pound out bass beats on the lower 88's. Man oh man!

"Who are you?" demanded a short stout woman in a low cut dress. She had an enormous bosom that defied gravity with the help of an undergarment that could only have been designed by the Army Corps of Engineers.

"I'm Hal. I'm a salesman."

She looked me over and sniffed. A sniff that said we are an exclusive establishment and you are tieless. I wasn't sure how snooty a whorehouse with a one-armed piano player could be but a thought occurred. A trick I learned in grammar school. It worked with construction paper, why not snaps?

I retrieved a crisp sawbuck from my pocket. The woman gave me a look indicating that if I attempted to insert the bill into her ample cleavage she would slap my face off. I retrieved another ten and folded it lengthways, and again. Then I took the narrower bill and knotted it around the middle of the wider bill. I tucked the thing inside my shirt collar.

"There. Any better?"

My twenty dollar bowtie did the trick. Madam bouncer giggled and took my hand. "I am Sofie. Sad to say all the girls are busy for the moment."

"That's oke by me. You're the one I want to talk to."

"To sell me what, Mister Hal the salesman?"

"I'm not selling tonight, Sofie my sweet, I'm buying."

"You are funny person."

"No argument there."

I handed her my bowtie and asked for a moment of her time, in private. She grabbed a bottle and two glasses off the bar and led me to a booth in the far left corner. I took the glass of Drambuie she passed me and took a sniff. It smelled like lighter fluid. Sofie downed hers like a dose of ipecac. I dug out the photo of Klaus Hilde and handed it over.

"I do not know this man."

"I gave you twenty dollars Sophie. Look again."

Sophie held up the photograph, closed one eye. "I do not know him," she said at last. "You must be talking to Eva. She knows everyone."

"Where do I find her?"

"She is upstairs. She is upstairs with your Yankee friend."

Sophie got up to answer the doorbell. How she knew Ambrose was my friend she didn't say. Funny she had pegged him for American despite his Irish brogue. What was it about us Yanks?

Two loud burly men stumbled in the front door, shaking snowflakes from their overcoats. Snow. In mid-May.

I bit my drink and winced. Lighter fluid, with sugar added. I thought about Col. Norwood. There had been rumors about queers in the OSS. It made sense when you thought about it. Who's better at leading a double life than a homosexual?

Which led me to a dark thought. Jimmy Streets, The Schooler's resident armbreaker, had baited an assault on me by the Mooney brothers. Jimmy's staged rescue was meant to win my undying trust and gratitude. Col. Norwood's rescue smelled likewise. Why else would two truckloads of Red Army troops turn tail for a bunch of tickets to a whorehouse? All right, the 300 Spartans at Thermopylae would have dropped their spears at the same offer. But why would the Soviet *Commander* agree to release two American gunrunners unless he had an arrangement with Col. Norwood?

Come to that how did the Soviet Commander know we were going to be at that loading dock at 10 a.m.? Col. Norwood said that Horst Schultouer's lubricated tongue meant anyone might have known. True enough. Anyone might. And most anyone wouldn't care. Our set up and rescue was an inside job engineered by Col. Norwood to win our undying loyalty and gratitude.

Wasn't it? Norwood wanted a source inside Global Commerce, he wanted a conduit to Bill Donovan. And he wanted to know what fugitive we were pursuing. Yet when I returned to his salon, ready to reveal the name, the Colonel couldn't be bothered.

I watched Sofie charm the loud men in a language I didn't recognize. I listened to the piano player bang out a very percussive version of "Our Love is Here to Stay." I felt seven kinds of stupid.

Chapter Seventeen

I was starting to feel sorry for myself, sitting alone in a brothel with a glass of lighter fluid and a head full of *huh*, when Ambrose and a young lady tripped down the staircase together, looking like they just stepped out of an Andy Hardy picture. She was a pretty young thing, strawberry blond with rosy cheeks and a lush figure. Ambrose took her hand and pulled her in my direction. I stood up from my table booth.

"This is Eva," said Ambrose, flushed and out-of-breath. "She has something she'd like to tell you."

"I'm all ears."

Eva wasn't quite a dewy young milkmaid on closer inspection. The rose in her cheeks was pancake rouge and she had hard-stamped wrinkles around her eyes. Ambrose nudged her forward. We made eye contact. I felt a flush of embarrassment. Her blue-green peepers seemed to look right through me.

"I have visit your Klaus Hilde," she said in a thick German accent. "I can take you to him when I'm done work."

"You're serious?"

Eva smiled most fetchingly. "I am very serious girl."

She was that. I showed her the photo of Herr Hilde.

"That is him, yes. But he has big beard now." Eva rubbed her cheek. "Scratchy."

I didn't know what to say to that. I didn't know what to say period. This was all too good to be true. A tell-the-rich-Yanks-what-they-want-to-hear con job maybe.

"He wants to know how you're sure Hilde is Hilde," said Ambrose, "since he wouldn't be using his real name."

Eva listened to Ambrose intently then turned to me. "I knew Herr Hilde from the wartime. When he was big man, General. He was my customer."

"And you recognized him after all this time?"

Eva held up both hands. "This was wrong to do?"

"No, no. I just wondered how you, well, no offense Eva but I imagine you've had a lot of customers and…"

"I am remember because Herr Hilde did not wanting to having sex. Not at first."

"What did he want?"

Eva mimed holding a baby to her breast.

"He wanted to suckle?"

Eva nodded. "And to sing baby songs to him."

"Baby songs?"

Eva sang a little lullaby.

"*Schlaf, Kindchen, schlaf / Ich gebe Dir ein Schaf / Und es soll eine Glocke aus Gold haben / Für Dich zum Spielen und zu halten / Schlaf, Kindchen, schlaf.*" Sleep, baby, sleep / I'll give to you a sheep / And it shall have a bell of gold / For you to play with and to hold / Sleep, baby, sleep.

Good Lord.

Ambrose waved his hand in front of my face. "Hey Chief, this is good news. Let's do something about it!"

"Right you are," I said with more enthusiasm than I felt. I gave Ambrose twenty bucks. "Go find Sofie and tell her Eva is done for the night."

They scampered off together. I chewed on what was eating me.

Good news. Col. Norwood's bordello was a bottomless font of good news. A basted Gestapo Captain runs his mouth about Yankee gunrunners, the Colonel rescues them from a fate worse than death the following morning, Ambrose Mooney visits the bordello later that day, is led upstairs and trips down an hour later with more good tidings. What luck!

Ambrose and Eva reported back. Eva was cleared for takeoff. I got up and dropped a pack of Luckies into the one-handed piano player's overturned hat. He grunted his thanks. The tune he was pounding out was "Too Marvelous for Words".

Yes it was.

We left by the side door, walked under the poplar trees, passed beneath the windows of Col. Norwood's noisy salon, crunched down the gravel drive and piled into the delivery truck on *Ernststraße*.

I took the wheel, Eva took Ambrose's lap, grabbing and giggling. I didn't get it. In my experience prostitutes will do just about anything but show affection.

"Where are we going?" I said to Eva.

"I don't remember street name but I know the house."

"What part of town?"

"Dahlem."

"That's the American Sector Eva."

"Yet he is there!"

I hung a U in the driveway of a boarded-up bungalow and drove west down the brick street in a cloud of fat snowflakes.

The villa was sealed off by a head-high brick wall. It was a four-chimney job with a grape arbor in front, a steep four-cornered orange tile roof snugged down like a rain hat and a small front balcony suitable for torch lit speeches. The villa wasn't two miles from the CO's residence, not to mention the Berlin Operating Base. Herr Hilde was hiding in plain sight.

The upstairs was lit. We watched for signs of life.

"Did Hilde have bodyguards when you visited?"

"Two men I saw," said Eva. "Very drunk."

"They carry guns?"

Eva screwed up her face in concentration. "I don't see them. Guns."

"What about Hilde? Did he carry a gun?"

"No. No gun."

I watched the upstairs some more, saw the brief silhouette of a male figure pass by an upstairs window as Eva and Ambrose nuzzled in the seat beside me.

"Eva when you visited Hilde here did he, uh, have a satisfactory experience?"

She had a very expressive face, Eva. At the moment it said she had no idea what I meant. I tried again. "You said he didn't want to have sex at first. Did you have sex later, and did he like it?"

Eva's face said I was a very naughty boy to ask such a question.

"Sorry, I need to know."

"Y-es. I think so."

"Was there an intercom at the front door? A radio, so you could call inside?"

"Radio. Yes I think so."

"Good."

"What are you cooking up over there?" said Ambrose. "Using Eva as a Trojan Horse?"

"Not to send her in. Just to get the drawbridge lowered."

Eva followed this exchange with narrowed eyes. "Speak English!"

It was a funny thing to say, we should have laughed. But Ambrose was cheesed off that I was putting his lady love in harm's way and I was cheesed off because Ambrose had broken the cardinal rule. They dress it up with fancy phrases like 'fraternization with civilian assets' but my instructor at spy school said it plainly. Poozle makes you stoopid.

"Eva I would like you to do me a favor," I said. "I would like you to go to the front door and press the button and say that you would like to speak to Klaus Hilde, or whatever name he used with you. Tell him you have to see him. Tell him you have never had a man like him."

"I think he will not believe this."

"Sure he will. Not a man alive that wouldn't."

Eva giggled. Ambrose glowered. I parked the truck down the block. We walked back to the front door.

I gave Ambrose my handkerchief. "Stuff it in his mouth after we grab him."

"What if he's got his gun out."

He would ask that. We couldn't shoot Germany's leading expert on the Soviet military no matter what. "He won't."

"What if he does?"

Poozle wasn't making Ambrose stoopid, it was making him cautious. And a cautious Ambrose was no good to me. He was worried that Hilde would shoot Eva in the moment after he poked his head out the door and we jumped out to dogpile him. I didn't want the charming Miss Eva to get plugged of course. But I wanted Brigadeführer Hilde more.

What can I tell you, it's a rotten business.

I was racking my melon for a quick fix when Eva said, "If he has gun I will say for him to put away. And he will do as I say." She said it with a great deal of confidence.

And that's the way the cookie crumbled.

Chapter Eighteen

We drove down the block with a bearded man in the bed of the delivery truck, bound and gagged with my belt and handkerchief. Another adventure in ad hoc espionage.

I needed to conduct an in-truck interrogation of our kidnap victim before we pulled up to the white brick mansion. Our snatch was unauthorized, and we had only Eva's word to guarantee that Klaus Hilde was Klaus Hilde. It wasn't that I didn't trust Eva – I didn't but it wasn't that. It's that all this good news was giving me a rash. The bearded man resembled the old photo of Hilde. Same long oval face, same oversized ears. But his eyes and nose were different. Plastic surgery. Or a look-alike impostor.

I turned south on *Koniginstraße* and dragged the delivery truck down the boulevard like a bucket of chum. Eva sat in the passenger's seat and Ambrose kept watch on our guest in the back. I checked the side view mirrors. I turned down a dead end lane. No one followed. I parked the truck and told Ambrose to remove the gag.

The bearded man took a huge draught of air, coughed, took another. I climbed into the back. I explained that we were American agents and apologized for the rough treatment.

"Where have you been?" he demanded in perfect English. "I have sent couriers to your headquarters, to your General Clay. They were turned away."

This squared with what the CO had told me about Hilde reaching out. I told him we didn't work for General Clay.

"Who then?"

"General William Donovan."

The bearded man hiked his eyebrows. I asked him his name.

"Klaus Hilde, as you know."

"Who was your intermediary in Karlsruhe?"

"He called himself Günter. He was to arrange my transport to Toulon, where I would catch a steamer to Lisbon. I was to hide in a manure truck!" The bearded man shook his head at the indignity of it all. "The NKVD had seen me even if your field agents did not. They were tracking me. When Günter contacted your operative it forced their hand. I was caught and captured."

I didn't bother explaining that the US didn't have any field agents. Too embarrassing. I didn't mention that I was the operative for the same reason.

"You were caught and captured and installed in a fancy villa."

Hilde shrugged. "I negotiated."

"If you wanted to reach out to us why didn't you? You were living in the American Sector."

"I was under guard. And they promised money for my family," said Hilde. "I was not a true believer. Hitler was a fool, I knew he would be defeated. It is why I kept my files."

He told a good story. But my neck itched. High value asset Klaus Hilde had got himself got awful easy. I pondered. An NKVD impostor would've been briefed about Karlsruhe. But he wouldn't know the details.

"Günter had something he wore that he was proud of. What was it?"

"I don't understand."

"Think about it."

The man stretched his spine, trying to get comfortable. I looked up. Ambrose and Eva were back at it in the passenger's seat. Christ.

"A medal," said the bearded man after a time. "A bronze infantryman's medal."

We had our boy. I climbed back into the driver's seat and swatted the two-headed hydra to my right. Ambrose returned to guard duty in the truck bed, Eva pulled down her skirt. I scratched my itchy neck and fired up the truck, thinking about one of my spy school instructor's pithy proverbs.

One coincidence is just that. Two are suspicious. And three are a conspiracy.

Col. Norwood had rung up two. His happy rescue of Ambrose and me. And the prostitute in his employ who just happened to know Herr Hilde's address. If Norwood operated a brothel to gather intel the first thing he would have asked his ladies was, 'Anyone have a line on Klaus Hilde?'

I drove back down the dead end lane and turned south on *Koniginstraße*. The Colonel said the Brits were sadly dependent on us cheeky Yanks. Could be Hilde was a gift to win us over, but Leonid said 'valuable information should be sliced thin and served sparingly.' Klaus Hilde was a full plate, with a side of hash browns. Hard to believe that Col. Norwood would be that generous.

"Pick up the pace, will ya?" said Ambrose from the back of the truck.

I looked at the speedometer. We were doing a respectable thirty. Kilometers per hour. I punched the gas pedal. The great beast gasped and gurgled and snapped my neck back.

Light snow drifted against the curb. I fished around for my string of thought. Oh yeah. What the hell was I going to tell the CO? We were shooting the breeze at the apartment when Herr Hilde stumbled by?

I turned right and drove past the white brick mansion at a good clip. The chain in the driveway was down. I took four right turns and approached again. No one cared. I pulled the truck into the driveway and had a talk with myself. Relax, Schroeder. You're just doing your job. If you get canned you can go back to Cleveland, and defrost.

I told Eva to remain in the truck, told Ambrose to cinch up the prisoner from behind.

The CO's face was a riot of conflicting emotions when we marched Herr Hilde through the front door. Anger at my insubordination, doubt that Hilde was the genuine article and barely suppressed eagerness to brace him and find out. He told Ambrose to take Hilde to the kitchen.

I gave Jacobson the full report, told him I had authenticated Hilde's ID, told him where Hilde was billeted, even told him how I came to find out, and braced myself for an ass chewing that didn't come. The CO had more pressing concerns.

We pushed through the swinging door to the kitchen and came upon an odd scene. Hilde was supine on the white tile floor, looking pained. Ambrose stood above him, pushing back on Hilde's raised right leg.

"Our Nazi pal's got back trouble," said Ambrose by way of explanation. "I'm showing him how to get the kinks out."

Ambrose lowered the right leg and started in on Hilde's left. The CO looked down upon the sweating and grimacing former *Abwehr* General. The OSS had used a number of creative interrogation techniques during the war but this had to be a first.

"Why are you still in Germany?" said Jacobson.

"I sent my family to Buenos Aires in '45. As you know."

"Answer the question."

Ambrose pushed back on Hilde's leg, hard. Hilde tried to roll over but the CO stepped on his hand. Hilde groaned, and talked in quick bursts.

"I had documents...Too many to transport...I reached out to you...I hid until my money was very small...I fled."

"And what of all the White Russian agents that have died and disappeared since your capture, agents you worked with before war's end? Know anything about them?"

Ambrose pushed harder. Hilde shuddered and squirmed.

"I do not...My hosts never asked about them."

"Why?"

"I can only speculate."

"Do so," said Leonid in his velvety baritone. Where the hell had he come from?

Jacobson removed his foot and told Ambrose to help Hilde up. Hilde dusted himself off and struggled to reclaim his dignity. He answered Leonid in clipped tones.

"Your White Russian agents are, after all, *Russian*. The Blue Caps know their identities. What they would want to know is their whereabouts at this time."

"You had been in hiding and have no current information on their whereabouts," said Leonid. "Is that your position?"

"It is not a position. It is the truth."

The CO popped the question. "Where is your cache of documents now?"

"The Blue Caps have them." Hilde tapped his head. "But I have a good memory."

"If the Russians have them why are you still alive?"

"There are certain matters of interest that I did not commit to paper."

"Such as?"

"Who gave me which document, and why."

"We have a more immediate concern," said Jacobson.

"I understand," said Hilde.

"What can you tell me?"

"I will need a chair," said Hilde, imperiously.

Ambrose dragged one over from the kitchen table. Hilde seated himself, stretched out his legs, straightened his trouser seams and rattled off all kinds of stuff. Stuff about Soviet military capabilities and orders of battle. He even claimed the Red Army had a well worked out plan for the seizure of all Germania, Operation LUNA, a plan they had been developing since late '44. He promised more details in return for an accommodation for himself and his family.

I stopped listening before he was done. This was all very important shit, but I was thinking about other things. Such as why Klaus Hilde was so easy to nab and so free with the very important shit.

It smelled. That Hilde said what we wanted to hear – Operation LUNA – made it smellier. A steaming pile of disinformation bought and paid for by the NKVD. Had to be.

And Col. Norwood? Well, there had been a lot of noise about Commies in MI6 but it was hard to figure. Norwood was an effete aristocrat with a degenerate lifestyle, a very unlikely Marxist. Of course in espionage to *seem* unlikely is entirely the point.

I asked a question when Hilde was done. "What happened to your guards?"

"I gave them a bottle when the young lady came to call."

"That's all it took to make them go away? A bottle?"

Hilde eyeballed Leonid with a leer. "They are, after all, Russian."

How Hilde knew Leonid was Russian I couldn't say. The little man's accent wouldn't raise an eyebrow in Omaha. But Hilde knew.

Leonid crossed to the kitchen sink and got himself a glass of water. He turned to face us and said, mildly, "There is a way to determine if Mr. Hilde is telling us the truth. A very simple way. If the extermination of our émigré agents ceases while he is in our custody we will have our answer."

Herr Hilde's smug leer lost altitude.

So. Here we were again. At the starting line, feet in the chocks, legs cocked. Ready. Set. Wait.

Chapter Nineteen

"We have to act as if everything Klaus Hilde told us is true," said Victor Jacobson to Ambrose and me.

We were seated in the parlor of the white brick mansion enjoying snifters of cognac and a roaring fire. Herr Hilde was cuffed to a bedpost upstairs, Leonid had gone home and poor Eva was still waiting in the truck.

Jacobson continued. "We can't wait to see if Hilde's the one fingering our White Russians, not after what he said about Operation LUNA."

"So what do we *do*?" said Ambrose.

The CO addressed himself to me. "Contact the leader of our network, code name MANTIS. We have a twice weekly blind drop, next one tomorrow, 1100 hours. If he's still alive he'll collect this note, instructing him to meet you at the *Lustgarten* at noon."

The CO handed me the sealed note along with a diagram of where to place it. A loose flagstone behind a bench in the City Hall plaza. He gave us an ask and answer code.

"What do we want to know?"

"Damage assessment, what is left of the network. Any new thoughts on the identity of the snitch. And any signs of mobilization by the Red Army. Anything at all."

"What about this Hilde fella?" said Ambrose. "We know anything about him?"

"No," said the CO and stood up.

Ambrose and I gulped our brandies. Jacobson escorted us to the door. I considered confiding my suspicions about Col. Norwood to the CO but I didn't have anything nailed down. Besides, the door was already closed behind us.

Ambrose and I drove to the *Rathaus* the next morning. The snow had turned to slush and a daylight moon followed us down the street. Must have been earlier than I figured. We needed to get a damn clock.

I parked a block away and we walked back to the City Hall. Yes, *Rathaus* is German for City Hall, *Fahrt* means journey and a *Schmuck Galerie* is a jewelry store. What can I tell you, it's a goofy language.

We hunted up the loose flagstone behind the park bench, I slipped the note underneath when no one was watching. Ambrose asked what we were doing here.

"We're here to contact MANTIS."

"You sure about that Chief?"

"What do you mean?"

"Well, did the old man chew you out? For going after Hilde without his OK?"

"He never mentioned it."

"Why?"

"Because we tossed him the most sought after fugitive in Europe'd be my guess."

"And one upped him pretty good. I don't know much, but I know that big shots don't like getting shown up by little shits like us."

"And you're thinking that Jacobson set us up here?"

"You're the spy Schroeder," said Ambrose, gesturing at the *Rathaus* plaza crowded with pedestrians and bicyclists. "This look right to you?"

I assured the goddamn bright-eyed Mick that Victor Jacobson would never sell us out. He took my word for it. But he was right about one thing.

A dead drop is supposed to take place in an out-of-the-way place where it can be deposited and retrieved in secret. A brush drop, where both parties know the appointed time and place, is usually conducted in a public place so both parties can enjoy the relative security of a crowd. The CO needed a spy school refresher course. This was a dead drop in a very public place.

The *Lustgarten* sat in the shadow of the blackened Berlin Cathedral. It was more of a parade ground than a park but it did have benches. A bell tower tolled the noon hour. We waited. And, no, *Lust* isn't lust. It's joy, delight. Same diff, Ambrose would say.

I was beginning to think MANTIS was another casualty of the NKVD when he strode purposefully towards our appointed bench. It was our guy, had to be. Broad shoulders above a gaunt frame, wild haunted eyes, long gray hair spilling down a long dark cloak, a bright purple scar on his forehead. A deposed count, or a cavalry officer sporting an old saber wound. He was as hard to miss as a house fire.

"That him?" whispered Ambrose.

"I dunno."

The man blew by us without a look. Our instructions were to wait until contacted. We waited. An old man with a black watch cap pulled down over his ears sat down on the bench a couple minutes later and crossed his legs.

"Would you know the time of day?" he said in an asthmatic wheeze.

"My wristwatch was stolen in Dusseldorf."

MANTIS stood up. "Let's walk."

He was a nimble old gent, poling himself along the parade ground on his cane. Ambrose and I had to lengthen our strides to keep pace. He answered my questions before I asked them.

"Our network is a ruin…Those still alive have fled west…or burrowed deep…I cannot say and do not know…the identity of our traitor…It matters little…I am all that remains."

He stopped and gulped air and gave us a dour look with rheumy eyes. I felt oafish, a well-fed American who doesn't know how good he's got it.

"The tree of freedom…is watered by the blood of martyrs," croaked the old man bitterly, reciting the popular Communist slogan. He poled on. We followed.

"You will want battle plans…something is afoot." We covered ten yards before I realized he was waiting for the question.

"How do you know?" We covered another ten yards before he answered.

"My military sources…were the first to die."

"Do you know the plans? Is the Red Army mobilizing?"

The old man shook his head and spat.

"No, they're not mobilizing? Or, no, you don't know?"

"I don't…" He stopped and leaned on his cane. "One question at a time!"

His cane slipped on the wet cement. Ambrose grabbed his elbow and held him up. MANTIS shook him off and stood erect.

"I have told you all I know." He turned around and started back the way we came. We followed.

"What will you do now sir?" said Ambrose.

"I will do…what I do…Search the camps for recruits."

"Is that difficult?"

"The new arrivals are farmers…conscripts…shopkeepers who lost all…They make poor spies…Still," he said, whistled, wheezed, "they harbor much hatred for the dam-ned Georgians."

We walked on in silence. The *Lustgarten* was almost empty. Had this been a downtown park in an American city the benches would have been crowded with old folks tossing bread crumbs to pigeons. But breadcrumbs were a valuable commodity in post-war Berlin. So were pigeons, come to think.

We returned to our initial contact point and sat down. The old man lit a Chesterfield, smoked it halfway down in two drags and coughed for the better part of a minute. He said he needed some money.

The CO hadn't said anything about a payment but the MANTIS looked like he could use a little extra. I slid my wallet across the bench. He could take what he needed.

The old man plucked out one bill with bony fingers and smoothed it on his knee. "President Jackson...Stonewall Jackson...This is correct?"

"Yes sir," said Ambrose.

The old man tucked the bill into his coat cuff and nodded. "You need such a President again."

And with that he was gone, poling himself across the wet parade ground in the shadow of the smoke-blackened cathedral.

"Georgians," said Ambrose with a furrowed look. "Why would they hate Georgians?"

"Its not our Georgia, *Dummkopf*, it's their Georgia. Part of Russia."

"Which part?"

"The part that Stalin and Beria are from."

We watched the old man's progress. His stride was more labored now. He kept his head down, as if he no longer cared if he was under surveillance. Or knew the NKVD no longer cared about him. The CO had summed it up succinctly, at our meeting in the *Bierstube*, when I asked him why he didn't think the CIG had been penetrated by the Soviets.

Why bother?

Chapter Twenty

Ambrose and I returned to the white brick mansion in Dahlem, met the CO in his cold damp garage and gave him our report. The émigré network no longer functioned, MANTIS didn't know who the rat was and something was up with the Red Army, exactly what he couldn't say.

Victor Jacobson digested our laundry list of bad tidings while sitting motionless at his desk. "They're *all* gone?"

I nodded.

"Which means we have no check on Hilde."

"How do you figure?"

The CO parked his chin on his fist and gave me a look that said I'm too tired to explain, you figure it out.

"Well, uh, let me see – according to Leonid, if the killings stop once Hilde's in our custody, he's the rat. But no more agents left to kill means we have no way to determine if Hilde's dirty."

Ambrose gave me an attaboy dig in the ribs.

"I have to decide about him," said Jacobson. "Without Hilde's cache of documents it's just his say so. And he's slick enough to have those rookies at CIG chasing their tails for years."

I was about to haul up my slacks and say my piece about Herr Hilde and Col. Norwood and so forth but Ambrose was vibrating next to me like a one man band, foot tapping, fingers drumming against his leg. The CO noticed. I suspected Victor Jacobson didn't much care for my wing man but desperate times require desperate measures. The CO asked him a question.

"What do you suggest Ambrose?"

"Well, you think the Russians are up to no good. You try to get the scoop but no go. The network is all balled up. Am I on track so far?"

The CO nodded. Ambrose continued.

"Hell, we're spies, right? Send us in, see what we come up with."

"The Soviets won't attempt to roll tanks without some excuse, some provocation. They can't use our snatch of Hilde."

Ambrose asked why not.

"The members of the four power *Kommandatura* that runs Berlin are required to report the capture of all fugitive Nazi officials. Our Soviet friends neglected to mention they nabbed Hilde. However, if they catch you boys nosing around, shooting snaps in a denied area you'll make the front page of *Izvestia*. And the headline will read 'Yank sappers plot munitions blast' or somesuch."

"So we can't spy on the Russians," said Ambrose. "And poor old MANTIS can't round up any new recruits till he knows who the rat is and *we* can't figure out who the rat is cuz MANTIS can't round up any new recruits to get knocked off so we know if we already *have* the rat. I got that right?"

"You got that right Ambrose. Mostly," said Jacobson. "The thing you need to understand is that spying on an enemy is simple. You get caught, you get executed. But spying on an ally is complicated. It's the reason we use émigrés."

"So what do we *do*?"

Jacobson dredged up a weary smile. "I'm working on that. Now leave me the hell alone."

Again with the abrupt dismissal. When was I supposed to say my long- winded piece about Herr Hilde, Col. Norwood and so forth? I puckered up my lips to speak.

"Henka's making potato dumplings in the kitchen," said the CO. We tumbled out the door.

They were succulent. The potato dumplings. And that's what we did. Suck them down, pork broth running down our chins. I had ideas about our next move. Could be my quick study Irish chum did too. First thing's first however. Making post-war Europe safe for democracy was an important undertaking, no question. But a distant second to inhaling a bowl of Henka the Polish cook's hot and buttery homemade dumplings.

I waited until we returned to our apartment to say my piece about Hilde. We parked the delivery truck near Heidelberg Platz at dusk. Spring had finally sprung. People were out in shirt sleeves, the makeshift refugee camp on the grassy plaza teemed with squealing kids, half-starved women watching them with arms akimbo. One of them likely a former tenant of our apartment. I chose not to think about it.

Ambrose and I climbed three flights and settled in to the mildewed sofa in the living room with a bottle of French brandy we had bought for a dollar. We gazed out the window, at the play next door. That's what it looked like. The top floor apartment, the one with the sheared off outer wall, had people in it. Electric lights too. Sonofabitch.

It wasn't much of a play, an elderly couple sitting in the parlor, he reading a book, she darning socks. Every once in a while she would say something and he would nod.

"You seen them before?" asked Ambrose.

"No, never."

"I bet I know."

"Let's hear it Einstein."

"They've lived there forever. Look how the old man fits that chair, like he was born in it. But winter comes, it's too cold with the open wall, they leave. Weather gets warm, they come back."

I raised my plastic glass of brandy. "To Ambrose Mooney. To his sharp mind, his keen eye and his big mouth."

We drank, deeply. I prepared to say my piece, Ambrose watched the old couple next door.

"Maybe they have a couple of daughters. Buxom daughters with blonde hair."

"Sure. Probably kootch dancers who come by so Mama can stitch up their flimsy costumes."

"You think?"

Ambrose was obviously in no condition to hear my well-reasoned analysis of the complex interconnections between our cast of suspicious characters. Another brandy and I wouldn't be in any condition to deliver it. Ambrose would like my conclusion however.

"We need to go back to the chalet on *Ernststraße*. Tonight. Any questions?"

"I got time to wash up?"

I drove the obstacle course that was the Berlin street grid, Ambrose rode shotgun. Berliners were out in droves, taking the air in twos and threes. I said my long-winded piece to myself.

Klaus Hilde said something that stuck with me, something that called up a picture I had seen. The something he said was, 'I was not a true believer.' The picture it called up was Joseph and Magda Goebbels' children - five girls, one boy - laid out in a row, dressed in white as if for First Communion, poisoned by their mother in the *Fuhrerbunker*. An act of mercy in her mind, sparing her children the misery of life without Hitler.

That's the way true believers think. True believers don't negotiate, true believers don't save secret documents just in case. Herr Hilde was no true believer, just as he said. Someone else had condemned a host of White Russian freedom fighters to their grisly deaths.

That was my opinion anyway. That was why we were taking a right turn on *Ernststraße*, or trying to. A city bus had stopped at the corner. A dozen soldiers piled out, tripping over themselves to get to the Colonel's bordello.

"She's not like the girls back home. She's been to Paris and knows about art and sculptures and shit like that."

"Who's that?" I asked, as if I didn't know.

"Eva!"

"Is that so?"

"And she can cook. French."

We watched the uniformed GIs, Tommys and Ivans troop across the street, pushing and shoving. Eva was going to be doing a lot of French cooking this evening. I parked the truck down the block. We walked back.

"You need any help up there?" said Ambrose, hiking a thumb at the Colonel's chalet.

"Nah," I said, indicating the brothel in back. "You?"

Ambrose winked. "I think I can handle it." Then he said something stupid. Poozle stoopid. "Somebody has to look after her."

And off he went, head down, determined to defend the virtue of a harlot.

"Stay out of trouble!"

Ambrose answered with a wave of his hand.

Chapter Twenty-one

The string of Chinese lanterns on Col. Norwood's chalet was unlit. I couldn't tell about the lights upstairs, the curtains were drawn. Had the Colonel retired for the evening? It was only…well, I didn't know what the hell time it was but it wasn't late.

I went to the front door and pulled the bell knocker. No answer. Norwood was probably out on the town. I pulled the clapper again and waited. And again. I took first prize once in my parish fund drive, selling candy bars door to door. I'm not easily discouraged.

Heavy footfalls on the stairs. An eyeball through the peephole. I grinned a cheesy grin. The door swung open.

Sedgewick was disheveled, ruddy-faced. "The Colonel," he snarled with jagged teeth, "is indisposed."

I've never been clear on what that word means. Ill? In a foul mood? On the crapper? "Sorry to hear that. I…"

"Who's *there*?" said the familiar voice from the top of the stairs.

"It's Hal Schroeder, Colonel. I have news but I can come back another time."

"No, no, come up, dear boy, come up."

I followed Sedgewick up the steep staircase. The Colonel had gone away. Sedgewick turned on his heel and went to the kitchen. I remained at the top of the staircase, an unclaimed parcel. I heard a toilet flush.

The Colonel appeared and greeted me in a paisley dressing gown and slippers that curled at the toe. His complexion matched his robe, swirls of pink and purple. Maybe indisposed was British for swacked.

Norwood indicated the chesterfield, the one draped with Chinese silk. We went there and sat down and looked at one another. The Colonel had washed his face and wet combed his hair. The room was very warm.

"How do you feel about Absinthe?" he said, reaching for a crystal decanter on the coffee table. "They say it drove a generation of French poets mad."

"Then it wasn't a long drive, was it?"

It was a half-assed quip by a guy who couldn't name a French poet with a gun to his head. But Norwood laughed as if I were the second coming of Oscar Wilde. He lit his pipe. It wasn't any pipe tobacco I was familiar with.

"I hear you have captured your much-coveted fugitive."

"That's true. With help from one of your ladies."

"Aren't they the dearest things?"

I nodded. "I was just curious why you hadn't asked her the question yourself."

"Whomever said I didn't?"

"Well, if you did ask your ladies about Klaus Hilde and one of them said that he…"

I gave up on my question. Norwood's dancing eyebrows told me I wasn't going to get a straight answer. But there was another question, a more important question I wanted to ask when the time was right. Soon. Before the Colonel placed his hand on my knee and I snapped his thumb. I looked at the tall glass of regret that Norwood had poured me. Absinthe, licorice in a glass. I took a pull and covered my wince with a tight-lipped smile.

"Feeling poetic, are you?" grinned Norwood.

"Not particularly."

"Then have another."

I drained the glass and rattled off a dirty limerick. The Colonel thought that terribly amusing. It went that way for half a bottle. Norwood thought he was getting me drunk but I'd done a lot of barstool training the last few months. He refilled my glass and scooted closer. I let him. Now was the time.

"I'm grateful to you Colonel, rescuing us and all. I feel the need to show my gratitude." Norwood liked that. He didn't like my clarification. "Especially my gratitude to the young lady who tipped you to our bigmouthed Gestapo Captain. I'd like to buy her a dozen roses."

I needed to know if there was any such lady. If not Norwood had learned of our sorry plight elsewhere, from the NKVD or Herr Hilde. Or the CO or Leonid or Eva or MANTIS for all I knew. Berlin's fluid network of allegiances made me pine for the clarity of war.

Norwood leaned in. "And what of the brave Colonel who saved your bacon? What does he get?"

I didn't flinch, didn't rear back, just met his gaze and said, "A hearty hand clasp."

Norwood made with his jolly laugh and sat back. Sedgewick was in the kitchen, washing dishes, loudly.

"Just having you off, dear boy. I'll see that the young lady is properly thanked."

"I'd rather do it myself."

"I understand, but we discourage gifts to the ladies. Stirs up jealousies."

"I could meet with her someplace else."

"Ah yes, but don't you see? She would just *have* to tell the other girls how the handsome young hero presented her with a beautiful bouquet."

Norwood was good, his made-up excuses made sense. I swabbed my forehead with my handkerchief and belched. Norwood thought me a shitfaced rube. Let him. There are three phases of drunkenness. I was only at phase one. Relaxation. I wanted to move on to phase two. Revelation. And I wanted the Colonel along for the ride.

I poured the rest of the decanter into two glasses and proposed a bottoms up toast. "To the eternal friendship of the Brits and Yanks."

We drank up. Why is it Europeans crave sugary booze? Hadn't they suffered enough? I chased this thought around my brain box for a minute or three.

Hey. Schroeder. You'd better get this done before you leap ahead to phase three. Regurgitation.

"Colonel, I'm all confused, just plain...bumfuzzled about Klaus Hilde."

"How so?"

"He claims he's a Clean Gene but Jacobson suspects he's the finger man, guy who peached out our White Russians and...and...those other guys we use."

"Ukrainians."

"Yeah. Them. Hilde says he couldn't have been the rat cuz he's been in a hidey-hole for a year and how's he gonna know?"

"Know what?" said the Colonel.

"Where the White Russians are hangin' their hats!"

I sighed. I hung my head. The Absinthe was burning a hole in my gut and the clanking heat made me woozy. TS. I would stay until Norwood took the bait.

The Colonel set his pipe down on its gnarled wooden holder and steepled his fingers. "You say Klaus Hilde claims to have lived in Berlin since the end of the war. Do I have that right?"

"Yes sir."

"Which would mean he was here from May to July when the Red Army had the run of the place, when they were dragging any Nazi they could find into the streets and executing them - soldiers, government clerks, young boys from the Home Guard. Yet Klaus Hilde, a German General, second in command of the Abwehr, survived?"

"You're sayin' Hilde's been in bed with the Rooskies the whole time?"

"I'm saying," said the Colonel, leaning on the g, "that Herr Hilde has either been very fortunate or very accommodating."

Well, crap. I had expected Norwood to point the finger at Hilde to deflect suspicion from himself. I hadn't expected his accusation to make so much sense.

"Then riddle me this Colonel. If Hilde's their boy, bought and paid for, why does he take off down the Rat Line?"

C'mon, you smug bastard, do your part! Say it was all a ruse to snooker us into believing him so Hilde could feed bad intel to Pentagon desk jockeys and State Department cookie pushers for the next ten years.

The Colonel shrugged, flicked his gold Ronson and lit his pipe. I took this to mean that there were any number of reasons for Herr Hilde to flee the NKVD and it was up to me to determine the right one. Christ Almighty. I was reading deep meaning into shrugs and pipe lightings, a bad sign. I hadn't gathered anything worth a damn and I was just this side of regurgitation. Time to go.

In a minute. One more try. I couldn't very well ask Norwood if he was a Commie but I might tease out a statement of his sympathies before I covered my shoes in puke.

"You said the Brits were defeated in victory, defeated by victory, somethin' like that. Makes no sense when you think about it but us too. And we won the damn war!"

I looked over to see Norwood's eyes at half mast. I spoke louder.

"I'm from Cleveland. Ohio. Factories there're running three shifts and would be four if they could find more hours in a day. The Russians lost twenty million in the war, their cities are all blown up and yet...and yet...they're the ones on the move and we're the ones in retreat. Makes no sense when you think about it."

"So you've said," said Norwood, wearily.

"Point is, Hilde's a survivor, blows with the wind. And the wind...at this peculiar time...is blowing east to west!"

I sat back, grinning, sweat-drenched, waiting for the Colonel to agree with me, to say you could hardly blame Hilde for selling out, to say it was really us, the Brits and Yanks, who were screwing up. Instead he thanked me for the visit and instructed his burly manservant to show me out.

Sedgewick braced me, back and elbow, at the top of the staircase and walked me down. I let him.

The door closed behind me with a thunk. I waited for the bitter cold Berlin spring to slap me sober. It did not. Berlin weather is for the birds. Freezing when you didn't have a topcoat, balmy when you needed a bracer. I staggered to the bushes and experienced phase three of drunkenness. Repeatedly.

I stood up and swabbed my mug with a handkerchief. Well done, Schroeder. Well done and executed. Could be the Colonel's right. You are a rube.

Chapter Twenty-two

I walked down the pathway west of the chalet, toward the two-story brothel in the back. I heard the one-winged piano player pounding out a percussive tune, I heard bawdy laughter, I heard loud grunts of exertion and a low groan of pain. I broke into a run, sober in a second, knowing what I would find and finding it. Ambrose duking it out on the front lawn.

The dumbshit had bit off a big chaw, two foes, one twice his size. British soldiers by their uniforms, drunken sots by their halting steps and wild swings. Ambrose was holding his own, darting in with quick combinations, dancing back, ducking, circling, boxing not brawling. I was suitably impressed.

Then the big man got tired of getting popped and lurched forward, arms wide. Ambrose jumped back but the big man fell and snagged his ankle. His pal bull rushed Ambrose to the ground. Shellacking commenced.

I let them get in a few well-earned licks before I waded in. I jammed a thumb deep under the smaller man's jaw and held it there. He went limp.

The big man rolled over to see what was what. I planted my heel on his testicles and said, "Fun's over. Go home."

Ambrose slithered out of his grasp and clambered to his feet. The big man had reached the fourth stage of drunkenness, the stage of not recognizing that your opponent has his foot on your nuts. He tried to get up and have at me. I bent down and gave him a quick piston shot, the heel of my palm right between his eyes. His head bounced off the grass. He groaned, and started back up.

I was beginning to get annoyed with this strapping Brit. A full-standing knee drop to the family jewels would serve him right. Ambrose intervened.

"Back off. I can handle this feckin' Limey."

"You weren't doing so hot a second ago."

"Just keep his pal busy."

"Won't be necessary. His pal is dead."

That took the starch right out of him. Ambrose looked over in horror at the facedown figure. The big man crawled over to inspect his fallen comrade. I hauled Ambrose away by the shirt collar.

"He's dead? You kilt him?"

"He had it coming, now pick up the pace."

We quick stepped around to the back of the building and ducked behind the stand of poplars. I chanced a glimpse around the corner. The big one had the smaller one's arm around his neck. They were making half circles in the dewy grass, lowing like cows.

"He's walking good for a dead guy," said Ambrose at my back.

"Yes he is. What the hell happened?"

"Nothing. I was at the bar, waiting my turn, mouth shut, head down. And this crumped-out yob starts in about Brunehilde with the big titties, what he's gonna do to her and..."

"Ambrose. He's a drunk. In a whorehouse."

"I know, but..."

"You took it outside?"

"Sure."

"The bouncer didn't toss you?"

"No. Not really."

I shoved the keys at him. "I need to see Eva. You go to the truck, pray your rosary, stay put!"

"Yeah, okay," said Ambrose, miserably. He dug in his pocket and handed me a stick of gum. "You smell of puke."

"Thank you, Ambrose. That's very considerate." I unpeeled the gum and bounced the wrapper off his mush. "Now go."

He went, walking backwards, spilling blarney. "She won't like you Schroeder. She only likes the wild ones."

I tossed a dirt clod at him and missed. Ambrose lit out down the pathway. She only likes the wild ones. I was a twenty-five year old off-the-books secret agent in the world capital of intrigue. Why wasn't I a wild one?

I walked around to the side entrance, knocked and waited. The bruiser who answered the door didn't like the look of me.

"I'm Hal Schroeder," I said with a smile. "Of the Gates Mills' Schroeder's."

The bruiser didn't like me any better after that. Did he think I was Ambrose? There was a superficial resemblance, that inscrutable thing that distinguishes Americans from Europeans, softer features maybe, from all the interbreeding that led Hitler to call us as 'a race of mongrels'.

"It's a pleasure to make your acquaintance," I said, extending my hand. The bruiser palmed the fin and held the door open.

The joint was a lot livelier this time. Fewer well-dressed older gents in the plush booths but a bar crammed with uniforms waiting their turn to climb the stairs. The one-armed piano player plunked out a tune that was either "Stardust" or "Somewhere Over the Rainbow." Ballads weren't his strong suit.

I looked around for Eva. No joy. She must be upstairs in the trenches.

"Mr. Hal the salesman."

I turned around. "Sophie."

She was gussied up this evening. Low cut velvet dress, flower in her upswept hair, wearing enough makeup to paint a steam yacht. She frowned her forehead. "Where is your bowtie?"

"In my wallet."

I took a step forward. Sophie took a step back, looked around for the bouncer. I was angry all of a sudden, disgusted with the shit I was wading through, swimming in, in a town where starved kids shivered in lean-to's on Heidelberg Platz.

I held out a ten dollar bill. "Tell me I am next in line to see Eva."

Sophie filled her enormous lungs, ready to put the upstart Yankee in his place and then some. I returned her look, and then some.

She tucked the bill into her brassiere. "In ten minutes. Room 4. Use the back stairs."

I nodded. She left.

The back stairs were outside, on the west side of the building. I climbed them, entered a narrow hall that smelled of spilt beer and jism. I killed time listening to soldiers relieve themselves. That's what the place reminded me of in my foul mood. A latrine.

The door to room 4 was closed. Had it been ten minutes? I stood there like a stooge. I listened at the door. A GI came bounding up the stairs and looked at me funny. I knocked on the door.

"It's Hal."

"Come in please."

I entered a small room with a big bed and a dirty window. Eva lay on the bed, scrubbing herself with a wet wash cloth under her unbuttoned cotton nightgown, rubbing her white skin pink.

"I am not here for sex, Eva."

"No?" she said, putting her wash cloth in a basin on the nightstand.

"No. I want you to do us a service. Ambrose and me."

Eva dragged a brush through her honeyed hair, winced at a snag. "He is good boy, Ambrose. I like him very much." She set down the brush. "But he is just a boy."

Eva put a dab of perfume behind each ear, drizzled more on her fingertip and ran that fingertip between her breasts. That she did this matter-of-factly didn't lessen its impact. She shook out her hair and leaned back on pillows and crossed her dainty ankles.

"I am ready now for you."

"Eva, I can't..."

"You can't?"

"No, no. I can, it's just that..."

"You want me for a service."

"Yes. It's very important. It concerns..."

"But I have already done...how you say?...a service for your working."

"Herr Hilde. Yes, great. Very valuable."

"And you want more now at this time?" she said, rising up off her pillows.

"I will pay you whatever you ask."

Eva leaned back and pouted most prettily.

I explained that I wanted her to canvas the other ladies in the brothel to determine if any of them had spent time with a drunken former Gestapo Captain who ran his mouth about a meet with Yankee gunrunners. Eva said it was against house rules to ask such questions.

"Will you ask them anyway?"

"No."

"Why not?"

"Because you will no have sex with me."

"Eva, you are...a very attractive woman. Very. But I can't..."

"You say that you could!"

"No. Yes. I can, but I..."

Eva giggled. She was messing with me. She patted the bed. She looked up at me with those blue-green peepers, gave me both barrels. "It is how I know who you are."

Crap on toast. It looked like I would have to take one for the team. And do it in a convincing manner.

Yeah, I know. Poor Harold, forced to frolic with Aphrodite. But it wasn't like that. I did my patriotic duty but I didn't enjoy it.

Not right away.

I gave Eva a gold sovereign when we were done. She tucked it away with a perfunctory *danke* and freshened herself up for the next guy.

"Know me now, do you?" I said as I pulled on my clothes.

"Oh yes," she said with a wink.

"Then you'll ask the other girls about the Gestapo Captain?"

"Yes, yes. Now you go."

I turned to her as I opened the door to the dank hall. She was scrubbing her armpits with the wash cloth. Prostitutes have a terrible job. I stepped into the hall and closed the door behind me. But being a john stinks too.

I clomped down the back stairs, a black mood in full pursuit. I had been weak, and stupid. Poozle stoopid. Ambrose would know. He would smell Eva on me. I could wash up in the washroom and he would still know. Was that why Eva had insisted? To send a message to Ambrose to back off? Or did she simply want to show the high and mighty Yank he weren't so high and mighty.

I didn't know. I did know that Leonid said the job description of a spy is contradictory - a person of impeccable integrity who is an accomplished liar. And I was neither.

I paused at the base of the stairs to clear my head and gulp fresh air and enjoy the simple pleasures of a Berlin spring. It was pleasantly warm, the one-armed piano player was thumping out "On the Sunny Side of the Street" and no one was getting shredded by artillery fire or pulverized by thousand pound grass cutters. I told myself to snap out of it. Everything was hunky dory.

Ambrose didn't ask me if I had seen Eva when I climbed into the delivery truck. We drove back to the apartment in silence. When we arrived Victor Jacobson and Leonid Vitinov were waiting for us on the musty couch.

Chapter Twenty-three

"Herr Hilde has upped the ante," said the CO when Ambrose and I had settled into chairs, facing our elders on the couch. We were young men out tomcattin' around town if anyone asked. Anyone didn't.

"He says there's something big brewing. Leonid doesn't believe him and I have my doubts."

"What's he say?"

"That a group of anti-Communists in town - White Russians, a few locals - have linked up. They call themselves the Committee to Free Berlin. They're issuing leaflets and dispensing cash. Hilde says they're a fly trap."

"Funded by NKVD?"

"So he says."

I had learned about false flag recruitment at spy school. It's when you recruit a source by disguising your true identity and affiliation, raising a false flag. This would be false flag recruitment on a grand scale. Not a double agent but a doubled organization.

"So," I said, "it's a front the NKVD can use to compile a list of enemies."

"And it gets worse," said Jacobson. "According to Hilde the NKVD are secretly arming this group, planning to instigate an attack on the Soviet armory on a date certain, with the intent of liberating a cache of heavy weapons. Whereupon the Committee to Free Berlin will be annihilated."

"Which gives the Red Army an excuse to blockade Berlin and seize the city."

"Which prompts a military response from us. At which time, according to Hilde, Operation LUNA gets underway."

Holy shit. Russian tanks across the Elbe. Brits and Yanks in full retreat. MANTIS, Colonel Norwood, Klaus Hilde, all singing off the same sheet. I was pondering these imponderables when Ambrose asked the obvious.

"And how did this Hilde sod come up with this blessed bullshit about this Committee, him being holed up for the last year and all?"

The CO smiled. He was warming to this scamp. "He won't say, not till we improve his accommodations anyway. But he figured to have a good hole card."

The well-draped Russian to Jacobson's left cleared his throat to speak. "This is a fairy tale that the NKVD told Hilde to recite to us."

Ambrose wanted to know why the NKVD would do that.

"Because they want to discredit this Committee, so that we do not offer them assistance."

Made sense. And double agent Leonid Vitinov ought to know. "The NKVD told you this?"

My question made Leonid angry. I know because he spoke with even less emotion than usual.

"I am not need-to-know on this matter."

"Then how can you be sure, Chief?" said Ambrose saucily, fist on his hip.

Leonid graced him with a thin-lipped grin. "If the plan that Herr Hilde described was legitimate I *would* have been need-to-know."

Leonid paused long enough for Ambrose and me to grope around in the murk and come up empty. He continued, with great forbearance.

"If the NKVD was supporting the Committee to Free Berlin, they would have instructed me to monitor and intercept any communications that pertained to the Committee in order to determine if we suspected that the Committee was a front." Leonid concluded with a smug tick of the eyebrow. "The NKVD has not so instructed me."

Ambrose said what I was thinking. In a roundabout way.

"I'm just an Irish eejit, I don't know about espionage and all that. But this, what I just heard, sounds to me like Sunday Mass. The priest always wants us to take his word for it, take things on faith, doncha know. How is this any different?"

Leonid looked droll, unoffended. "Such a mistrusting young man."

I asked the Irishman's favorite question. "So what do we *do?*"

"There is a meeting of the Committee to Free Berlin in two days time," said Jacobson. "You'll go as reporters for Stars'n'Stripes. If they're a political group they will welcome you. If they have a more sinister agenda they'll keep their distance."

I liked it. Ambrose too from the look of him. We looked to the slight, silent Russian, waiting for his curt dismissal of this plan as a waste of time. Leonid did not oblige. I wondered why.

Came a small knock at the door.

"Don't answer it," said the CO. The small knocking became small thumping, heel of the hand or sole of the shoe. Jacobson drilled me with a look.

"I think it's the boy who used to live here."

Jacobson glowered. He had given me explicit instructions not to open the door. The thumping continued. Not loud, but it built up a great tension in the room. Jacobson seemed unsure, not wanting to break his own rule.

"*Wer ist da?*" I said through the door. Who is there?

"*Der Junge mit dem Topf.*" The boy with the pot.

"*Was willst Du?*" What do you want?

"*Der Deckel für den Topf.*" The lid to the pot.

"Hold the artillery," I said as I unlatched the door.

He was leaner and more foul-smelling than I remembered him. More dog than boy. I told Ambrose to fetch the lid to the cooking pot. He went to the kitchen and clattered through cabinets.

I crowded the little bugger but he bunged around trying to catch a glimpse of the men behind me. He saw the person to my right and bunged left. He saw the person to my left and froze. Dead. I turned to see who that person was. Leonid.

Ambrose returned with the lid to the cooking pot. I took it and turned to face the kid but he was halfway down the stairs.

The CO gave me the time and place of the Committee to Free Berlin meeting. Then he and Leonid went away. Ambrose and I nipped at the brandy bottle and ate Zwieback crackers.

Ambrose kept his manner light but I could tell what was on his mind. So I apologized for having sex with a prostitute.

I could've told Ambrose that Eva called him a boy and insisted that I jump in the rack with her but I'm not that kind of heel. I said I was weak and I said I was sorry and both were true. Ambrose growled, called me a motherhumping son of Satan, drained his brandy and said, "What's next?"

"Eva agreed to canvas the ladies, see if anyone got an earful about Yankee gunrunners from our Gestapo Captain. If there ain't no such lady we'll know the Colonel got his information elsewhere."

"Where elsewhere?"

"The Soviets. Where else?"

"How'd they know we were gonna be there at the loading dock? The Soviets."

"From Horst Schultouer I guess."

"The Gestapo Captain? Why he tell 'em? Isn't he s'posed to be a Commie hater?"

"Supposed to be. But in the spy game there's sometimes a long stretch of road between what's supposed to be and what is."

Ambrose chewed, swallowed and digested this pearl of wisdom along with a Zwieback cracker. "Why did the kid run away like that?"

"He recognized Leonid, was afraid of him."

"Why? What's it mean?"

"I don't know."

Ambrose poured himself another slug of brandy. "You're not very good at this are ya?"

I laughed. What could I say? The intemperate young son of the Old Sod was right.

"What's on the slate if Eva finds that Horst didn't blab to the ladies?"

I smiled, I grinned. I had a plan!

"We return to Col. Norwood's late night salon and play a bit of nick and nack."

Chapter Twenty-four

The hard-working Miss Eva was doing okay for herself. She had a private telephone line. Ambrose had the number. We stumbled out at something o'clock the next morning to locate a working phone box.

No such thing. So we ducked into a sweet-smelling *Konditorei* where all the customers spoke English and all the prices were in dollars. We borrowed their blower for a buck. Ambrose called Eva while I ogled a tray of apple *Kuchen*. It was a thing of beauty but not what I needed at the moment. I was overhung. I needed a big hunk of *Schwarzwurstl* dipped in Tabasco sauce. I settled for a cup of black coffee, straight from the jar.

We ankled out. Ambrose ran it down.

"She talked to all the girls. Not a one of them knows Horst whatzisname and nobody heard nuttin' about any Yankee gunrunners."

"She's sure?"

"One hundred per cent."

"That's it then. Colonel Norwood's a lying sack."

Ambrose shrugged. Aren't they all?

"Seems like everyone and his uncle knew we were going to be at that loading dock in the Soviet Sector," I said. "We were on the Lubyanka Express till Norwood rode to the rescue. And now we're going to a meeting of a possible Soviet front organization with fake credentials. The NKVD might be there to greet us."

"How they gonna know we're comin'?"

"I don't know. I don't know shit from Shinola as you've pointed out many times."

"I only count one."

We stopped at a street corner. "I was in the war, funny boy. World War II, maybe you heard of it. It was horrible, bloody and everything in between. But it had one thing going for it. You knew who was on your side and who was not. *This...*", I said gesturing around at the jumble of caved-in buildings hard by bustling cafes, "This is..."

"Bloody confusing?"

"Yes!" I said, shouted, abusing my parched brain casing. A young girl standing nearby clapped her hands to her ears in fright. We crossed the street. "Now let's find some goddamn sausage before I die of hunger."

Ambrose accompanied me down the sidewalk. "Got another question for ya Chief."

"Okay."

"If we know the Colonel's a lying sack, why tell him? Why not keep it under our hat?"

The Irishman had a point. We had superior knowledge on the old queen.

"Because I need to know just how dirty he is," I said after a moment. "If he's peddling a little gossip to keep himself in fine wine and Darjeeling that's one thing. If he's a Soviet double agent it's another."

"And you think our little song and dance in front of a room full of people is going to tell you that?"

Once more with feeling. "I don't know."

The plan was for me and Ambrose to crash Col. Norwood's late night salon and tag team him about his ride to the rescue. How he knew to be there, the real story this time. I'd be the soft spoken diplomat, Ambrose the loudmouth Mick. The theory was that Norwood loved to hold court, prized his salon above all else and would fess up to a bit of fun-loving subterfuge with the Rooskies in order to make these embarrassing questions go away. The more polished his story, the less likely it was to be true.

That was the plan as Ambrose and I waded into a jam-packed jamboree that evening in the chalet on *Ernststraße*. We had to bide our time, wait for things to quiet down to a dull roar. The Colonel was in top form, working the crowd like a ringmaster, clad in a double breasted white dinner jacket and a necklace of beaded shells where the black tie should have been. The hooch and the groaning sideboard of good eats took their toll eventually.

People flopped down to sip and mumble. Ambrose and I did our song and dance.

The plan didn't work out as planned. Col. Norwood purpled with rage at our impertinence and instructed Sedgewick to toss us down the stairs. Ambrose got his Irish up. Fisticuffs were about to commence when a wan young man spoke up.

"*I* was the one that Horst Schultouer told his secret to."

I asked him what secret.

"He said that he was a freedom fighter. A freedom fighter who was meeting some arms merchants from America the next morning."

I asked why Horst Schultouer would tell him that.

The young man got all kinds of embarrassed. "I believe he was trying to win my affections."

I thanked him, apologized to the Colonel and pulled Ambrose down the long steep staircase. He wanted to know what the hell that was all about. He didn't understand. I was surprised I did. I was a long, long way from Youngstown, Ohio.

"The young man is a male prostitute."

Ambrose shook his head as we pushed through the front door. "Bloody wankin' Anglicans."

We returned to the delivery truck, tails between our legs. "You drive," I said, tossing Ambrose the keys. I wanted to think.

"Bloody shame, that," said Ambrose with a tick of his head as we drove past the chalet and its brightly-lit Chinese lanterns. Raucous laughter spilled from upstairs windows opened to the warm night. I pictured Col. Norwood holding forth, sending up the bumbling Yanks.

"Feckin' Brits are worthless in every way but one."

"What's that?"

"Roast beef. They were carvin' up a rib roast back there, nice and bloody like. And I didn't get a lick."

"We've got a can of pea soup at home. Some Zwieback left."

I was preoccupied, I didn't intend my remark to be funny. I guess it was. Ambrose certainly thought so.

Ambrose and I trudged up the three flights of stairs to our apartment with all the enthusiasm you'd expect of two humiliated men about to share a dinner of crackers and canned soup. I kept an eye out for the German boy, hoping to ask him why he ran away. But the hour was late and the stairs and corridors were empty.

"I'm all in," said Ambrose when I keyed open the door.

"No soup?"

"Nah."

Had I said good night this story may have had a different ending, but I eyed the brandy bottle on the coffee table. Four fingers left.

"Have a quick snort with me. I want to kick it around a minute."

"Sure 'nuff, Chief," said Ambrose gamely, plopping down on the musty couch. I took the wobbly chair across from him.

"The brandy's yours," he said, pulling a sterling silver flask from inside his coat. "I'll have a nip of Bushmills." He unscrewed the flask and poured a dram in the cap. "Gift from me brothers on me 21st. Says so right here." He showed me the engraving across the front.

"Very handsome."

"They're good lads."

We clinked. The almost empty bottle to the silver flask. The brandy went down quick. I felt a pang of guilt for dragging Ambrose away from his family. Felt a pang of envy too, him with two brothers and me with none.

"I keep coming back to it, not sure why," I said. "The difference between a traitor and a snitch."

"Which is?"

"A snitch snitches for money or advantage. A traitor acts from conviction."

"I dunno. People do all kinds of lousy things for money."

"You're right, no question. You and I robbed a bank. What did we do afterwards?"

Ambrose looked away. He didn't like it that, now that we were semi-respectable espionage agents, I had dredged up our sordid past. "We ran like hell."

"Yes we did. The person who ratted out the émigrés did not. He hung around and guided the NKVD to their moving targets over a period of many days. Which doesn't sound like Herr Hilde to me. It's not that he *wouldn't* sell out innocents for money - he admitted the Blue Caps spared him because he told 'em who gave him which document and why - but Hilde's like a skiff, tacking with the winds. Winds that blew him from the Third Reich to the Soviets to the US of A. Hilde's not a true believer. Lying to the us about a phony NKVD plot buys him nothing but a jail cell when it doesn't come true."

"You say something Chief?"

"You heard me. Shithead."

Ambrose sniggered and poured himself another dram. "What if Hilde doesn't *know* it's a phony plot? Meant to keep us from backing this Committee. What if the NKVD didn't tell him?"

"That's the only way they *would* tell him."

"What is?"

"The only way the NKVD would tell Hilde about the Committee is if it *is* a phony plot. So he could pass it along, as disinformation."

"Okay, say the NKVD *didn't* tell Hilde about the Committee. How's he find out it's a front?"

I shrugged, I mumbled. "He's a career intelligence officer, must have a few contacts left."

"Whasamatter Chief? You look funny."

"I just said something I should have known."

"Whuzzat?"

"I said *so he could pass it on*. Hilde. Pass on the disinformation. Leonid pissed all over Hilde's story about the Committee being a front, said it was a fairy tale *that the NKVD told Hilde to recite to us*."

I hiked my eyebrows. Ambrose spun his hand.

"Why would *Leonid* assume - that the *Soviets* assumed - that Herr Hilde would have a *chance* to pass it on to us? Hilde was in Soviet custody."

"You're givin' me a headache here Chief."

"Hilde fell in our lap awful easy. You see what I'm saying?"

Ambrose mulled it over. "You're sayin' Leonid knew in advance that we'd bag Hilde?"

"Sure looks that way."

"But how the hell did Leonid know that we'd meet Eva and she'd tell us where to bag Hilde?"

"I'm not saying Leonid knew how. Just that he knew or suspected that the NKVD wanted Hilde found."

Ambrose sat up, eyes blazing. "You sayin' Eva's in on it?"

"No, not at all," I replied with more conviction than I felt. Ambrose settled down. I changed the subject.

"Here's another thing. Leonid told me that Lavrenty Beria, head of the Soviet secret police, had his mother under house arrest. That's Beria's pressure point. Leonid's mother."

Ambrose stretched out on the musty couch. "Piss poor hole card, you're sayin'. An old woman. What happens when she croaks?"

"Yes. Correct. Very good. If Beria wanted a real hole card he would have taken Leonid's wife."

Ambrose nodded agreement and yawned.

"*Plus...*" Ambrose put his finger to his lips. I lowered my voice. "Plus, Leonid said Hilde's story about the Committee to Free Berlin was a crock, yet he didn't object to the CO sending us in."

"Why should he?"

"Because he's an arrogant little shit! An arrogant little shit whose superior knowledge had just been ignored. He should have bitched to the CO. But he didn't. Not a groan, not a mumble."

"We got any toothpicks?"

"I don't think so."

"Then how'm I s'posed to keep my eyes open?"

"Ha ha."

"I get yer drift Chief. You think Hilde's a snitch. You think Leonid's a traitor. Now what do we do about it?"

"We find out if it's true. Before we wander into that Committee meeting."

"How?"

"I have no earthly idea."

Ambrose rolled his eyes and shut his lids. His breathing grew heavy. I got up to make soup.

"Leonid's wife fancies you," said Ambrose with his eyes closed.

"She does?"

"At the reception, my first day on, we shot the breeze. Name's Anna I think." Ambrose yawned for a good ten seconds. "She fancies you."

"I heard you the first time."

"She does, I know it."

"How so?"

Ambrose feigned sleep. I kicked the musty couch.

"The CO poked you in the back. You walked away. And her eyes followed you all the way out of the room."

I struggled to dredge it up from the murky depths, conjured only a faded image. A pale slender woman who said little. And declined to shake my hand.

"You sure?" I said. But Ambrose was asleep.

Romancing another man's wife is chancy under the best of circumstances. Romancing the wife of a Soviet agent who either was or wasn't working our side of the fence and was doubtless paranoid in the extreme was - what would you say? Daunting? Risky? Nuts?

There is an old German saying, *Frauen behalten die Geheimnisse.* 'Women keep the secrets.' It never made much sense to me but maybe it's different in the Old Country. We have a different saying stateside, about the three best ways to spread the word. Telegraph, telephone and tell-a-woman. Women know the secrets, let's put it that way.

Anna would know if her husband was double dealing. It was up to me to find some way to pry it loose. Was I that charming and irresistible? Not so's you'd notice. But I had a distinct advantage. If I had things right Anna was married to a cold fish whose sole passion was the advancement of the people's revolutionary struggle against capitalist oppression of the workers. Unless she shared this passion Anna would be lonely. And bored.

Did she share his passion? Not likely. Fanatics are almost always male. Women know better somehow. Women know there's more than one answer to every question.

Finding Leonid's address was the next order of business. I wasn't going to ask the CO and I didn't picture tailing the little man home in a three ton truck. The only half-assed lead I could put my finger on was the café where I met him for the first time. Café Gestern. They knew him there, he probably lived nearby.

The stern *Grossmutter* with the pulled back hair might oblige me for a fiver.

Fat chance. She hadn't outlived the Nazi regime by disclosing privileged information at the drop of a fin. I would have to find another way.

Chapter Twenty-five

Ambrose and I slept in late the next morning. Almost blinded myself when I snapped open the blackout shades. We had two single beds in the small bedroom. A kid's room, the boy and girl in the family photo. Where had the parents slept?

Ambrose buried his groggy head under a pillow. I padded to the kitchen and put a pot of water on the stove. Could I get away with combat hygiene? A shave and a pit wash over the sink? Or would I have to huddle under the rusty pipe that passed for a showerhead and shrink my gonads into raisins? Buck up, Schroeder. With any luck you've got a heavy date.

I did my patriotic duty. It was worse than I expected. Brutal, bone chilling. Two years previous I would have considered it a luxury to stand under cold running water and soap off the clay dust and oil smoke. Like most of America I had gone soft in a fat hurry.

Ambrose and I walked the two miles to Café Gestern on *Bundesalle* just south of the *Kurfürstendamm* in the British Sector. The block was broken but unbowed, save for an array of brick buildings across the street. A National Socialist Institute of Something or Other that the Allies had taken particular care to blow to bits.

The entry bell tinkled merrily as Ambrose and I swept in at something o'clock in the late morning or early afternoon. The gas lights flickered low and smoky, the few patrons scattered, old, alone.

We parked our hind quarters at the petite bar. It had lace doilies for coasters. We angled around for the barkeep. No target acquisition, as the fly boys like to say. We had a plan. A plan that required the jolly bartender. Where the hell was he? I remembered him from my first visit. He reminded me of my Uncle Jorg, a beefy character with fleshy jowls that jiggled when he laughed. I grew up with first generation Krauts. They came in two flavors. The melancholy Germans and the jolly-jolly Germans. The barkeep, like my Uncle Jorg, was a jolly-jolly German. Kind of guy who would sing the *Schnitzelbank* song at the drop of a hat and he'd drop the hat. When the barkeep was properly lubricated Ambrose and I would conclude that our pal Leonid wasn't coming, worry that he hadn't showed and wonder should we check on him? He lives right around the corner, doesn't he? At which time the jolly barkeep would set us straight.

That was the plan. Unfortunately the jolly barkeep had the day off and his fill-in was a pinch-faced old geezer who did not imbibe. He *did* enjoy a smoke now and then. Camels were his preferred brand but he would make do with Lucky Strikes. Two packs.

Leonid and Anna lived one block south and two blocks east, on *Spirchenstraße*. We found the building that the barkeep described. A big pearl gray stucco structure with a high arched entryway and large apartments with balconies that faced the street. The repairs had been extensive, nary a bullet hole to be seen.

Ambrose and I camped in a doorway across the street, hoping to spot Anna coming or going and bump into her, accidental like. We burned half an afternoon that way. When the shadows of the western buildings crept halfway across the street I told Ambrose I was going in.

"You don't know the apartment number."

"I'll think of something. Keep an eye out for Leonid. Waylay him if he shows."

"What the feck does that mean? *Waylay*."

"Delay, interrupt. Say you need to talk to him."

"About what?"

"About...me. You're worried about me."

"Why?"

"Because...I don't *feckin'* know, that's your lookout! Just don't let him in that door."

Ambrose didn't take offense. Or didn't show it. But I came to regret the rudeness of my remarks.

Chapter Twenty-six

There were twelve mail slots in the foyer of the pearl gray building on *Spirchenstraße*. Eleven of them had nameplates, none said Vitinov. The mailbox for apartment K was unmarked. I counted upward. Top floor, facing the street. That would be the one.

The glass paneled inner door to the lobby was locked. Jimmy it with my blade, or press the intercom button and try to talk my way in? Jimmy it. Too easy for Anna to say no to a disembodied voice.

I examined the cylinder lock in the lobby door. A pin and tumbler deadbolt. A Schlage, as in Walter Schlage, fellow Kraut American made good. Not what I wanted to see. I wouldn't be jimmying the tongue out of the latch, not with a deadbolt.

I tried raking it, sticking the tip of my knife all the way to the back of the cylinder and yanking it out hard while twisting the door handle. It bounces the pins up. Sometimes you get lucky and they stay up.

Not this time, not with a ten pin Schlage. I had a full set of lock picks thoughtfully provided by the CO but it was late afternoon, residents would be returning, and tumbling this sumbitch would take some time. I could smash one of the glass door panels but Leonid would notice that when he came home. Time for plan Z.

I went to the buzz board and pressed buttons for the second floor, got an answer from apartment H. One Frau G. Unkel.

"*Lieferung für Frau Unkel.*" Delivery for Mrs. Unkel.

She wanted to know what it was.

"*Es ist ein Paket, meine Dame.*" It's a package, ma'am.

"*Woher ist das Paket?*" Where is the package from?

How the hell did I know? Think, genius. What package would any and every woman in the Western world open the door to receive? Oh, yeah. I had dug deep one time and made a big hit with Jeannie on her birthday.

"Von Godiva Schokoladen in Brüssel." From Godiva Chocolates in Brussels.

Frau Unkel buzzed me in post haste. I crossed the marble floor, passed the brass-trimmed elevator and hunted the fire stairs, saying a silent apology to Frau G. Unkel, Apt. H, 1832 *Spirchenstraße*. I would send her a box of Godiva chocolates when all this was done. I would!

I found the stairwell in the back right corner of the lobby, next to the fire door. Now there's something you don't see every day. Carpeted fire stairs. Leonid had himself a swank scatter.

I climbed two flights of stairs and walked down the corridor to apartment K, wondering what the hell I was doing with every step. If Anna told me to take a hike I would be in deep Dutch with Leonid. I knocked anyway.

No answer. I knocked some more. The door opened against a chain lock. A woman said something in a soft voice, something in Russian. I looked through the crack in the door, saw no one.

"It's Hal Schroeder Mrs. Vitinov. We met before. I work with your husband."

No response. Did Anna speak English? I couldn't remember, couldn't recall if we had exchanged a single word. I tried Deutsch.

No response, no face in the door crack. But the door didn't close. I said the only word I knew that Anna would recognize.

"Leonid."

A pale frowning face in the crack of the door. "No Leonid here."

I nodded. "I know, I understand."

"What is he?"

Good question. She meant 'where is he' maybe. Or 'Has something happened to him?'

"Leonid is fine. O-kay. *Fein*."

Anna understood. Leastwise she smiled, a quick mechanical curl of the lips seen through a crack in the door. A sad smile.

"Why here are you?"

Another good question. Anna moved closer to the door, peered at me with one pale gray worried eye. She was a wounded bird, this one.

"I was nearby, close by. Café Gestern."

The pale gray eye watched me.

"I wanted to apologize, to say I'm sorry." I bowed my head in penance. "When we met," I said, pointing to her, pointing to me, "at the party, in Dahlem, I was rude to you."

I made a mean face. No sign of comprehension from behind the door. I droned on, with a lot of gestures.

"We talked, we had pleasant con-ver-sa-tion. And then I turned away, walked away without saying goodbye. So long, *auf Wiedersehen*."

Anna understood the last part. I know because she said "Goodbye" and shut the door in my face.

It was the way she said it that kept me standing there. Softly, reluctantly. And the way she closed the door. With a click, not a slam.

Ambrose and I had a date with the Committee to Free Berlin the following evening. A date or an ambush. We would show up either way, two gobs on a job as the swabbies like to say. Would be nice, however, to know what we were in for and up against. Nice to have a chance to prepare.

I knocked again, gentle but insistent.

The door opened against the chain. I got both eyes this time. They were angry. I put my hand against the door jamb and met her look and smiled. Easy like, not too cocky.

We had an odd moment just then. A back and forth with eyes and eyebrows and unsaid words. Ambrose was right. She liked me for some reason. She also feared me. How to tip the balance?

Act human, act stupid. *Speak*.

"I just had a long lunch at the Café Gestern with a friend of mine. Ambrose, you met him at the party. And we had a couple steins of *Bier* and now, well, I need to go to the bathroom," I said, mincing about. "Water closet. *Toilette.*"

No response, no reaction. I pulled a face and raised my hands in prayer. "Please?"

This coaxed a tiny smile and an opened door.

I said thanks in several languages and followed her through the parlor to the head. The apartment was spare, stark. The only touch of warmth were several framed watercolors. I closed the bathroom door and tapped a kidney.

Anna was standing by the open front door when I returned to the parlor, ready to usher me out.

I pretended not to notice, studied the watercolors on the walls. They were good, bright and lively. A plump cat curled up in a basket, one eye open. A bunch of dark cherries in a yellow bowl. A blazing late autumn maple missing half its leaves. The tree leaned sharply to one side and called to mind an elegant society dame at the end of a long night.

I wondered who the artist was. Then I didn't. The plump cat in the portrait wandered over and hissed at me. Though it pained me deeply I leaned over and petted the little bastard. I'm allergic to cats, in more ways than one.

"Your paintings are very beautiful." Anna lowered her eyes and flushed ever so slightly. She understood English well enough. "You must be very famous." She squinted at my last word. "Famous, well known. Like Rembrandt."

Anna put a blue-veined hand to her face to cover a snort. Prettiest hand you ever saw.

"Could we have some tea?" I mimed a sip, my pinky in the air.

Anna fought a smile to a standstill. But she shut the door and went to the kitchen. I sat down on the only upholstery I could find, a gray couch stiff as a parson's collar. I put my foot up on the coffee table – a large green metal ammunition box stenciled

CCCP. Charming. Anna entered a short time later with a tray. I stood up to help her, a guest now, not an intruder.

Anna perched on a wooden chair with the bow-backed grace of a ballerina. She crossed her wrists. Thin as spun sugar. The fat cat bounded up on the couch and settled in my lap. Never fails. Anna scolded the cat in Russian. The cat paid her no heed. His name was Ivan. I stifled a sneeze.

Well. Here we all were. Hal, Anna and Ivan the Terrible.

"I am also very talented Anna. I am, I'll show you."

I know exactly one magic trick, one Uncle Jorg taught me. It's a variation of The French Drop. You hold your right hand palm upward and place a coin between thumb and forefinger. You move to grab the coin with your left hand. Just before the left hand closes you let the coin drop to the palm of your right hand, making a big show of snatching the coin with your left hand as you palm the coin in your right.

You then display your empty left hand to astonished gasps and *find* the coin in your pocket with your right hand. The Schroeder variation involves finding the coin in your nose. It's a big hit at taverns. Anna liked it too. Ivan got bored and wandered off.

We settled back into silence. Anna was a proper lady, she wasn't going to respond to pointed questions about her husband. Yet her loneliness was palpable.

I knew the feeling. It gets worse over time. The last few months of my behind-the-lines OSS service I occasionally entertained the notion of surrendering at a German checkpoint just to have someone to talk to. I'd heard tales from senior agents who had been captured and held in solitary for months. They would scream and misbehave in any way they could just to get some human contact, just to get a beating.

So. Play the loneliness angle.

"This is a nice apartment, nice building. You must have many visitors. *Besucheinen.*"

Anna gave me a quick dismissive shake of the head.

"What about your parents? Your *Mutter und Vater*? Do they come to visit?"

Another head shake.

"What about Leonid's parents? His mother and father?"

"Leonid father, no more. *Tot*. Leonid mother..." Anna lowered her voice to a grim whisper. "*Lubyanka*."

"That is what Leonid told me. He told me that his mother was held by Lavrenty Beria in the *Lubyanka*. So that Beria would have control, complete control of Leonid. Do you understand what I'm saying?"

Anna did not respond.

"Forgive me, Anna, but I don't see why Beria would do that. Hold Leonid's mother in prison."

Anna stood up. It was time to go. I thanked her for the tea and company. She walked me to the door.

We squared up, two inches apart. Her gray eyes had flecks of purple in them. They lit on mine and flitted away. And again. I managed to keep my hands to myself. Anna kept hers out of trouble by knotting them together at her waist. She was strangling those graceful delicately-tapered fingers purple!

"Don't do that," I said and put my hands on hers. They were surprisingly soft, her skinny hands. And warm. "I would like an answer to my question."

Anna reclaimed her mitts and opened the door. She eased me out with a hand on my back, just above my belt. Her touch was firm, no nonsense.

"*Eine Ehefrau kann ersetzt werden, eine Mutter nicht*," she said and closed the door behind me.

A wife is replaceable, a mother is not.

I glided down the carpeted stairs, enjoying the springy feel of them. Or was that just me, walking on air? I hadn't felt the like for quite a while. Not since Jeannie.

I indulged these adolescent yearnings all the way down to the lobby then made a beeline for the front door. Progress had been made. Anna's explanation about Leonid's mother made some sense. Russians were famously sentimental about their mothers. Could be Leonid was on the level.

I made it out onto *Spirchenstraße* without incident. Am-brose was not where he should have been, huddled in the doorway across the street. Which meant he had to see a man about a dog or he'd waylaid Leonid. Not a problem. Ambrose was nearby in either case. I positioned myself across the street and down the block. By the wreckage of the National Socialist institute of Something or Other.

I watched and waited. And waited.

Ambrose did not appear. I searched every *Bierstube, café, Kneipe* and *bistro* in a four block radius. Checked every barstool, toilet stall and back room, returned to the spot on *Spirchenstraße* and waited till night fell.

Ambrose was nowhere to be found.

Chapter Twenty-seven

I double timed it back to the apartment, hoping Ambrose had got bored and gone home, not believing it for a second. Ambrose hadn't ditched a merry life of Dublin pub crawls to come to Berlin and be a punk. I bulled my way down the crowded sidewalk, scattering cripples and old ladies, wondering what I should do if he wasn't there. Call Eva? Call the CO? Call Wild Bill Donovan?

No. I would play it close. If Ambrose wasn't at the apartment, if Ambrose had been snatched.

Stupid of me not to tell him to find better cover while he kept an eye out for Leonid. Whatever side of the fence Leonid was working the Blue Caps would keep watch on his residence. I bust in, they snatch my sentry. And why do that? Make some sense, Schroeder!

But someone had. Snatched my sentry. I climbed the three flights two stairs at a time. The apartment was empty.

I stripped off my clothes and stood underneath the rusty shower pipe. The water pressure was good at this hour. The frigid gusher beat back the waves of guilt welling up inside me. Why hadn't they bagged my sorry ass? I had signed up for this. I had something to gain. Ambrose didn't know a Communist from a Rotarian. It wasn't goddamn fair is what it wasn't.

I climbed out and sat on the toilet and shivered. I left the mangy gray towels where they were. I think better when I'm cold.

The NKVD wouldn't risk snatching a low value target like Ambrose. Not now. They had the USA right where they wanted us, fast asleep. But Leonid wouldn't have been able to snatch Ambrose by himself. Gun or no gun, Ambrose would have wiped the floor with the little man or died trying. Leonid had help. He must have convinced his superiors that Ambrose was a hothead who was threatening to go public about the Committee to Free Berlin.

Or something like that.

Take a breath, Schroeder. Take another. Don't outrace the facts for once. Nail it down. You have a lot of questions on your tick list. The only one you've checked off is how Col. Norwood came to know that you and Ambrose would be on that loading dock and even that answer stank of rank convenience if you thought about it which you are not going to do right now because you need to answer more immediate questions.

There was only one. Okay two. Ambrose and I had hoofed it, meandered, tarried, doubled back. We hadn't been shagged. How did Leonid know we would be paying a visit to his wife on this particular afternoon?

That was the second question which in some corkscrew way led to the first. Why had the German boy, demanding *der Deckel* to his family's *Topf*, suddenly bolted down the stairs at the sight of Leonid Vitinov?

Stand up, Schroeder. Stand up, towel off and nail it down.

I got dressed and went to the kitchen, grabbed the lid to the cooking pot. I scrambled down the stairs and headed for the Heidelberg Platz. And stopped. I needed a peace offering. The pot lid wasn't enough and a sawbuck was too brashly Yank. I needed something real.

Meat. I had passed a butcher shop a couple blocks down. I went there.

The blinds were drawn, the door locked. I didn't know what time it was but it wasn't late. Six o'clock at most. Goddamn Krauts are so one way. My old man would lock the door of his candy store at the tick of six every night even though he could have sold *cartons* of cigs to well lit factory workers stumbling home from the corner tap. They would tap on the porthole window after closing time, waving dollars. And here I was, tapping on the porthole window after closing time.

A small brown man with a mop in his hand looked up. A Spaniard or a Portugee. He waved me off, then recognized what I had pressed to the glass. The international badge of American authority in all matters great and small. A pack of Lucky Strikes.

The door swung open. Miguel had plenty of raw bratwurst and knockwurst he was willing to trade me but that wasn't what I wanted. It took some haggling but he came across with the good stuff. Two pounds of smoked bockwurst. He wrapped it in butcher paper, I stuck it in my coat.

You can bomb a city down to the nubs but you can't keep songbirds quiet in spring or dogs from barking at the setting sun. The lone surviving tree in Heidelberg Platz was hung with drying laundry and the air was thick with the smell of baking potatoes. Spuds were the staple now, dumped on street corners by US Army trucks as payment to the *Trummerfrauen*. They sat around fire pits, the rubble women, roasting potatoes on long sticks, watching their children chase each other across piles of rubble sprouting dandelions.

It was a stirring testament to the resilience of the human spirit and so forth but I had a little Kraut peckerneck I needed to find and pronto. I advanced toward the piles of rubble. The kids saw me coming and took off.

I approached the fire pits. The women kept their heads down. I wandered around like a dope, my *Deckel* in my hand. So to speak. I was looking for the matching *Topf*. I found it.

"Ich glaube dies gehört Ihnen." I believe this belongs to you.

She looked up at me from underneath a curtain of dirty hair. Was this the boy's mother? Or grandmother? She looked old as the hills, save for her eyes. Her eyes were young. She made no move to take the pot lid. I set it down on the grass next to her, squatted down and gestured to the bubbling stew of potato chunks and grass clippings.

"*Es sieht dünn aus.*" It looks thin.

The woman grunted. No shit.

I removed the precious parcel from inside my coat and took my time unwrapping the butcher paper, fold by fold, to reveal the luscious contents within. The woman watched me closely but without expression. I sliced off a hunk of bockwurst with my folding knife, eyed the pot. "*Darf ich?*" May I?

The woman's look said this was a very stupid question. I plopped the chunk of sausage into the pot, cut up some more and did likewise. The aroma of rendered pig wafted out over the Platz, quieting conversation, drawing hungry stares.

I had an apology I wanted to make to this woman about displacing her family from her apartment, how it wasn't my idea and all that. But I flushed it. This woman had had a bellyful of the pieties of men. I told her I needed to talk to her son, that he wasn't in any trouble but he had seen something and I needed to talk to him about it.

She looked away. "*Was hat er gesehen?*" What did he see?

I said I believed he had seen a stranger enter my apartment. Her apartment. The apartment on the fourth floor.

"*Wer ist dieser Fremde?*" she said with a shiver. Who is this stranger?

I scratched an ear and said I plumb didn't know. Which is why I needed to talk to her son.

My Huck Finn act bought me a look of utter contempt and why not? I was the Yankee Doodle Dandy who had commandeered her apartment, banished her to a lean-to in a public park, bombed her husband to smithereens and likely her fair-haired daughter too. There were two parents and two kids in the family photo above the stove, but only two beds in the apartment. Best guess the boy was all she had left. She wasn't going to put him at risk for a slice of sausage.

I told her that I had been dispatched to Berlin by the President of the United States to help prevent a Russian takeover of the city. The woman kept her head resting on her tented knees for that part. She raised it up after the second part. The part where I said her son was in grave danger.

"*Falls der Mann den Mann gesehen hat, von dem ich denke, das er ihn gesehen hat.*" If the man he saw was the man I think he saw.

She shot to her feet and called, sharply, "Martin."

Martin came trooping up a moment later, arms at his sides, head down. He had raw red spots on his scalp. His mother instructed him to answer my questions. She said it sternly. Martin nodded his hung down head.

I held out my hand. "*Martin, ich bin Hal.*"

Martin took hold of my forefinger. We shook. I cut a piece of bockwurst, speared it on my knife and handed it over. He gnawed the sausage in small bites, savoring it. I told his mother that Martin and I needed to talk.

"*Von Mann zu Mann.*"

She nodded her consent. Martin and I walked toward the lonely birch tree draped in drying laundry. I waited till he finished eating. Our conversation went as follows. In Deutsch.

"Martin, you came to the apartment yesterday, asking for the lid to the pot. And then you ran away before I could give it to you. Why did you do that?"

"I don't know."

"I think you do know. Did you see something that frightened you?"

Martin took my measure and stated his terms. "I want a cigarette."

I looked left and saw why. His pals were watching from atop the rubble mound. He wanted to show off.

"I can't give you a cigarette in front of your mum. But I'll slip you an entire pack of Lucky Strikes once we're done."

Martin's dirty mug lit up like Christmas Eve. We stopped beneath the birch tree. The clothes hanging from its branches weren't fit for dusting rags. He answered my question.

"I ran away because I saw him."

"Who?"

"The little man. I saw before."

"When?"

"Two days before."

"At the apartment?"

"Yes."

"What were you doing there?"

"I was coming to knock."

"What did you see?"

"The little man. Coming out of the door."

"Did he see you?"

"Yes."

"What did he do when he saw you?"

"He grabbed me and asked who I was."

"What did you say?"

"I was a beggar boy and could I have a cigarette."

"What did he do then?"

"He said that I must not come here," said Martin and stared at his shoes, if you could call them that. The leather uppers were shredded into strips. Call them sandals.

"Is that all he did? The little man?"

"No," said Martin, watching his toes wiggle.

"What else did he do?"

"He slapped me in my face and knocked me down."

Nice, Leonid, classy. Jimmy Streets beating the crap out of a cop tied to a chair, Hitler sending Panzer tanks against the Polish cavalry. They're always like that, the wrong numbers. They never pick on anyone their own size.

I thanked Martin for answering my questions. He put his hand out for his pack of butts. I shook it, and imparted some fatherly wisdom. "Always get your payment up front."

Martin went from crestfallen to awestruck when he saw what I had placed in his palm. He turned it over and ran his grubby fingers across its raised surface. A shiny gold sovereign bearing the likeness of George V.

"Tell your mum to find a place far away from here. Do you understand me Martin?"

Martin nodded and ran off to show his mom. I walked back toward the apartment, feeling pretty good about myself. I had confirmed my suspicion about Leonid and done a good deed in the bargain. Yes, I was walking tall. A dapper little Russian would soon have to deal with someone his own size and then some. I was looking forward to that encounter when Martin chased me down.

I was about to tell the little moneygrubber to buzz off when he did the strangest thing. He fell to his knees and kissed my hand, like I was Pius the XII or something!

I retrieved my mitt from this embarrassment and walked on, feeling pretty lousy about myself.

Chapter Twenty-eight

I didn't find what I was looking for when I got back to the apartment. The hidden microphone that would explain how Leonid knew we would be paying a call on his wife.

I'm not a complete idiot, just a lazy one. I hadn't searched the apartment for a bug when I moved in because audio surveillance requires round-the-clock engineers and I wasn't anywhere near that important. But maybe a round-the-clock crew wasn't necessary. Could be the eavesdropper knew when we would be home and when he wanted to listen in.

What I found was a ventilation box, in the parlor, on the far wall next to the radiator. I unscrewed the perforated cover. The box was a phony. No duct pipe, just a tiny wire-sized hole. And something else. A wad of spirit gum that plugged the hole. I pried it loose and rolled the gum between my thumb and forefinger. It was still fresh, pliable.

Cute. Leonid had heard all he needed to hear and removed the microphone. The wad of gum was his little taunt, his thumb in the eye to prod me to make wild accusations, accusations the CO wouldn't buy. Not without something more solid than a wad of gum. Turning NKVD Major Leonid Vitinov was the CO's one unqualified success in Berlin. I point the finger at Leonid Vitinov now and I was on my way back to the States in steerage.

Well screw Leonid, I wasn't going to play that way. I wasn't going to make wild accusations just yet. I would convince the little man that I didn't suspect him of kidnapping Ambrose.

No, that wasn't right. Ambrose had disappeared outside Leonid's apartment building. I had to suspect Leonid, while somehow convincing him I didn't know about the hidden mike, didn't know for certain that he was guilty as sin.

I wasn't sure how to pull that off but I knew that Leonid already thought me one lamb chop short of a mixed grill. I would do my best to confirm that opinion.

I put the wad of spirit gum back where I found it, replaced the cover to the ventilation box and had a terrible thought. I had something more solid than a wad of gum. I had a phony ventilation box that hid a wire hole. I had Ambrose getting snatched outside Leonid's building. Why was I so reluctant to make my case to the CO? Victor Jacobson was a dour rigid s.o.b. but no one could question his patriotism. He was as gung ho as they come. Wasn't he?

I thought about it for a minute. Yes, everything I knew about the CO said he was a straight shooting Clean Gene. And everything I knew about post-war Berlin said there was no such animal.

I went to the musty couch and stretched out, tried to get comfortable. I sat up, lied down, squeezed my head between my hands. It was 1944 all over again. Behind enemy lines. On my own and devil take the hindmost.

With one key difference. This time I had more than my own hide to worry over. I had a comrade in arms under hostile guard.

I had a lousy night. Fitful sleep and dark dreams. Wide awake at the slightest sound, hoping to see Ambrose stumbling home drunk. He didn't oblige.

I cooked up a can of Campbell's pea soup in the morning and ate it from the pot, wishing I had been a little less generous with the bockwurst. Pig and pea soup are made for each other. I washed out the pot, filled it with water, heated it on the stove and hauled it to the bathroom for a shave and a pit wash. I brushed my teeth, combed my hair, put on a clean shirt and set sail, a man with a plan.

First stop was the sweet-smelling *Konditorei* for some coffee and a phone call. There was one last tiny remaining shred of a possibility. Fevered thoughts of Eva had driven Ambrose to abandon his post. I sincerely hoped he had been that stoopid. I drank a cup of coffee. It was so bad I drank another.

I wondered if Eva could be working the other side of the street. She *had* led us to Herr Hilde awful quick. I slurped some mud. There wasn't enough time on the clock or Nescafe in the jar to answer that question.

I borrowed the phone for a buck and called the number I had committed to memory. Could Eva's phone be tapped? Not likely, didn't matter. I wasn't going to say anything the other side didn't already know. I got a groggy hello on the fifth ring.

"Eva it's Hal. Sorry to wake you." Drowsy noises on the other end of the line. "I seem to have lost track of Ambrose. Have you seen him?"

Eva was instantly alert. "No. What has happened?"

I spilled it. "I think he's been kidnapped, captured. By the Soviet secret police."

"*Mein Gott,*" she said in a voice that conjured images I had kept at bay. Ambrose strapped to a chair. Two goons taking turns. I shook it off. Not now.

"I would like to hire you Eva. I will pay whatever you like to help me find him."

A moment's silence, then a hearty "Screw you" echoed down the line.

"I don't understand, Eva, don't you..."

"I sell my body, not my heart," she said angrily. "My heart comes free."

Well. Okay then. I said a muted thanks and asked her to ask around about Ambrose. She agreed. I lowered my voice and cupped my hand around the mouthpiece, as if that would keep a phone tapper from overhearing.

"None of my business Eva but do you have any customers that work for the secret police, the NKVD?"

"No, no."

"How can you be sure?"

"Why they would come to us? We are costing them money!"

"I don't understand what you're saying."

I could almost feel the spray on my ear as Eva blurped her lips contemptuously. "I am saying, Mister Hal, that Blue Caps have their own place where to go."

I thanked Eva, told her I would call her tomorrow morning and rang off.

Capitalists take note. The Union of Soviet Socialist Republics is fully committed to the cause of world domination. The NKVD has their own brothel.

I drove the delivery truck to Dahlem. The trees had grown leaves all of a sudden and scattered yellow and red tulips stood to attention along the way. Also daffodils and some purple flower I didn't know the name of. Bulbs, buried deep. Can't keep 'em down.

I arrived about noon, parked down the block. I hadn't so much as looked in the side view mirror on the drive over. Why bother? My life was an open book. I hiked to the white brick mansion, down a block hung with fragrant blossoms on knobby-limbed trees, a lucky man in an unlucky world.

The jug-eared GI who'd picked me up at the airport answered the door. He wore civvies but had an Army-issue .45 holstered on his hip. He greeted me by name. I said I needed to see Victor Jacobson. He asked me to wait in the parlor.

Was Jug Ears a real GI on loan from the Berlin Operating Base, here to stand guard on Herr Hilde? Or was he a Global Commerce operative with a khaki uniform in his closet, next to his Navy dress whites and his Army Air Force bomber jacket? Maybe a penguin suit in case he had to impersonate a waiter.

I waited in the parlor. The swinging door to the kitchen was closed but Henka the Polish cook was up to her elbows in dumplings again. I smelled chicken fat, and a pungent smell that carried me back to the tiny kitchen of a row house in Youngstown. Liver. Henka was cooking up a batch of liver dumplings. The heartless witch.

I held my position. I have my pride. I wasn't going to barge in, my tongue hanging out like a big slobbery dog. I wasn't going to. I wasn't going to all the way across the parlor to the swinging door, which banged open, knocking me back.

"Look what the cat dragged in" said the CO, in a jolly mood for once. Liver dumplings will do that to you.

I paused, wanting Leonid present when I delivered the bad news. Doubtless he felt the same way. I sensed movement behind me and turned to look. Sure enough, there he was, standing in the hall by the front door, hands folded at his crotch.

I backed up to triangulate the situation. "I haven't seen Ambrose in twenty-four hours. I believe he's been taken hostage."

"Where? By whom? How in the hell?" demanded Jacobson.

"It happened outside Leonid's apartment building," I said, watching the little man to see if this brought any reaction. A minor wrinkling of the brow was all.

"We had a beer at the Café Gestern. The bartender recognized me from my meet with Leonid, which struck me as a little too observant. So Ambrose and I had a couple, pretending to be waiting on Leonid. When he didn't show we asked the barkeep if Leonid didn't live nearby. As a matter of fact he did. One block south, two blocks east."

"And then?"

"As a career snoop I felt duty bound to drag Ambrose over there to reconnoiter. That's when the beer caught up to me, I went off to find a *pissoir*. When I came back Ambrose was gone. And, yes, I've checked everywhere."

The point of telling this lame ass story was to bait Leonid, see if he would chastise me for making a public scene with the barkeep about Leonid's place of residence. This was unprofessional behavior. As our counterintelligence officer Leonid should take me to task. Unless he didn't want to ask the real reason I went looking for his building.

"You should never have gone there," said Leonid. "The building is under constant surveillance."

"Who by?"

"Interested parties."

"Who's interested?"

"Who is not?"

Answering questions with questions. The Napoleonic little prick wasn't going to call me out.

"Leonid, forgive me, but I'm the suspicious type. That Ambrose got himself got outside your building has me thinking all kinds of terrible thoughts."

I let that stinkeroo hang in the air for a moment. "Like, for instance, Leonid knows we're loitering around his living quarters so he calls in an NKVD snatch of Ambrose to teach us wisenheimers a thing or two."

"How would I know such a thing? That you and your friend were outside my building?"

This was it then, my cue, my *let me show you this wad of spirit gum* moment.

I let it pass. I shook my head, slowly, sorrowfully. "I don't know Leonid, I'm sorry. I guess I just don't want Ambrose's disappearance to be my fault."

The CO took the floor, said stuff about how we're all in the same boat on rough seas and need to pull together and so on and so forth.

I nodded, watching Leonid. He was a difficult read, his face never betrayed him. I couldn't tell if I'd put it over. Leonid would have preferred wild accusations that got me sent home in steerage but I was offering him another way to go. A manageable truce with a bumbling hick. Question was, did he buy the act, think me too stupid to search the apartment for a hidden mike?

Leonid plucked a plump oval cigarette from his gold case and said, "Do not blame yourself Harold. We will find your friend."

Yes he did.

I made a pious face and thanked him for his kind solicitude. I was over. He thought me stupid. And in the spy game being thought stupid is a wonderful thing.

Leonid promised to check with his NKVD handlers to see if Ambrose had been swept up 'by mistake.' The CO pledged to alert the proper authorities, whoever they might be. This was all gas and no flame of course. I would have to locate, and rescue, Ambrose by myself.

Leonid left the room. The CO slumped in an upholstered chair. "He better not be shacked up with some *Fräulein*."

"He's not."

"You know the Committee to Free Berlin meeting is tonight. Twenty hundred hours, *der Admiralspalast*, Soviet Sector."

"But isn't that where..."

"That's where it is Schroeder."

"Then I'll be there. With bells on."

"Good. Because we still have Hilde, upstairs."

"I understand."

"Your report will go a long way toward determining his future."

I snapped a snappy salute. "I'm on it sir."

Jacobson chuckled. "Get the hell out of here." I marched myself toward the front door.

"Not that way." The CO pointed his chin toward the kitchen.

I stopped. I sniffed. "Yes sir!"

Chapter Twenty-nine

I climbed into the delivery truck and cranked the ignition. The engine coughed and sputtered. I feathered the accelerator until it settled into a happy thrum. They say an army marches on its stomach and now that I had a belly full of liver dumplings I was ready to engage the enemy. The question was how.

Why not measure for measure? Swap Leonid for Ambrose.

Not bloody likely. The NKVD would wash their hands of the little man once they knew his cover was blown. It would have to be personal. I would have to kidnap Anna.

I'd do it in a blink to save Ambrose. But Leonid wouldn't care. Not enough to compromise his precious all-important principles. True believers don't compromise. Ask the murdered children of Joseph and Magda Goebbels. Ask Leonid's parents, come to that. Denouncing a family member was a sure way to curry favor with the Party. It would explain why Leonid's father was dead and his mother in custody. And why Lavrenty Beria trusted a White Russian. There was no way short of death to defeat a true believer.

Unless I could turn Leonid's handlers, turn the Communist Party, against him. Leonid's mission was to disinform the US about Soviet plans and capabilities, not difficult since the US didn't know squat. But Herr Hilde, he knew plenty.

The NKVD was counting on Leonid to discredit Hilde. The Soviets installed Hilde in the American Sector with two stumblebum guards. They *wanted* us to capture Hilde after they'd finished their purge of the freedom fighters, so he could take the blame and deflect suspicion from Leonid. More than that. The Blue Caps knew Hilde had reached out to us, that he would tell us secrets he would keep from them.

God, it was brilliant. The NKVD wanted *us* to conduct the interrogation of Brigadeführer Hilde for them, with Leonid acting as their stenographer.

Hilde couldn't have known the precise whereabouts of our émigré informers. But Leonid could have. As our CI officer he would have had reason to meet with them in order to determine their credibility. And as a fellow White Russian he would have won their confidence. Which meant, it seemed to me, that Leonid was the Judas, not Hilde. Leonid was the one who targeted our freedom fighters for death.

I glanced down at the fuel gauge. It was just above *L* which is Kraut for empty. *Leer.* I pulled away from the curb and thought deep thoughts as I drove the rumbling delivery truck north towards downtown.

If Leonid could not discredit Hilde, if the *Amerikanskis* were to begin to act upon Hilde's intelligence, or give that appearance anyway, Leonid might become expendable to the NKVD. Which might make our True Believer into a Doubting Thomas. At which time he might agree to divulge Ambrose's location.

Christ Almighty, it was a *long* way from here to there. What I really wanted was to grab the dapper little shit by the scruff of the neck and snap his digits one by one till he came clean. It's what I would have done in 1944. But things were more complicated in 1946.

It sounds like treason to say it now but most fighting men in the European Theater weren't big fans of Ike and Monty, the four-star heavyweights of the Allied Supreme Command. We considered them back-and-fillers, politicians almost. Our boy was George S. Patton, the human half-track with no reverse gear. He was one hellacious good General. In wartime.

I had a new appreciation of Ike and Monty now, understood that sometimes you've got to put it in neutral, wait and watch and pick your spot. Ambrose wasn't on the Lubyanka Express, not yet.

Leonid said his Berlin Bureau Chief was a rival to Beria. The Bureau Chief would want to keep Ambrose in his vest pocket as long as possible. But every day that passed increased the odds that the headstrong Mick would do something stupid and get himself killed.

I stopped at a corner in Wilmersdorf to fill the tank from a young street vendor with a hundred liter drum of black market petrol and a rubber hose. He employed the suction method we teenage hot-rodders used to use to steal gas. He was good at it. I paid him ten cigarettes and drove on, picturing the young man lighting up a Lucky and exhaling a ten foot flame.

The sidewalks were crowded with ragtag locals out to enjoy the late-arriving spring. Most wore kerchiefs across their mouths. I'd been foolish to grouse about the constant rain. A spike of wind sprayed brick dust across the windshield. I rolled up the windows.

The Committee to Free Berlin meeting was fast approaching. Time for a mirror read. The CO said, in Leonid's presence, that the Committee would keep their distance from a newcomer if they were plotting violence. Which meant I would be welcomed by a friendly Blue Cap in order to demonstrate that the Committee had nothing to hide. If all went according to plan I could sabotage Leonid with his handlers tonight.

Then what? Wait for him to repent the error of his ways? I would need more and better leverage on the little man. I didn't know where to find this better leverage but I knew where I wanted to start.

I hadn't thought much about Anna since our meeting in her apartment. I had tried not to think about her anyway. Mostly because I had sweet talked her into opening the door when her husband was elsewhere. She would have suffered the consequences. I had to see her again. To apologize. And to tease out some kernel of incriminating evidence I could take to the CO, thereby putting Anna in further jeopardy.

What can I tell you, it's a despicable profession.

I drove north toward the pearl gray apartment building on *Spirchenstraße*, pondering just how despicable I was willing to be. I would do whatever it took to break Leonid and rescue Ambrose. But I didn't have to destroy Anna in the process. I was a well-heeled Yank with friends in high places. If Anna played ball I would give her a way to flee Leonid and the NKVD. Unless Anna was a co-conspirator. Unless Hal Schroeder had gone poozle stoopid. She *had* let me in to the apartment. And somewhere along in there, while we were sipping tea, Soviet goons grabbed Ambrose.

I thought about it long and hard but it didn't click. Anna seemed as transparent as her blue-veined skin. Horns honked behind me. I geared up and drove on.

I would need a different way in. If the apartment building on *Spirchenstraße* wasn't under constant surveillance before it was now. The front door was out. Ditto the rear fire door. But there had to be a coal chute. It would be on the alley to the north of the building. I could slide in that way in the dead of night, bide my time and knock on Anna's door the following morning, looking like Al Jolson in *The Jazz Singer*.

I racked my noggin for another way to go. No joy. It was a miserable night in a coal bin for old Hal.

I drove north, across the *Kurfürstendamm*, the hoity toite shopping district before the war, bullet-riddled signs and busted-out plate glass now. The Red Army would have taken particular pleasure looting decadent bourgeois Kraut clothiers. I pictured weather-beaten Ivans parading down the Ku-damm in vicuna topcoats and double breasted blazers, the more acutely inebriated sporting ladies' hats and feather boas. Must have been a hell of a party.

Shoppers buzzed in and out of a ten story building topped by blackened steel girders. A department store, just like Higbee's in Cleveland. Except this one was missing the top two floors. I parked the truck and went inside. I needed an overcoat and a hat that didn't make me look like a goatherd.

I returned to the truck with a black wool topcoat and matching fedora and renewed respect for the almighty dollar. I had gotten change back from a ten.

I drove east on *Bismarckstraße*, through the treeless Tiergarten, past the sidewalk vendors and head-high nettles and a clump of refugees clustered around a fire pit where something meaty crackled on a spit. A rabbit by the long ears. Or a dachshund.

I passed through the Brandenburg Gate, the hammer and sickle snapping in the wind high above. I turned left on *Friedrichstraße* and hunted *der Admiralspalast*. I found it just north of the train station.

It was a big old thing. Half a block long with a peaked roof, four Doric columns embedded in the marble façade. It had suffered some surface damage but looked to be in one piece. I'd thought the CO was mistaken when he told me this was the site of the meeting of the Committee to Free Berlin. Seeing this grandiose old *Grande Dame* of a theater up close didn't change my opinion.

der Admiralspalast was in the Soviet Sector for starters. And it had been, just last month, the site of a big deal meeting of Germany's two new political parties. The democratic socialist SPD and the Communist KPD. A confab where the two parties had agreed to merge. The English language newspaper suggested it was a shotgun wedding, with Papa Joe holding the twelve gauge.

Why in the world would anti-Commie freedom fighters choose to meet here?

I drove on, looking to park the delivery truck out of sight of the building. I found a spot three blocks north, on a street that hugged the twisty banks of the Spree. I parked behind a donkey cart piled high with combustible material, splintered joists, torn-out paneling, chunks of asphalt. The cart driver had gone off somewhere. I killed the engine and watched and waited. Nothing happened.

The Commies were doing something right, here in the Soviet Sector. Two miles to the west displaced persons would have stripped this unattended cart clean by now. And dug a fire pit to barbecue the donkey.

The meeting of the Committee to Free Berlin was scheduled for eight p.m. My internal astrolabe calculated the angle of the fading sunlight against the vertical polarity of true north and told me, with admirable precision, that it was somewhere between late dusk and early evening. I climbed out of the truck and set off to find a clock. Preferably one behind a bar.

I found a corner tavern a block away. The old fashioned kind with stand up tables and no barstools. The cuckoo clock said seven-twenty. I ordered a stein and nursed it and asked myself a question.

Herr Hilde said the Committee was a Communist front, a fly trap set up to snare unsuspecting freedom fighters. Leonid said that was pure Commie propaganda meant to keep the US from offering assistance to the fledgling group. I preferred the Herr Hilde version. But why would the secret backers of the ruse, the NKVD, permit the meeting to be held in a gaudy showplace in the Soviet Sector?

I sipped some suds.

The NKVD were smart, that's why. They could rally the rank and file with 'Let's march into the Soviet Sector and dare the bastards to shut us down', knowing the Soviet authorities would keep clear. And they could silence any skeptics with 'If we were a Communist front why would we advertise the fact by holding a meeting in *der Admiralspalast*?' They had it covered coming and going.

I drained the last of my stein. I didn't need another as the cuckoo clock reminded me, eight times. But a shot of schnapps to smooth out the wrinkles wouldn't kill me. I asked the barkeep. Peppermint was all he had. I declined. Nobody needs a drink that bad.

I paid up and ankled out, took my time strolling down *Friedrichstraße*. I wanted the crowd settled in.

The lobby of the theater was a neck-craning sweep of sleek Art Deco curves, adjoining an empty cloakroom big as a roller rink. The place was clean but smelled bad, smelled of soot and burnt cork. Conventional bombs leave a cordite smell. *der Admiralspalast* had been hit by incendiaries.

The doors to the auditorium were closed. I could hear a loud voice declaiming inside. The curtain was up, the production underway. I got my reporter's notebook in hand and barged in.

Chapter Thirty

The auditorium was immense. About a thousand floor seats, a big mezzanine above and two balconies above that. Ritzy too. Crushed velvet seats and gilded loges that towered above the stage. The Committee to Free Berlin - the charter members sitting behind a long table on the stage, maybe forty supporters in the audience - looked dwarfed, silly, out of place. The stage was lit, the house lights dim. The man who had been declaiming in a loud voice shut his yap as I came into view. Everyone turned to follow his look. I doffed my fedora in greeting.

"*Bitte nehmen Sie Platz*," said the man on stage. Please take a seat.

"*Danke, aber ich habe bereits eins!*" Thanks, but I already have one!

All right, it was a lame joke. But even Groucho would have been hard pressed to tease a smile from this school of trout.

I sat down, in an aisle seat. I sat and listened to a series of speeches by the charter members. They hit the high notes, called for democratic self-determinism and such but nobody in the gallery said boo. The meeting had all the rough and tumble of a show trial.

Good. I wouldn't have to stand up and make a fool of myself. I'm a spy. We do our best work offstage. And if you think I'm lousy at adlibs you oughtta hear me give a speech.

This was wishful thinking, of course. I had come here to sabotage Leonid with his handlers. That required getting up on my hind legs and addressing the group.

The charter members droned on about multiparty coalitions of coagulating interests, best I could make out. When the chairman thanked the last speaker and asked if there were any questions I got my feet organized underneath me and stood up.

I introduced myself as a reporter for Stars'n'Stripes interested in doing a story on the Committee to Free Berlin.

Glacial silence.

I said I was a German-American who had fought against the Nazis, said I wanted to see the land of my ancestors return to the democratic ideals of the Weimar republic.

Pin drop silence.

I said I wanted to tell their story, said I was interested in interviewing any and all members of the Committee and their supporters.

The Chairman banged his gavel. Show over. The actors left the stage, the audience streamed toward the exits. I stood and watched them go. Herr Hilde's intel was accurate. This was a group no longer open to outsiders.

I returned to my aisle seat and waited, confidently. I had played my part. The NKVD had heard me. They would come calling, on orders from Major Leonid Vitinov.

No one showed.

I got up and walked toward the lobby. How was I supposed to sabotage Leonid with his handlers if I didn't get to speak to them? Had Leonid outthunk me on this? The CO dispatched me to the Committee meeting to see if Herr Hilde's allegations against it were true. Leonid heard him. Therefore, ergo, ipso facto, Leonid would dispatch one of the NKVD infiltrators to give me a face to face regarding pertinent circumstances.

Unless I was wrong about the Committee. Unless Hilde was the lying sack, not Leonid. No, Leonid was definitely a lying sack. Which didn't mean that Hilde wasn't also. Christ.

I pushed open the door to the lobby. A blond man about thirty held it open for me. He looked more like a boy scout than a Blue Cap. He needed a knife scar across those apple cheeks maybe, more squinty calculation in those bright blue eyes.

"I wanted to apologize to you on behalf of the members of the Committee," he said in English. English with a German accent.

"Why is that?"

The man released the door and walked with me toward the exit. "My name is Gerhard Dunkel. I am a founding member."

"Good for you," I said and kept walking.

"We have charted a noble, yet dangerous, course."

"Yes you have."

"The members of the Committee are shy about publicity."

I stood still and looked around at the gaudy Art Deco lobby of the biggest theater I had ever seen. "Hell of a spot to turn bashful."

Gerhard's eyes followed mine. He waxed nostalgic. "I saw a show here one time, in '34. My 21st birthday. It was a revue." He waggled his eyebrows. "Naked ladies."

"What fun."

Maybe this guy really was German. He sure looked it. A Kraut Blue Cap? How did that work? I asked a question.

"What was it about, the Revue? Who was in it?"

Gerhard shrugged. "It was a long time ago." I resumed walking. "If you would like I can arrange a private meeting with some of our members."

A man in a custodian's uniform pulled a janitor's cart on the other side of the lobby, emptying ashtrays that didn't need emptying.

"That won't be necessary. And you don't have to apologize. I expected a cool reception."

"Why is that?"

I reached the exit door and put my hand on the push bar. It budged. I would be able to drop my bomb and blow.

"Because, Gerhard, I have heard that the Committee to Free Berlin is a Communist front organization." I stood toe to toe. "Any truth to that?"

"Of course not! Who would say such a lie?"

"I wonder."

The blond man's breath came in little gasps. He was all kinds of upset.

"I know what you're thinking Gerhard. If I believe that why didn't I say so? Why didn't I stand up like a man and make my accusation to the group?"

"Yes indeed! Why did you not?"

I pushed open the panic bar, felt cool spring air on my face. The custodian wheeled his cart in my direction. Time for my exit line.

"Call it a professional courtesy. Comrade."

I walked out the door and beat feet. No one followed.

Spirited back-patting propelled me down the sidewalk for about two blocks. I had done what I came to do, with a touch of style if I do say so. Gerhard the phony Kraut would now tell his NKVD superiors that Leonid wasn't doing what he was paid to do – debunk and defang Herr Hilde's intelligence. Gerhard would do this right away.

And he wouldn't risk a phone call.

Crap on toast, Schroeder. The man can lead you right to the target, right to the top secret NKVD hideout where Ambrose, for all you know, is being held in chains. Tail him!

I ran the two blocks to the delivery truck, kicking myself all the way. I jumped in and drove back to the theater.

der Admiralspalast had an underground parking garage, the exit next to the front door. I parked half a block shy and watched and waited. I waited and hoped and waited some more.

God did not smile. Gerhard was already gone. I had screwed up.

I told myself all was not lost. I told myself that so long as we had Leonid we had a way to find Ambrose and set him free. I told myself all kinds of crap, even believed some of it.

I drove south down *Friedrichstraße* and fought back urges. The urge to get stinking drunk. The urge to blast my way into the pearl gray apartment building, kick the door to Leonid's apartment and beat him to a clotted pulp. These were good solid All American urges, don't get me wrong. But they would have to wait. I had a late night date with a coal bin.

Chapter Thirty-one

The coal chute was shut tight. It didn't have a handle or any way short of a crowbar to pry it open. And there's never a crowbar around when you need one.

I was huddled in the dark alley north of Leonid and Anna's apartment building, unfollowed and unobserved, best I could tell. I groped around for a lock cylinder, found it on the side of the chute cover. A crude contraption fit for a skeleton key. The coal chute was locked, not sealed. I whipped out my folding knife and poked and prodded. It was the simplest lock imaginable and it took me a sweaty ten minutes and a busted blade tip to tumble it.

I opened the cover slowly. It creaked. It creaked like Dracula's coffin lid.

I listened for approaching footsteps, heard none. I studied the coal chute in the moonlit dim. It was narrow and it didn't plunge straight down. The chute had a bend in it. A twist. Like everything else in this town.

I weighed my options. It had to be after midnight by now. No one had come running at the sound of the creaky cover. Odds were slim that the front and back doors of the building were still under active surveillance.

Tough shit. The chute was big enough to accommodate me, provided I stripped down and covered myself with hog grease. Jimmying my way in the front or back entailed an extra measure of risk. Not just to me, the hell with me. The risk was to Ambrose. And to whatever noble half-baked enterprise we were embarked on here in post-war Berlin.

I shrugged off my new coat and stuffed it down the coal chute. I braced myself with my right hand and held the chute cover with my left as I stuck my legs inside and questioned my sanity. I pushed off with my right hand and swung the cover shut with my left as I plunged downward.

I made it through the bend in the chute with a great deal of wriggling and muffled curses, then dropped like a rock into an empty coal bin. My topcoat cushioned the fall. Sort of. The chute cover was creaky because no one used it. The apartment building on *Spirchenstraße*, I noted as I climbed out of the coal bin, slowly, in stages, had acquired a shiny new gas furnace.

I shook the coal dust from my coat and searched out a utility sink. I was gritty as a ranch hand and wanted to wash up. Which risked the groan of old pipes. I had made enough racket for one evening. I found an empty crate, turned it over and sat there all night long.

I killed time by asking myself questions for which I had no answers. How to talk my way into apartment K this time? How to determine if Anna was a co-conspirator? If she wasn't a co-conspirator how to convince her to give me something tangible to prove to the CO that Leonid was dirty? And, if she did that, how to give her a way to flee and where to?

Shit, what a tangle. I looked on the bright side. If Anna refused to open the door I was free to drive back to Dahlem, drag Leonid into the bathroom and shove his head in the toilet.

A pleasant prospect.

But not one worthy of Wild Bill Donovan's fair-haired boy. Wild Bill's fair-haired boy was expected to find a way to rescue Ambrose while exposing the perfidy of Leonid and the Committee to Free Berlin, thereby keeping the Soviet tank divisions that were supposedly gunning their engines on the eastern banks of the Elbe from shifting into gear and starting World War III.

How was that fair?

When the local bell tower tolled nine a.m. I washed up in the sink, dried my hands on the seat of my pants, waited another precautionary half hour then started up the basement steps. I listened at the door at the top of the stairs. It wouldn't do to step out just as Leonid strode through the lobby, late for work.

Nothing to hear. I stepped into the lobby. The coast was clear. I hurried to the rear fire stairs and started climbing.

My late night noodling had yielded one nugget. Leonid knew, from monitoring our conversation, that Ambrose and I would pay a visit to his apartment while he was away at work. He would not have needed to inform Anna of this, not needed her to invite me in for tea. He would have known I'd post Ambrose as a street sentry, known his goons could snatch Ambrose before I made it halfway across the lobby. Anna was not necessarily a co-conspirator.

I walked down the corridor to apartment K, passing the open door to the apartment next door. I heard a small dog yapping.

Keep it up, Fido, give me cover. Yap your fool head off till I talk my way into the apartment.

Fido did. He caught my scent and chased me all the way down the hall, yapping his fool head off. He was one of those fluffy rich-lady dogs. I shushed him as I knocked on the door to apartment K. He didn't pay the least attention.

I carried all the gear that the well-trained espionage agent is supposed to carry – counterfeit credentials, a gun, a folding knife, lock picks, a pen light. I even had an L pill stashed in my wallet somewhere. But my spy school instructor had never said anything about dog biscuits.

I squatted down and made nice. "Hey there, buddy, what's all the fuss?"

Fido's yapping intensified. I tried Deutsch. "*Hallo, Kumpel, Was soll die Aufregung?*"

No go. I grabbed for the little mutt's yapper but he jumped up, bit me right on the schnozz and didn't let go.

Man, that smarts. I had to employ top secret ju jitsu disabling techniques to persuade the little fiend to unlock his jaw. Then I reared back and heaved him down the hall.

This did not go unobserved. Fido's owner, a plump matron in a bathrobe and hairnet, shrieked in horror at the sight of her precious pooch tumbling ass-end over teakettles.

She tried to scoop him up but damned if the little fiend didn't scramble to his feet and race back down the hall for another go at me, his owner chasing frantically behind, her bathrobe becoming unhinged in the process.

A bloody Yank under attack by a rabid Pomeranian and a shrieking half-naked neighbor was the charming tableaux Anna beheld when she opened the door in her painting smock.

It wasn't a complete disaster. I wouldn't have to invent some clever reason for Anna to let me in. I only had to, as the little fiend tore at my ankles and his owner paused halfway down the hall to reassemble herself, turn to Anna, blood streaming down my chin, and say, drolly, "This is the last time I will ask to borrow your bathroom, I promise."

Anna didn't say no. She didn't say anything. She was at a loss for words maybe. I entered her apartment. She bent down and spoke to the little fiend, sharply, in Russian.

He shut his yap.

Chapter Thirty-two

Anna marched me to the bathroom matter-of-factly, pushing my chin up so I didn't drip on her nice clean floor. It worked. The blood from the puncture wounds in my nose sluiced behind my ears and down my neck and made my shirt wet.

She sat me down on the pot and swabbed me with gauze and isopropyl. There are few things in the life more pleasant that being ministered to by a beautiful woman, even one who was...*ouch*...ticked off.

"You haf brought me much trouble," she said, clamping a compress to my beezer with a bit more force than absolutely necessary.

"I am very sorry Anna." I sounded like Bugs Bunny. "And now, forgive me, I am here to bring you more trouble."

She stood back and laughed at me, a pearly little trill in the back of her throat, pretty as birdsong. "You haf *more* trouble?"

"Yes I do."

Anna left the bathroom and went to the parlor. I followed, holding the compress to my nose. Anna stared out the window and waited for me to say what I had to say. It was another odd moment between us. Domestic, familiar. Why didn't she just march me out?

"Anna I believe that Leonid had my partner Ambrose kidnapped, taken prisoner. Leonid did this while you and I shared cups of tea the other day." She turned towards me. I mimed a cup, my pinky in the air. "Is there anything that you would like to tell me?"

Anna had a stark face, all planes and angles, nothing round. A Russian face. One seriously pissed off Russian face.

"You think I can do such thing?"

"I don't want to think so Anna. But I don't know you very well."

Anna gave me a defiant look and turned around and pulled her painter's smock up to her shoulders to reveal a pale naked back pocked with deep purple bruises and a semi-circular abrasion at the base of her neck. Leonid had pressed her face to the floor while he worked her over.

I had seen a lot worse, but it got to me. The methodic nature of it, like he'd been following one of those Arthur Murray dance floor diagrams. How miserably sick did you have to be to do that to your wife?

Anna lowered her painting smock to its proper place and turned to face me. I had an unforgivable, burn-in-hell-for-all-eternity pang of regret when she did that - shook her smock back in place before turning around. Anna wasn't wearing a brassiere. And I so wanted to see her breasts.

Yeah, I know. When did I say different? And now I was going to ask Anna to betray her husband and put herself in the crosshairs.

I couldn't do it. Not yet.

"Anna you must leave here. You must go away, you can't live like this. You must leave." Anna hugged herself and looked at me, her eyes filled with tears and resignation. "I can help you. I can, I have money. I am rich *Amerikanski!*"

Anna didn't smile. She did pucker her lips a bit, as if considering.

"Do you have somewhere you can go? Someone who will shelter you, take you in?"

She scraped a tear from her cheek with her fist. When she spoke she was barely audible.

"I haf cousin, Sasha, who will take me."

"Great, that's great. Where does Sasha live?" Anna inclined her head. "Where does she live, reside?" She frowned. I used the only Russian noun I knew. "Where is her *dacha*?"

This brought a fleeting smile and a starry gaze and three words, whispered, as if in prayer.

"New York City."

I fought to keep my encouraging smile in place. New York. How in hell was I going to pull that off?

Anna noted my frozen smile and started in on her fingers again, strangling them. I don't know why that bothered me so much, but I would have moved mountains to keep Anna from strangling her pale delicately-tapered fingers purple.

"Yes Anna. *Da*. I will arrange for you to travel to New York City."

Anna's muffled sobs and hiccupping thank you's were gratifying, but she had ceased her violent hand wringing, that was the main thing. I approached and took those glorious digits in mine and squeezed them, gently. She squeezed back, with a ferocity that shot bolts of pain up to my shoulders.

We were face to face now, blood pumping, untoward things begging to happen. I told myself not to misbehave and meant it and forgot it a second later. I bent down to kiss her. She backed away. I tasted why. Salty blood was streaming down my face.

I pressed the compress to my nose. Anna guided me to a chair, took hold of the compress and clamped down. I had to brace my feet to keep from sliding off the chair. Not a hundred pounds dripping wet yet strong as a stevedore. God only knew what horrors she had survived in wartime Russia. She was a woman to be reckoned with.

I sat still and waited for my blood to clot. The silence between us was easy, companionable. Ivan the cat slinked over and jumped on my lap. My eyelids drooped. Time to speak up.

"Anna I need your help now," I said, my words echoing through the foggy chambers of my head. I stifled a yawn. "I need your help to...bring Leonid to justice, to show, to *beweisen* to my boss that Leonid is a *schlecht Mann*. Do you understand?"

Anna shook her head, then nodded just as quickly. "I know what you say, not what you ask."

"What do you mean?"

"Leonid tells me nothing."

"Nothing at all?"

"I do not, even, to meet his family."

Family? "I thought that Leonid's only living relative, his only family, was his *Mutter*."

Anna looked down at me with a curious intensity, then crossed to a dresser drawer and dug deep. She returned with a framed photograph, a professional portrait of two young children dressed in their Sunday best. A young boy with fine features holding his lace-swaddled kid sister on his lap. Their love for each other was unmistakable.

"Leonid's sister? *Schwester*?"

Anna nodded. Leonid had told me he was an only child, doubtless told the CO the same. Not a big lie but one I could prove.

"Is she still alive?"

"Yes, yes. She is living closely."

"Do you know where? Her address? *Ansprache*?"

Anna pouted, sorry to disappoint me. "But she is not so far. They meet on some evening."

"Leonid tells you this?"

"No. But he is happy after. And he is never happy."

Well. Here we all were again. Hal, Anna and Ivan the Terrible. I had done well, the pieces had fallen nicely into place. Which made me nervous. Was there any possible way in hell I was being played here? Could Leonid have somehow anticipated my intent to pay a second visit to Anna and ordered his beaten submissive wife to play along with whatever I proposed? Could Leonid be that good?

There was the slightest glimmer of half a chance he could be. And it didn't matter. If Leonid was that good I may as well turn Commie because the Soviets would overrun all of Continental Europe while we poor dumb Yanks took a victory lap.

I'm not sure if I thought this or dreamed it.

I woke to the sound of a shrill scream. I was on my feet before my eyes opened, digging for my gun, stumbling forward, ready to do battle. Anna laughed at me. And took the whistling tea kettle off the stove.

I slumped back in the chair and tried to wake up. The cup of black tea helped. I had no idea how long I'd been asleep. Fast asleep in the apartment of my mortal enemy.

Anna had been busy. A big leather-strapped suitcase sat by the front door next to a wicker basket. I was wondering what was in the basket when a trapped angry mewl answered my question.

I stood up. "We can't leave the building together."

Anna nodded her understanding. Now what? My good intentions had outraced my planning once again. I had no safe house to send her to. But Anna was a step ahead. She wrote down an address in Kopenick, southeast of the Central City, in the Soviet Sector.

"Tattia, she is my friend, *gut* friend."

"Does Leonid know her?"

"No, no."

Which didn't mean he didn't know about her or where she lived. What the hell. I didn't have any better ideas.

"How will you get there, to Kopenick?"

"*der Straffenbahn*," she said. The streetcar.

"Okay. But you might be followed. Be careful, keep watch. Do you understand?"

Anna gave me a droll look. "I am wife of spy."

"Right, of course," I said and pointed toward the door. "But you can't take the suitcase." Anna pretended not to understand. "*Der Kaffen is verboten.*"

"*Aber ich werde es brauchen!*" she replied. But I will need it!

"*Nein, es ist zu gefährlich!*" No, it is too dangerous!

Anna glared at me. I glared back. We hadn't set foot out the door and we were already spatting like an old married couple. An old German couple!

I stepped forward and stood close. "Take the damn cat if you must, take Ivan, but the suitcase stays put! Stays here. Does-not-leave."

Anna's stark glacial face remained that way. Mulish to a fault, just like Jeannie. Why are all the best gals the world over so goddamn stubborn?

"Okay," I sighed, "I will smuggle your suitcase out of here somehow. Take your damn cat in a basket and go."

Anna smiled up at me, then wrapped me up in a steaming hug that squeezed every ounce of air from my lungs. It felt good. I looked about the room, at Anna's vivid watercolors on the walls, surprised she hadn't crated them up too.

Anna caught my look and answered with a shrug. "I will make more."

"Attagirl!"

"I am sorry?"

I told Anna I would see her in Kopenick tomorrow morning and pushed her out the door.

Chapter Thirty-three

They had separate bedrooms, Leonid and Anna. His the spacious master with French windows that opened onto the street. Hers a small windowless maid's quarters, walls cluttered with watercolors, pencil sketches and oil portraits in that modern style where the heads look like they'd been chopped to pieces with a meat cleaver then wedged back together.

I tossed the joint. I searched behind the wall hangings for a wall safe and inside them for documents stashed in the matting. I did this in each room. I pulled up rugs and looked for a floor safe or a trap door or a loose floorboard. I checked the furniture for hollow legs and secret panels and docs taped to seat bottoms. I looked in the bathroom and kitchen cabinets. I yanked the cushions from the couch and flipped it over and dumped out every bureau and kitchen and desk drawer I could find.

This netted me nothing of interest. Okay. Due diligence done. Now the fun part.

I went to Leonid's clothes closet and pulled open the folding doors. Dozens of custom-tailored suits hung in a precise seasonal progression from black and navy blue wool, to brown and tan tweed, to pale linen. Silk ties hung light to dark on a yard-long tie rack. The shirts, starched and cardboard-collared, were tucked away in the drawers of a built-in cedar cabinet at the end of the closet. Heckuva wardrobe for a selfless champion of the proletariat.

I didn't bother the shirts. But Leonid's suits would need a thorough going over. I waded back down the long closet, through the forest of topcoats and sports jackets and the hanging vines of silk until I came to the summer linen. I flicked open my folding knife and did to Leonid's pretty suits what I wanted to do to him. Sliced them up one side and down the other. Methodically.

I took hold of a blood red cashmere blazer. It had a gold monogram on the breast pocket, LAV. I sliced it off and stuck it in my pocket for future reference. Then I tore the coat off the hangar and stepped on it and grabbed the back vent and pulled with all my might. The suit coat split all the way to the collar.

Good, Schroeder. Well done and executed. You've shown Leonid's wardrobe who's boss. Now, how do you exit the building in a stealthy manner while carrying a suitcase the size of a hay bale? The Blue Caps would have their tails down and their ears up. You'll be scooped up the moment you step outside.

I told my brain to shut its yap. I knew what to do next. Start a fire. One with a lot of smoke. A swank joint like this had to have a fire alarm. Yank it and race down the fire stairs and out the back door with the rest of the tenants, their hastily-packed suitcases in hand.

But I needed a hat, a snap brim I could pull low across my brow. Just like the one I had recently purchased and left in the truck. Leonid had hats on the top shelf, plus a little step stool to reach them. I selected a gray felt number. It perched atop my melon like a Girl Scout beanie. I sliced a vent in the back of the hat band and tried again. It would have to do.

What to torch? Something dense, something that would burn a long time and throw off a lot of smoke. A red cashmere blazer for instance. I snatched up the coat from the floor of the closet, went to the kitchen, grabbed the largest pot I could find and took a bottle of Drambuie from the liquor locker. I crammed the blazer into the pot, doused it with booze and lit it with a kitchen match.

Drambuie's good for something. The coat caught fire.

I waited until the kitchen filled with smoke, threw open the front door and fanned smoke into the hallway with a kitchen towel. I pounded on doors and yelled *Feuer* as I hauled Anna's two-ton grip down the hallway.

The fire alarm was halfway down the corridor. I busted the glass with the little hammer on a chain and yanked the handle. A great clanging commenced.

The neighbor lady threw open her door. She had changed into a housedress since our last meeting. She had Fido clutched to her bosom and wet panic in her eyes.

I offered to escort her down the stairs. The neighbor lady accepted. We fled down the carpeted fire stairs, our ranks swelling at every landing until we spilled out the back door, a tumbling cascade of terrified refugees.

That's the way it was supposed to work anyway. Unfortunately the back door didn't open. I kicked it and slammed a shoulder against it and it didn't budge. The door had been barred or shimmed shut, a bad sign. It meant the Blue Caps would be waiting as we funneled out the front. I could join the panicked tenants streaming out the entryway and take my chances on getting lost in the crush. Or I could try to blast my way out the back door with my Walther.

I surprised myself. For once in my life I didn't blunder forth. I slunk back down to the basement instead, closed the door behind me, found my overturned crate and sat down and considered the possibilities. Harry Houdini couldn't wriggle his way up a folded coal chute while hauling a suitcase but there were two windows up at ground level. Transom windows that vented in, at an angle too narrow to climb through. I would have to use my burglar skills. Provided I could get up there.

I looked around for a ladder. Every basement has a ladder somewhere. Every basement except this one.

I scavenged up crates and storage boxes and laddered them against the wall and climbed up to the window that faced the alley. I placed my coat against a window corner and tapped at it with the butt of my Walther, creating a small spider web of cracks. I did this all the way around the window frame. Then I took my knife and sliced through the perforated glass. This was the tricky part. You have to start at the bottom and tease the pane inward as you unzip the window from its frame. I wrapped the glass in my coat and climbed down my makeshift ladder. I shed the glass, shook out my coat, donned it, grabbed the heavy suitcase and climbed back up. Slowly, cursing Anna with every step. I gathered my strength and shoved the suitcase through the window frame. Which caused my jumbled staircase to collapse.

I grabbed the window sill and hung suspended for a painful second. I hadn't cleared away all the glass shards.

I dropped to the floor and took a quick minute to wash my bloody mitts at the utility sink. There was an ancient zinc mirror above the sink that I hadn't noticed before. And a mug in the looking glass I couldn't have identified in a police blotter. He was wearing a grey felt hat two sizes too small, had dried blood stains on his swollen beezer and bags under his eyes you could pack a lunch in.

I laughed at him and doffed my hat.

I reassembled my rickety stairstep, climbed up to the window, cleared away the glass shards and squeezed, gingerly, through the busted window.

Chapter Thirty-four

I walked down the side alley toward the rear of the building at a deliberate pace, not looking back, listening for footsteps or the sound of an engine, hearing neither. The Blue Caps had outfoxed themselves. I should have been spotted by the rear door watcher as I turned left down the back alley. But the NKVD had sealed the rear door and posted the sentry out front. Leastwise no one objected as I ankled down the back alley and into the sunlit spring, Anna's suitcase in hand.

I fired up the delivery truck and drove south on a side street, toward Dahlem, keeping an eye on the mirrors.

I had misread Leonid, it seemed to me. What kind of fanatical true believer in world Communism has a wardrobe that Cesar Romero would kill for? Leonid was, it seemed to me, first and foremost, a fanatical true believer in Leonid. It would explain something that had been marinating in that catch basin just above the spinal cord where unanswered questions go to sit and stew.

Why did Leonid have Ambrose snatched?

Ambrose and I didn't have anything solid on Leonid, he didn't need to throw down the gauntlet. A true spook, a *true* true believer would have done nothing but keep watch, confident in his superior knowledge. But we had offended Leonid by daring to suspect him.

So. Leonid was an egotist. That was good. Egotists are a soft target. Egotists have something that can be taken hostage. Their pride.

I would need to set it up just so. Get the CO to play along, listen in as I confronted his counterintelligence officer. Busting the little man wide open would be the easy part. I would explain how hayseed Hal had chumped the sophisticated superspy by betraying him to the very NKVD agent Leonid had instructed to greet me. Leonid wouldn't like that. If need be I'd slide the gold monogram from his red jacket across the table and let him follow those rails to the station.

None of which would matter if the CO didn't agree to co-operate. I had been a bad boy. I had undertaken operational initiatives without prior authorization. I would have to confess my sins to Victor Jacobson and then, if he didn't can me on the spot, convince him to eavesdrop on his prized double agent.

Hoo boy. I did have one piece of solid evidence though. The photo of the sister Leonid claimed not to have.

Shit.

I curbed the truck in a panic. Where was the goddamn photo? I patted my pockets but that was stupid. I hadn't removed the photo from its frame before I dozed off in apartment K. The suitcase sat on the passenger's seat. I unbuckled it, pledging my undying fealty to Anna if she had done as I hoped.

She had, God bless her devious soul. The photographic portrait of young Leonid and his baby sister had been removed from its frame and rolled up and tucked into an elastic shoe pocket.

Anna had done something else as well. Taped a piece of sketch paper to the back of the portrait, a deft pencil drawing of a woman with an angular face and thin lips that curled up, impishly, at one corner. I returned the smile. The smartass. She knew that I was going to carry her grip out of the building.

I fastened the suitcase and drove on. A sudden rain spattered the windshield. Traffic slowed to a stop as we approached a major thoroughfare. I got nervous, sitting there. I checked my mirrors. No vehicles behind. My training said I should take a circuitous route, play hide and seek. My gut said get to Dahlem as soon as possible, make my case to the CO before Leonid learned that his building had been evacuated and his wife had flown the coop.

Did the Blue Caps know for sure that I had paid another visit to the apartment building on *Spirchenstraße*? I had entered the building undetected and left the same way, that much I knew. Everything in between was open to interpretation. Anna's exit with her basket, the sudden fire alarm and the stream of fleeing tenants. The Blue Caps couldn't trace those back to me with any certainty. No they couldn't.

Not till they discovered that the smoldering fire was set in apartment K thirty minutes after Anna left the building. They wouldn't misinterpret that.

Traffic remained stalled. I opened the door and stood tiptoe on the running board. The rainfall made it hard to see. It looked like a flatbed truck had taken too sharp a turn and dumped empty pallets all across the intersection ahead. The truck driver was arguing with somebody while horns honked. Five'll get you ten that similar scenes were being acted out along the thoroughfare, to the immediate west of the apartment building on *Spirchenstraße*. A search perimeter quickly improvised to capture a solo escapee. Me.

Time for evasive action. I checked my sideview mirror. Past time. A big black sedan was closing in behind. The kind of vehicle you'd expect a bunch of NKVD goons to drive. I shoved the truck into reverse and tromped on the accelerator, keeping my eyes on the sideview mirror.

I noticed my mistake a moment too late. The big black sedan was full, but not with Blue Caps.

The sedan hit the brakes. I did likewise but the truck had a head of steam. I skidded backward on the wet pavement and plowed into the sedan's front grille.

A bald noggin punched a hole in the windshield on the passenger's side. The horn blared as the driver hit the steering wheel. The other passengers careened around inside the car like bowling pins.

Five men. Wearing Roman collars.

I jumped out to lend assistance, saw the familiar circular logo on the driver's side door. *National Conference of Catholic Charities.*

Good Lord.

Catholic priests can be a tiresome lot. For every good shepherd tending to his flock there are two who mumble through Mass and fall asleep in the confessional. Still, they are trained to expect the worst of humankind, and dole out forgiveness. Which is what the good fathers from the National Conference of Catholic Charities did once I apologized profusely and donated my last two gold sovereigns to the cause. I explained that I'd thought they were a carload of Russian spies. They found that amusing.

Their injuries were minor, mostly. The bald priest whose head hit the windshield, well, there must be a lot of vessels up top because he looked like bloody murder. I mopped his dome with my hankie and offered him a pack of Luckies. He offered me absolution. We parted on good terms.

The traffic jam at the intersection had melted away. The flatbed truck was gone, the pallets cleared. I had wasted enough time looking over my shoulder. I climbed back into my barely dented delivery truck. It started up without complaint. I drove due south - hot, straight and normal, as the submariners like to say.

I felt good despite my recent idiocy. I felt ready for action. Let the Blue Caps try to stop me and my brawny delivery truck. Just let 'em try. We would teach them the error of false pride.

As I like to say.

Chapter Thirty-five

"What the hell happened to you?" said Victor Jacobson, looking up from his desk in the garage. He had a phone cradled to his ear and a cigarette in his hand. I waited until he finished his call.

"Bit by a dog sir."

"On the nose?"

"It's a long story."

The CO didn't ask further, which was jake by me. "How did the Committee meeting go?"

"Very well."

"What did you learn?"

"A good deal."

Jacobson blew smoke through his nostrils. "Well?"

"I learned that the Committee to Free Berlin is a Soviet front just like Hilde said it was. I learned that because a founding member greeted me warmly after the meeting adjourned."

Jacobson balled up his cheeks. "If the Committee's a front they'd keep their distance."

"They did. They acted like I smelled bad. All except this founding member."

The CO stubbed out his cigarette. You could have bought a small house in the country with what was in that ashtray. Something was up.

"I don't have time to play Twenty Questions Schroeder. Bill Donovan is flying in tomorrow. And it's not a social visit."

Wow, Wild Bill himself! Wanting a full report from his fair-haired boy no doubt. I hadn't smoked in years but I bummed one and took a drag.

"Sir, in my opinion, the founding member approached me because Leonid instructed him to do so, to defuse any suspicions of the Committee we might have. Leonid did this, in my opinion, because Leonid is working for the NKVD, not us."

"Based on what?" said the CO, just like that. No fireworks, no hard stare.

I laid it out. The evidence of a hidden mike in our apartment, the phony ventilator box, the fresh wad of gum over the wire hole, then the snatch of Ambrose based on intel gleaned from the hidden mike. The CO smoked and listened. Hearing myself run it down I realized how thin my case sounded, how circumstantial.

Ah, but the photo. I had somehow remembered to bring the photo of young Leonid and his little sister. I placed it on the desk.

"Leonid told me he was an only child. What did he tell you?"

Jacobson studied the photo. "Anna give you this?"

"Uh, yeah. Yes she did. She said the sister lives nearby."

"You went *back* to Leonid's apartment?"

The CO's angry stare said don't bother repeating that cock and bull about how you haven't been in her apartment before, how you'd wandered off to drain the snake when Ambrose got snatched.

"Yes sir."

"Are you nuts?"

"Not to my knowledge," I said, woozy with nicotine, adding my half-smoked butt to the pile in the ashtray.

The CO addressed his desk blotter. "This is an extremely serious allegation Schroeder."

"Yes sir."

"One based on fraternization with the wife of your superior, a fraternization conducted *in his home*."

The CO looked up. His stare was no longer angry. It was cold.

"I don't see how Leonid rates as my superior, sir, but I agree that my comportment stinks. To high heaven. But I'm right about Leonid, I know I am. I just need you to know it too."

Jacobson spun ribbons of cigarette smoke above his desk. Get to the point.

"I need to confront Leonid in a neutral location. Not here but someplace secure, someplace he's comfortable."

"Tall order."

"There's more. I need..."

"You need, you need, you need, you need! You need me to listen in. You need me to hide in a closet and eavesdrop while you try to pry some admission of guilt from our counter-intelligence officer, a seasoned professional who will tell you nothing! Is that what you *need*, Schroeder?"

I bit my lip while Jacobson had a brief talk with himself, jaw working, right hand flicking ashes, left hand punishing his receding hairline, every gesture saying *why did I ever sign up for this*. I realized I had been foolish to question the CO's loyalty, even in passing. The guy bled red, white and blue.

"He *will* tell me something sir."

"He had better," said the CO grimly, chain lighting a fresh Lucky.

"If I don't strip the dapper little man naked in your presence you will have my letter of resignation on your desk in the morning."

Victor Jacobson wasn't listening. I didn't take it personally. He wasn't answering his ringing telephone either. I let him cogitate while I stared at the hairline cracks in the plasterboard that Leonid had found so interesting a week or a month or a year or so ago. Time flies when you're having fun.

"The back room of the Café Gestern has an armoire. The employees hang their cloaks there." The CO cleared his throat, and again, like a cat coughing fur. "I could squeeze in, I suppose."

Yes.

"And how do we go about luring Leonid to the Café?"

Victor Jacobson looked up and smiled, happy to pass the baton of insoluble dilemmas to his underling for once.

"You *invite* him Schroeder. He's in the Comm Center last I looked."

Chapter Thirty-six

The Communications Center was upstairs in the back, in what must have been the master bedroom of the white brick mansion. It looked like a big time bookmaking operation. Banks of telephones, clanking teletypes, a blackboard chalked with columns of numbers. Hell, it *was* a big time bookmaking operation. Only Wild Bill's green eyeshade boys were charting the odds on something more important than Gumlegs in the third at Pimlico.

Nobody noticed me when I pushed through the door, the reception desk was unattended. Beyond the desk a shortwave operator hunched over his set, headphones on, transcribing furiously on a clipboard, code book at his elbow. An analyst, his desk buried in periodicals and press clippings, was head down in the latest cable dispatch. Phones rang off the hook and no one to answer them.

Data collection and analysis are not my cup of wax. Rearguard wool gathering is what it is. Still, I thought as the missing receptionist I had seen before brushed past me and clickety clacked her high heels over to the bank of phones, the Global Commerce Comm Crew looked to be gathering a lot of wool this afternoon.

The shortwave operator got up from his desk and crossed to a tin wall-map of Europe. He moved two numbered red magnets west in the Soviet Zone, placing one just north of Hamburg and the other just south.

I studied the map. Red magnets were arrayed all along the eastern bank of the *Elbe*, from Hamburg in the north to the Czech border in the south. No wonder Bill Donovan was coming to call.

Now, where the hell was Leonid? There wasn't any big desk in a corner that he wasn't sitting at. There wouldn't be. Leonid wasn't a big desk in a corner kinda guy. He'd want privacy, with a way to keep an eye out. An adjoining office, with a peephole.

The far wall. A pane of smoked glass in a wall of cheap wainscoting that didn't go with the rest of the room. That would be Leonid's office. Where the hell was the door? And what in the hell was I going to say to the little creep when I found it?

The red-headed receptionist gave me a nod and a smile when I approached her at the phone bank. I returned the nod and waited till she completed her call.

"Busy day," I said.

"Very."

"Will you please tell Leonid that Hal Schroeder is here to see him?"

"Certainly Mr. Schroeder," she replied in a Scottish burr. "Though I must tell you, he is not one who takes kindly to interruptions."

I assured her it was important. She pressed an intercom key and did my bidding. Leonid replied with an obscenity.

I scanned the wall for a door hinge or handle. No sign. Must be a pocket door.

It was. Leonid appeared in the doorway, in silhouette, backlit by some kind of superwhite light. He saw me and gestured, hand open, palm up. *What?*

I gave him a merry wave and held my ground.

Yeah, I know. I'd sworn off winging it at the last minute in favor of dutiful preparation. But there's one drawback to dutiful preparation. Just ask French Defense Minister Andre Maginot, *Saint Patron* of the Maginot Line. You can get locked into a plan that doesn't fit the shifting circumstance.

Red Army divisions were crowding the *Elbe*, Wild Bill was flying in for an emergency consultation, my appearance at the Committee to Free Berlin had not gone according to Leonid's plan. I wasn't going to lure the little man to the Café Gestern. He would smell a rat. It was here and now, or never.

I bent down and huddled with the redhead. She didn't like Leonid any more than I did apparently because she agreed to my muttered request to get Jacobson up here, and have him eavesdrop via the intercom.

I squeezed her arm in thanks and approached Leonid at a deliberate pace. I entered his office. He slid the door shut.

The room was long and narrow, not six feet side to side. The smoked window was one way glass, offering a clear view of the Comm Center. A large window on the opposite wall looked out on the backyard and the garage. And the door to the CO's office. A perfect perch. I would have to command Leonid's attention to insure he didn't spy Jacobson hurrying out of his office. And find a way to get my mitts on the intercom key.

There was only one chair in the room. His. One of those fancy leather jobs that wheel and swivel. I took it, and put my feet up on his desk for good measure.

"What...do you think...you are doing?"

"I think better with my feet up," I said, amiably.

Leonid blinked under the bright light that came from some sort of vapor lamp behind his desk. The lamp shutters were crimped so that the glare was focused forward. He blinked again. It must have been disorienting for him, poor dear, his inner sanctum invaded by a cocky jerk twice his size.

"Aren't you going to offer me a libation?"

I had never seen Leonid imbibe but he was Russian, he had a bottle somewhere. I asked for a drink to distract him while I keyed on the intercom. And to give my false bravado a little boost. Yeah, Leonid's small, but so's a pit viper.

The intercom was a small keyboard of toggle switches. I pushed down the switch labeled *CC* while Leonid rummaged in a steel cabinet on the wall behind him. The switch popped back up when I released it. I cast about for a way to pin it open.

Leonid found what he was looking for. A dusty bottle of clear liquid.

I did too. A pencil thick as a forefinger. I depressed the switch and wedged the pencil stub between the keys on either side. Leonid returned to the desk. The pencil rolled out.

"I'm not a complete savage Leonid. I use a glass."

Leonid muttered something vile in his native language, Russian being well suited to that sort of thing, and returned to the steel cabinet. I crammed the pencil back into place and gave it a stern look. It held.

Leonid plunked the bottle and a glass down on his desk, stepped back and crossed his arms. He looked like a cheap hood in a B movie.

I poured two fingers of Russian vodka into the glass and down my gullet. I looked up and x-rayed the little man.

"Aren't you s'posed to say something tough and hardbitten here Leonid? Something like, *This had better be good mister?*"

I held my look. Leonid returned it, his deep, liquid peepers frosted over, flat as buttons.

When I figured the CO had had enough time to get to the intercom, I started in with, "How's your sister?" That backed Leonid up a step.

"I do not have a sister."

"No? I thought you did."

"Why?"

"Oh, things I've heard. Here and there."

"I do not have a sister."

"Okay. Glad we cleared that up." I tossed back another shot. Leonid no longer looked angry, just very, very alert. I asked another question.

"Any idea where Ambrose might be?"

Leonid waved me off, dismissively.

"No? Because I'm pretty sure you had him kidnapped."

A contemptuous snort from the little man.

"It was just a coincidence Ambrose got snatched outside your building?"

I laid off the 'while I was romancing your wife' part because I didn't want a knife fight just yet. Leonid wasn't heeled that I could see but he had a neck slicer tucked in the pocket of trimly tailored pants.

"My building is under constant surveillance, by many parties."

"Yeah, so you've said. I remember that now. I guess I owe you an apology for what I did."

Leonid's eyes got slim. I ground my back molars to a halt. He would have to ask if he wanted to know. And he wanted to know. I knew that the moment he didn't knock my legs off his desk.

It burned his ass but Leonid managed it. "What did you do?"

"I told Gerhard Dunkel, the friendly founding member of the Committee to Free Berlin, that I knew his group was a Commie front."

Leonid kept his cool. Not a peep, not a frown. Not good. I kept at it. "It's what we in the spy game call a mirror read. That's when you..."

"I know what a mirror read is," snapped Leonid .

The gritted teeth were good. But I was still a long way from home. A thought occurred.

"I have a question for you Leonid." I leaned back in the leather chair and waggled my feet on his desk. No reaction. Buster Keaton could take lessons from this guy.

"We Yanks were blessed with great Generals in the war. Eisenhower, MacArthur, Patton. Superb leaders, brilliant strategists. We lost 300,000 on our way to VE Day while single-handedly defeating the Empire of Japan. Your side lost twenty million. So my question to you is, who were the great Russian generals of World War Two? *Were* there any?"

I paused. Leonid's deep, liquid eyeballs had defrosted, his pretty purple lips were squeezed thin. I was rounding third and headed for home.

"Leonid, Lenny, if I may call you that - we Yanks are crazy for nicknames - I have a follow-up question, something I've been puzzling on. Why would a smart operator like yourself, given the opportunity to work for the greatest and most powerful country in the world, choose to throw in with a bunch of dumbshit Commie *Unter Menschen?*"

Leonid put his hands on his hips, leaned over the desk and spat his reply.

"We will *destroy* you Yankee."

I held my position, feet up, smile on. "That's not much to brag about Lenny" I said, hoisting another shot, "I'm half-destroyed already."

I drank it down, and belched loudly for emphasis.

That's what did it. It was the belch, the crude insult to his sense of his Old World decorum that got Leonid's neck-slicer out of his pants pocket.

I guess they call it blind rage for a reason. Leonid darted around the desk and took a wicked cut at my goozle with his folding knife. He got real close, I felt the wind on my neck.

Fortunately for me, unfortunately for him, he had neglected to extend the blade. Leonid realized his mistake and stopped to flick it open about the time I pushed back, jumped up, cocked my arm and put my fist in his right ear and about halfway through his head.

It was one of those once-in-a-lifetime Joe Louis haymakers where everything lines up just so and you're very impressed with yourself for a minute until you think, *Shit, did I just kill someone?*

Leonid crumpled to the hardwood floor and stayed there.

Chapter Thirty-seven

Victor Jacobson opened the pocket door and stood there like black doom. The redheaded receptionist and the green eyeshade boys formed a neck-craning chorus behind him. Good scene for an opera. I went to one once, as my mother's date. The old man refused to go. It was one of those dark Germanic jobs where the head man discovers his trusted confidante has betrayed him and sings a mournful aria in a thunderous baritone.

Victor Jacobson didn't burst into song. He just slid the door closed behind him and surveyed the carnage, eyes lingering on the open knife that lay on the hardwood floor two feet from Leonid's outstretched arm.

A pronoun had saved me. Had Leonid said, '*I* will destroy you' instead of '*We* will destroy you' the CO might have concluded that Leonid was simply defending his honor. Leonid's confession had been a very near thing.

I hadn't killed the little man. He was snoring peacefully on the hardwood floor. I hooked him under the armpits, hauled him backwards and dumped him in his leather chair. He didn't resist. I wheeled his chair away from the desk in case he had a gun stashed in a drawer. And I removed the pencil from the intercom keys.

Leonid muttered a Russian curse when he saw me do that. He was back with us.

"What a sad little group we are," said Victor Jacobson. "A traitor, a hothead and a dupe. Of the three, I believe I am most disappointed in myself."

Leonid tried to speak, coughed, tried again, croaking out something that sounded like what do you want?

Jacobson spoke with quiet menace. "I ask, Leonid, you answer."

Leonid rubbed his ear, gingerly.

"As you know, Leonid, we do not trade. Not for Ambrose or anyone else. What I can offer you is the life of your sister."

This remark cleared away all the cobwebs for the little man. "You have no cause to threaten her! She is an innocent. You betray your own ideals!"

"We will not threaten her, harm her or imprison her," said the CO. "What we will do if you don't co-operate is make it known that you have crossed over, and let the NKVD take their vengeance where they will."

"They would take my wife, not my sister."

I declined to tell Leonid that his wife was no longer available. The poor guy had suffered enough for one day. But the CO got in a good lick.

"Your handlers know you better than I do, Leonid. And even I know you don't love your wife."

Leonid hoisted himself up off the chair, wobbled, sat back down. He didn't speak.

"You know me to be a man of my word," said Jacobson. "I will not place your sister in jeopardy if you instruct your handlers to release Ambrose."

"They will not. Not unless I instruct them in person."

The CO shook his head. He wasn't going to risk that. "Then you will tell us where Ambrose is being held."

"I do not know."

"I believe that you do."

"On my sister's life I do not."

The CO stepped closer and picked up the vodka bottle from the desk. "Dovgan. This used to be your poison, didn't it Leonid? Quart a day or so?" Jacobson unscrewed the cap. "As I understand it cirrhosis is a chronic disease. Once you've got it, it's yours to keep. No more booze, ever. Isn't that right?"

Leonid didn't say. Jacobson set the bottle down gently on the desk and then - BAM - stunned the little man with a vicious slap to the face.

Leonid rocked back and struggled upward. I jumped forward and snagged his wrists, pinning his arms behind the chair. The CO grabbed the bottle and waded in.

"Where is Ambrose being held?"

"On my sister's life I don't know."

The CO clamped a big mitt below Leonid's jaw and strangled his mouth open.

Being force fed premium vodka was not a form of interrogation I would have found particularly unpleasant but Leonid sure didn't go for it. Jacobson forced almost half a bottle down Leonid's throat as the little man squirmed and writhed and hacked and hawed.

"Where is he weasel?"

Leonid spit bile at the CO by way of answer. Jacobson scraped it off his cheek and stood up. He set down the vodka bottle, replaced the cap, then picked up the bottle. By the neck.

This was a fight that was about more than it was about, a long-simmering conflict between bitter rivals. Time for ref Hal to intervene. I dragged Leonid's chair back out of bottle-clonking range and stood him up. I applied a one-wing choke hold from behind, his neck in the crook of my left elbow, my right hand hooked inside the back of his shirt collar. I tightened my elbow and hauled Leonid six inches off the floor and held him there.

He clawed at my arm. There are countermeasures to a one-wing choke hold of course – a thumb to the eye, a punch to the groin – but even trained veterans tend to forget the finer points when they can't breathe.

I returned Leonid to his chair and loosened my elbow. I let him have one lungful and cinched him up again.

"Where is Ambrose being held?"

Leonid didn't respond. Possibly because I had my forearm jammed against his windpipe. Could that be why? I pondered this question for a good thirty seconds as Leonid tore desperately at my arm.

Yes, my forearm was indeed the problem. I relaxed it enough for our kidnapper to suck a straw's worth of air.

"Tell me what I want to hear, Lenny," I said, "tell me now!"

"The Soviet Armory," he croaked, "on *Blummenstraße*."

I removed my arm and stood up. Leonid slumped to his chair and sucked wind. The CO grimaced.

Leonid had said a very bad word. *Armory*. Dollars to donuts the Soviet Armory that held Ambrose Mooney was also the target of the ill-fated freedom fighters of the Committee to Free Berlin. It would be teeming with well-armed troops.

"Watch him, I'll be right back." The CO went to the outer office and closed the door behind him.

I stood behind Leonid in the chair and felt oddly hopeful. We had a way forward, we just had to work out the tedious death-defying details. Leonid wasn't an all-knowing, all-powerful superspy after all. I wouldn't have to turn Commie.

He was a handful though, give him that. Leonid had used his bent over gasping as cover to retrieve a nasty little Exacto knife snugged in his sock garter. He was drunk, disoriented. I had the tactical advantage, standing above and behind him. How then did I have to jump back at the last moment to avoid a swiveling knife thrust aimed at my temple?

It was that goddamn chair is what it was. The little prick was using it as a shield now, wheeling it side to side.

"Hey, Lenny, I'm not going to shoot you. Not here. So why not come out and play?"

Leonid shoved the chair aside and smiled all the way up to his ghoulish gums. He extended the blade another two inches.

I frowned.

"Four inches? Christ, Lenny, is four inches the best you can do?" I reached into my coat pocket and held up the severed gold monogram from his red blazer. I waved it at him.

"No wonder your wife was so glad to see me."

Leonid bolted forward with blood in his eyes. I had fraternized with his wife in the privacy of their apartment. Worse, I had violated his finery!

He held the knife low, in between his legs, blade up. He would. A knife thrust from below is far more perilous than a thrust from above. If the attacker misses your noggin on the way down he is shit outta luck. If he misses your gonads on the way up, however, he still has a shot at your neck and chin.

So I was happy to see Victor Jacobson return to the office about then, take stock of the situation, and shoot Leonid in the back.

Chapter Thirty-eight

Victor Jacobson shot Leonid Vitinov in the back with a dart gun. Leonid would hate that. It broke his 'no gadgets' rule. I bent down and cleared his airway and turned his head sideways. He had much more he could tell us. With any luck I would get to ask the questions.

The CO nodded approvingly at the state of affairs. He looked a new man, all doubt and anxiety washed away. I was surprised to see him so chipper, what with a major career embarrassment sprawled on the hardwood floor and General Bill Donovan inbound tomorrow. Victor Jacobson would have some Fancy Dan explaining to do. He returned to the outer office, leaving me alone to guard the prisoner. And chew my cud.

I sat down in the fancy leather chair. I was hell bent to spring Ambrose now that I knew where he was being held. But Wild Bill and the CO would have other concerns. Like how to keep the Committee to Free Berlin from assaulting the Soviet Armory and starting World War III. They had a point. I didn't want World War III on my resume either.

It went contrary to my most deeply-held beliefs but I would risk getting my head blown off to short circuit the NKVD's plan. They say that soldiers don't crawl out of their foxholes to assault an enemy pillbox in pursuit of an abstract ideal, they do it to save their buddies.

They're right. I would risk getting my head blown off, I was right, ready and gung ho. So long as springing Ambrose was part of the plan.

And quick. The Blue Caps would be cranked up after Anna's quick exit and the apartment fire. When Leonid didn't return home that evening they would know he'd been blown. They would know that we knew the Committee to Free Berlin was a Commie front.

The NKVD would assume we knew the Committee was planning an assault on a Soviet target, assume we knew the time and place. They would assume we knew everything. Edict one in the spy biz. Assume the worst and work backwards.

The Blue Caps would be hard pressed to change the location. There was only one Soviet Armory in Berlin. But they would sure as hell move up the go date, try to hit quick before we could make a plan. The only silver lining I could glim was that modifying an operation of this importance would need clearance from on high, from Stalin himself. If the Soviets planned to use the attack on the Armory as a pretext to seize Berlin all the pieces had to be in place.

72 hours? That sounded about right. We had 72 hours to head off the Committee to Free Berlin and rescue Ambrose. And save the world. I sat down in the fancy chair and didn't think about it.

Ring ring.

Brainstorm for Mr. Harold Schroeder, plee-ase hold.

I held, waiting for the no-nonsense PBX operator who resides in the upper reaches of my cranium to patch the lines together at her plugboard. I haven't mentioned her before because I was afraid you would think me nuts but she does exist. Her name is Gertie.

Here is your party.

I waited, I listened. A faint watery echo down the line. It sounded like reverse the order.

Thanks a lot, Gert. Some brainstorm. Reverse the order of what?

Oh.

Yeah.

We didn't have 72 hours to head off the Committee and then rescue Ambrose. It was the other way round. I could no longer march into a Committee meeting and present my case. MANTIS wouldn't expose himself in such a public forum. Ditto the CO.

Only one sad sack Yank could turn the tide of history with grim details about what awaited the Committee members at the Soviet Armory. Ambrose Mooney.

Excellent. Now all I had to figure was a way to bust him out. They do it all the time in Westerns, it's easy as pie. You just tie a rope around the bars and yell giddyap! The bars rip loose every time.

"Good news, bad news," said the CO when he returned to Leonid's office. The little man remained on the floor, sawing logs. Jacobson looked down at him. "The tranq dart lasts about three hours."

I asked him what the good news was.

"I get to get shed of Hilde. He's been a pain in the ass."

"Where will you send him?"

"Now that he's proved his worth General Donovan will carry him off to the Pentagon."

"What's the bad news?"

"I'll have to install Leonid in Hilde's room upstairs."

"Why? Hilde's old news. Leonid knows field agents, current ops, codes, drop points."

"Hilde's a former second in command of the Abwehr, a big-map guy. The Puzzle Palace will love him. Leonid's just a low level operative. That's the way we play it."

"Play it? To Wild Bill Donovan?"

"Yes Schroeder. If you're thinking I'd rather not have General Donovan know how badly I screwed up on Leonid, you're right. But I'll tell him when the time comes. We hand out truth on a need to know basis. Donovan and the Whiskey Colonels are too far removed to make good use of what Leonid knows. That's my job for now."

"I'm happy to comply sir, provided you consider my proposal to short circuit the Committee to Free Berlin."

"I'm listening."

"It needs Ambrose."

"Why?"

"He's been there, the Armory. He can give them the birds-eye lowdown."

"Why would they believe him?"

"Because, before I free Ambrose from his cell, I will snap photos of the Armory fortifications, which photos will be developed and enlarged and circulated among the members of the Committee by Ambrose at their meeting tomorrow night."

The CO sighted down his nose. "Got any thoughts on how to gain entry?"

"Not a one sir. I was hoping you'd tell me we have a mole in the Soviet Sector."

Jacobson gave out with a bitter snort. "Leonid Vitinov was our mole."

"What about Colonel Norwood? I'll wager he has Soviet contacts."

"I thought you considered him a snitch?"

"I changed my mind," I said without further explanation. The CO would have heard all about our embarrassment at the chalet. "But he hates me now."

The CO coughed a laugh out his nose. "The only person John Norwood hates is Winston Churchill, who declined to tender his name for knighthood following the Colonel's wartime service in the Balkans, no explanation given."

I remembered the humidor in Norwood's display cabinet, the one with Churchill's initials. What was that? A consolation prize?

"Norwood will love it if you come crawling back. Just be prepared to eat some shit."

"Yes sir." Jacobson's pinched look indicated he might like to serve up an extra portion. I stood ready, I had it coming. My tip off to the Committee's founding member was insubordinate in the extreme.

But the CO said only, "The NKVD knows we suspect the Committee by now, so it wouldn't hurt to talk dirty about them at Norwood's, get the word out."

"And Ambrose? The Armory?"

"Norwood might know a way in. But keep that discussion private."

"And I keep mum about Leonid?"

"Have you?"

"I'm sorry?"

"Kept mum about Leonid?"

I cast my mind backward. I knew what the CO was after, a cross check of who told what to whom so he could have all loose ends tied up when Wild Bill came to call. I told him what I remembered to the best of my ability, addled as I was by vodka and exhaustion. "I have no idea."

The CO grumbled, extended his hand and hauled me out of the fancy chair. "Get some sleep. Stay patient, and stay sober. The Colonel has a form of interrogation uniquely his own."

As if I didn't know.

"This is critical stuff, Schroeder," said Victor Jacobson, quietly. "We're counting on you."

"Yes sir."

Chapter Thirty-nine

I drove to the French Sector after a home cooked supper of Zwieback and Dinty Moore stew. The weather was raw, a tin sky venting gusts of jagged wind. I cruised past the chalet on *Ernststraße*. The Chinese lanterns burned brightly and the gravel driveway was jammed with cars. Excellent.

I hadn't arrived empty-handed this time. I had stopped to buy a bottle of champagne. A big one, a jeroboam they call it. A peace offering.

I parked down the block, in front of a car repair shop. A skinny brown mutt prowled a yard full of rusted heaps next door. He snarled and threw himself against the chain link as I passed by. I like dogs and don't like cats. Odd they held the opposite opinion of me.

I slung my gallon of bubbly over my shoulder and walked down the block and up the front walk of the chalet, the entryway for uninvited guests. I was well scrubbed and well dressed, the dog bites on my beezer scabbing over nicely. My champagne wasn't chilled but the Colonel would have one of those sterling silver ice buckets. The kind I'd seen at Mushie Wexler's Theatrical in Cleveland, where the waiter turned the bottle every two minutes, rattling ice and whetting appetites.

I stopped at the door to the steep staircase and pulled the knocker. I recalled Victor Jacobson's advice as I waited my turn to join the tumult. 'Stay patient, stay sober'.

The Colonel probably didn't glean many deep dark secrets at these jamborees but there are other confidences that can be had in the proper setting. Not a human made who doesn't want to be considered in the know. In Berlin especially. Not sure how the

Colonel worked it but if it was me I'd bait the source with a false statement of fact and wait for a smug correction.

Now there was an idea. Why not use it on Colonel Norwood and his merry band of men? Might work, you never know.

Sedgwick answered the door wearing white tie and tails. I was crashing a hoity toite party this evening. I held up my carbonated peace offering. Sedgewick took it from me.

"I will ask the Colonel if he wishes to receive you," he said and trooped up the stairs.

I waited a long minute. Then another, wondering what sort of assortment the Colonel had gathered this time. The Victrola was playing chamber music.

And who was I supposed to be? I had neglected that little detail. I had posed as a salesman on a previous visit. Nobody cared. But I was poised to ask impertinent questions this time around. Why? Who was I? A reporter for Stars'n'Stripes? A conversation stopper if ever there was.

Heckfire, I was who I was. Personal adjutant to General William Donovan, sent to Berlin on a fact-finding mission. The enemy was mobilizing. It was time to show the flag.

Past time. Hard to know without a wristwatch but it felt like ten minutes past time. Screw it. I climbed the long steep staircase and stood in the entryway. Sedgewick ignored me from the kitchen. Colonel Norwood was in the parlor, showing off Churchill's humidor. I cleared my throat, loudly.

"There you are dear boy. Come join the fray."

Some fray. It looked like a congress of church deacons. The men wore rumpled old-fashioned suits and bowties and the two women guests were even drabbier. They didn't laugh when Norwood crooked me around the arm and introduced me as his illegitimate son.

He was working hard tonight, the Colonel, wearing a dress blue uniform he had outgrown, beaded sweat on his temples, his jolly booming voice laboring to find the right pitch. I shook hands with the guests and let Norwood do the talking.

The visitors were deposed dignitaries by my guess. Former legislators or cabinet ministers or somesuch. One white haired old gent wore a clerical collar. A somber bunch. My bottle of bubbly sat unopened and un-iced on the coffee table.

When we had finished making the rounds I apologized to the Colonel for my rude behavior on the previous visit.

"Gone and forgotten dear boy. And I do appreciate the giggle water."

"Least I could do Colonel. What's the occasion this evening?"

"No occasion," said Norwood, surveying the crowd with a jaundiced eye. "Just a group of self-important expats who expect us to drive the Red Army back to Minsk so they can reclaim their positions of power and privilege."

"Ah. Is that all."

I tried my bait and switch idea. "Colonel, Klaus Hilde suggests the Red Army is about to head in the other direction." Norwood hiked one considerable eyebrow half an inch. "I think it's a crock, a cheap ploy to keep us interested. But Hilde says the Committee to Free Berlin is a Soviet front."

I stopped there. The Colonel waved me on without comment.

"A Soviet front planning an assault on a military target in the Soviet Sector, which the Red Army will use as a pretext to seize the city."

"First I've heard of it," said Norwood, "though it does sound like Beria. Devious little bastard, to the cloak and dagger born." He gave me a brusque once over. "What do you intend to do about it?"

I shrugged, surprised the Colonel hadn't dismissed Hilde's theory. Maybe I could trust the old queen. "We don't have much leverage. The White Russians on the Committee don't trust us for some reason."

I wanted to do as the CO suggested, throw open the discussion, get the word out to the dignitaries. They were Eastern European anti-Communists. They had to know somebody who knew somebody on the Committee. Better if Col. Norwood delivered the message, however. The White Russians had a perfectly good reason not to trust us. Most all of their Yankee collaborators had been murdered.

I said it again, louder this time. "I just don't understand why the White Russian freedom fighters don't trust us!"

Heads turned, conversation quieted. The Colonel was off like a shot.

"It's quite a good reason act-tu-ally. You bloody Yanks hold yourselves aloof. We Brits like to jump in up to our nellies, mix it up with the natives and all that. Which is why, as any of these good people can tell you, that we are so universally revered!"

This brought a titter from the starchy group.

"You Americans suffer, if I may say so, from 'top down' thinking," said the Colonel with a saucy wink.

"How so?"

"Well, dear fellow, there's a reason the MI6 call American agents bat boys."

"I assumed it was a baseball reference. You Brits are the sluggers, we Yanks just hand you the bats."

"It's worse than that I'm afraid."

I nodded for the Colonel to continue, not that he needed any encouragement.

"It seems that General William Donovan, wartime head of the OSS, once proposed a peculiar plan of sabotage."

Col. Norwood paused. One of the dignitaries had the bad taste to cough. Norwood paused until order had been restored.

"The General had been informed, incorrectly as it turns out, that the Japanese populace were deathly afraid...of bats. Based on this misinformation the General – they call him Wild Bill – conceived a plan. A plan to sow panic and chaos amongst the enemy. A plan to drop thousands of live bats on the Empire of Japan!"

Uneasy mirth from the dignitaries.

"A test run was arranged. How and where the bats were gathered I am not at liberty to say."

The Colonel mugged at his guests to indicate that this was a laugh line. They obliged.

"Comes the day. A B-24 holding steady at 20,000 feet above the Arizona Territories, Army Air Force cargo monkeys scrambling to drag the crates into position, the bats keening against the light as the bomb bay doors are breached, the top of their crates prized open with crowbars, then yanked free by fifty foot lanyards when the crates are pitched into the wild blue yonder!"

The Colonel had done a good deal of physical business during this speech, dragging crates, yanking lanyards and such. The dignitaries were right there with him, in the cargo hold of the B-29 high above the Arizona desert. Heck, me too, though I knew that Wild Bill's silly bat scheme never made it past the talking stage.

"The crates are ripped apart, and the captive bats spread their wings in newfound freedom above the parched landscape far below!" The Colonel threw out his arms. "And promptly freeze to death at the high altitude and drop like rocks."

The dignitaries groaned. They didn't like the sad conclusion to this amusing anecdote. I didn't much care for it myself.

The Colonel changed the subject. "Ladies and gentlemen, our American friend brings word that the Committee to Free Berlin is a Soviet front bent on mischief. Can anyone confirm this?" Shrugs and head shakes all around. "Well, pass it along if you have a mind to."

I got the distinct impression I was being screwed with. As in, *Anyone care to do the bidding of these balmy Yanks?*

The Colonel kept at it, grabbing a copy of Collier's from the coffee table. "Allen Dulles proposes, in this issue, that Berlin be left for dead as fitting tribute to the Nazi horrors." Norwoood shook the magazine at me and grinned. "This is wrong thinking!

We need you cheeky Yanks to stem the tide of Communist domination."

"I agree Colonel," I said loudly, then leaned in. "Is that why you let us grab Herr Hilde instead of taking him for yourself?"

The Colonel bulled ahead at full volume. "I set you a task old thing! To see if you could track Hilde down, to see if you were worthy. We pitifully outnumbered Brits didn't amass the greatest empire in history by doing all the scutwork ourselves. We selected our allies carefully, then tested them in battle."

The Colonel turned to the crowd and boomed, "Our friend Hal, you'll be glad to know, passed with flying colors."

The dignitaries weren't. Glad to know. They were miffed that their concerns were being ignored. The Colonel seemed not to notice, seemed, in fact, pleased as punch. I would have chalked up his erratic behavior to too much Absinthe but he had no scorched purple patches on his cheeks, had nothing showing but plain toothy malevolence.

What the hell?

Sedgewick entered the parlor from the kitchen holding a silver serving tray with both hands. The Colonel made the announcement.

"Fresh picked *Spargel*, ladies and gentlemen. Steamed, chilled and served with lemon and hand-whisked mayonnaise."

The dignitaries crowded round the tray. I joined them. I was cheesed off nine ways to Sunday but I wasn't about to pass up home-cooked grub.

Spargel is Kraut for asparagus, that much I knew. It's considered a German delicacy, served up from cans at Christmas and Easter. Why then were the long spears on Sedgewick's silver serving platter white? I grabbed one and slurped it down.

The Colonel appeared at my elbow. "Delightful, aren't they?"

"Very. But I thought asparagus were green."

"They are. German *Spargel*, however, are white. The master race of asparagi you might say."

This was some sort of an insult to my Kraut heritage I supposed. The Colonel's flaring brows and licking lips said he was waiting on my response. I stayed patient, stayed sober. Entirely too sober.

"Colonel Norwood," I said, putting my hand on his shoulder, "I think we need a drink."

"I thought you'd never ask," said the Colonel and pulled me through the throng of dignitaries. "Sherry drinkers," he said under his breath. We shuddered in unison.

Norwood walked me to his bedroom and pushed through the door. Its hydraulic pump pulled it back into place. When the door clicked shut Norwood turned on his heel and backed me up against it. His voice was low, his breath foul.

"I know why you are here Schroeder. You expect me to say the word and set your odious Irishman free from his captivity."

"Actually I..."

"Shut up!" I did so. The Colonel continued, so close I could count his nose hairs. "I cannot. And I will not."

"Sorry to hear that," I replied without pointing out the obvious. If you can't, it doesn't much matter what you won't.

"I have already saved your miserable hides once this month, that should be sufficient largesse on my part."

"You're coming through loud and clear Colonel. Now, didn't I hear something about a drink?"

"Of course," said Norwood, instantly the genial host.

He was all over the place this evening. Hail fellow, sarcastic wag, snarling attack dog and back again. The Colonel crossed to a black ceramic end table next to the bed. He pushed a button. The top of the table parted like a two-span drawbridge and a spring-loaded cocktail tray rose up and presented itself. Impressive. Very.

"I have gin, vodka and Scotch," he said, tinkling around in the joy jumble. "And a bottle of that American rot the Whiskey Colonels drink."

The Colonel held up a bottle of Jack Daniel's Tennessee sippin' whiskey. Holy cats. "A double, on the rocks."

The Colonel poured mine with great care, using ice tongs to add four cubes, a crystal jigger to measure out three fluid ounces. Then he glugged a big splash of gin into a highball glass, no ice, no tonic, rimmed the glass with a wedge of lime, placed the wedge in his mouth and noisily sucked it dry.

I hadn't spent much time with aristocrats. Were they all this goofy?

We drank, I noodled. Norwood said he'd already saved our miserable hides once this month. True enough. It was the second part, the 'that should be sufficient largesse' part that kept burping up like the taste of Dinty Moore stew. Real allies don't ration their largesse when a life is at stake.

When our glasses were empty and Norwood was refilling them I asked a question that I shouldn't have, not if I was here to recruit the Colonel to help free Ambrose. Norwood had made it plain he wasn't in a co-operative frame of mind, but we were knocking back cocktails in his boudoir. His mood figured to improve. So I should have kept my yap shut maybe, done what I had to do to save Ambrose. But a spy's first allegiance is to the truth.

"How did you make the Russian platoon go away that time you drove up in your Rolls?"

Norwood sipped gin and looked offended. "Winston Churchill has a fond adage that you might find instructive."

"I'm all ears."

"No one asks hard questions of good fortune."

I nodded and smiled and kept my powder dry. If Churchill did say that saying the Colonel had misunderstood it. Churchill wasn't saying one shouldn't ask hard questions of good fortune, just that no one bothered to.

I asked my question again. Norwood answered, grudgingly.

"Sheer luck. I knew their commanding officer. Knew him, and his vices, rather better than he cared me to, if you take my meaning. If it had been another squad, or the Blue Caps, you and your Hibernian would now be dead. Or worse."

I offered my thanks and gathered my wits about me. Col. Norwood had already rung up two coincidences to his account. One of his ladies just happened to know Herr Hilde's address. And Norwood just happened to have that male prostitute handy when Ambrose and I confronted him about how he knew we'd be at the loading dock. Two coincidences are suspicious, three are a conspiracy. I now had three. Col. Norwood just happened to know the big Russian commander.

"Here's how I see it, Colonel." I took a bite of Jack and plunged ahead.

"Your rescue was an elaborate charade you arranged with your Russian friend to win our trust and gratitude and that of Victor Jacobson. And Bill Donovan. When I returned to your salon to answer your question about which fugitive we were chasing you couldn't be bothered. That made me trust you all the more. But could be you already knew the name of the fugitive. Could be Leonid told you. Like he called to alert you to our surprise visit, so you could arrange more playacting, by your queer young man. After Ambrose and I slinked off you returned Leonid's call, told him to monitor our conversation, listen in to our speculation about the identity of the traitor, now that the good Colonel had been cleared."

I took a good pull, swishing it around like mouthwash before I swallowed. That the Colonel hadn't laughed in my face or slapped me silly by now told me all I needed to know. "Any truth to that?"

"Preposterous dear boy."

"Really."

"Yes, as you say, really. Now I have guests to attend."

I remained standing in front of the door. "I want Ambrose. By morning. Or I have a talk with General Donovan. He arrives tomorrow."

This was news to Norwood. He cast his eyes about like Leonid in his hidden office, wondering what had happened to his snug little world. He recovered nicely however.

"Talk to him all you like. I know the General personally, squired him about Bletchley Park in '42. A crazy Harp but aren't they all?" The Colonel drained his glass. Patches of scalded purple brightened his cheeks. "You have nothing but speculation to present to him. Dear boy."

I didn't say different, just stood there and looked like I knew more than I was letting on. Norwood remained calm, unruffled, not one to be intimidated by the likes of me.

"It shouldn't be difficult," I said, pleasantly. "Now that Leonid's been blown the Blue Caps won't care to keep Ambrose. He was Leonid's prize, not theirs."

"Just as you say," said the Colonel. "But they will want an exchange, Leonid for Ambrose."

"I don't think so. Swapping a kidnapped Yank for a Russian spy? That would be an admission of dirty doings by our stalwart allies."

The Colonel paid attention to his gin and no tonic.

I didn't have anything solid on him, just as he said. I had a dim glim of an idea how to get that something but it would have to wait. Col. Norwood prized one thing above all, his status as Berlin's well-connected all-knowing salon keeper. And I held the key to something he coveted. A sociable visit to the Norwood salon by the legendary Wild Bill Donovan.

"Bring the General here tomorrow, nine p.m. For cigars and cognac, he's partial to both," said the Colonel, regarding me with squinty distaste. "And I will present to him your bloody Irishman."

"Thank you sir."

The Colonel nodded curtly. I held the door open and let him return to his guests, saying I needed to use the head and would be along shortly.

The hydraulic bedroom door scissored back and clicked shut. I got to work.

Chapter Forty

I had about five minutes. Five minutes to toss the room before the Colonel got antsy and returned to check on me. Ten minutes if Norwood got on a roll with the sherry-sippers. Okay, five minutes.

Very unlikely Col. Norwood kept any incriminating work documents in his place of residence. But he might have some personal items he wanted to keep close.

I had interrupted something during my unannounced visit two visits ago, something I had chosen to ignore. Sedgewick disheveled, red-faced. The Colonel gone to the loo and returned with his face washed and his hair combed. I had interrupted something all right. Gawd. Norwood and Sedgewick were lovers, lovers of long-standing. Which meant there would be memorabilia.

I searched a bookcase against the far wall, found a leather photo album embossed John and Nell. I paged through quickly. Norwood and his wife at their wedding ceremony, at the christening of a child, at a military fete, at their anniversary party. I checked the pockets of the leather album. No joy.

The clock was ticking. The dignitaries weren't laughing. Col. Norwood would soon be wondering. I removed the leather bound volumes on either side of the album and shook them out. No luck. I shook out more. Nothing doing.

Time to get brilliant Schroeder. The Colonel's a jokester, right? What would a jokester do? He would hide his secret behind his proper façade, behind the handsome photographic portrait of John and Nell and their daughter that hung above the bookcase. I pried off the backing with shaky fingers. It was awful quiet out there.

I got lucky. I found an 8x10 photo that would have been shocking if it wasn't so funny. And vice versa.

An Alpine vacation, the Matterhorn in the background. A much younger Norwood and Sedgewick in ski gear with their arms around each other. Nothing scandalous, save for Norwood's tongue in Sedgewick's ear and Sedgewick grinning like a chimp.

The shot was poorly framed, indicating a camera on a timer. Even if they had developed the film themselves it was a dumb thing to do. And keep. Ditto Leonid and his childhood portrait with his sister. Love doth make fools of us all.

I didn't know if the photo was enough to get the Colonel cashiered from MI6, though homosexuals were considered blackmail bait. Didn't matter at the moment. What counted was that I could use the photo to make the good Colonel do my bidding.

A devious thought occurred.

I yanked out the photo album again and removed another 8x10 and slipped both pix into my coat pocket. I hurried to the door and pulled it open just as Col. Norwood was reaching for the handle. He spilled into the room, I grabbed his arm and held him up.

"My apologies Colonel. I took a minute to raid the liquor locker."

The Colonel wasn't interested in my blather. He made a beeline for the cocktail tray, poured a stiff gin and drank it down. "These are the dullest humans ever assembled."

I chuckled. Norwood said "Think it's easy, do you?" and propelled me through the door.

I stumbled out into the parlor. The dignitaries turned towards me as one. They looked glum, abandoned by their master of ceremonies. My appearance didn't cheer them up any. Entertaining the stuffed shirts wasn't my never mind but I had more I wanted to do here this evening. Might as well pitch in.

I chose something all the Western World had in common. American movies. I did Jimmy Cagney in "The Roaring Twenties." I did John Wayne in "Back to Bataan."

The dignitaries observed me with a sort of grim fascination. All right, time for the heavy artillery. I summoned my lisping bug-eyed Peter Lorre from "The Maltese Falcon," the scene where he calls Sydney Greenstreet a fat oafish bloated *idiot!*

They liked that. So much so that Col. Norwood crept from his lair to see about all the ruckus.

The evening rolled on from there. Norwood, his manhood challenged, cranked into high gear, spinning anecdotes and gossip and ribald stories into one long spell-binding monologue that had even the elderly cleric flushed and giggly.

I watched him work, fascinated. Was this why he was playing both sides? The Colonel said the Brits were defeated by victory, called the U.S. commitment to the struggle half-assed. A seasoned operative might conclude it was time to hedge his bets. But could be it was simpler than that. Could be Norwood just had an overpowering need to be the center of attention.

Was that it? Was international high-stakes power politics just another playground game where ego and bragging rights trumped all? See: Vitinov, Major Leonid; Norwood, Colonel John; Hilde, General Klaus. And Schroeder, Harold M. for that matter. I only took the job because I wanted to be a hero.

I had been a fake hero in Cleveland of course, a newspaper hero. A real hero does what needs to be done and hang the consequence. A real hero doesn't negotiate with the enemy in order to obtain a happy outcome built on sand. Col. Norwood serving up Ambrose to Bill Donovan tomorrow evening for instance.

After which I would be up to my eyeballs in hock to the old whore, expected to keep my yap shut as the Colonel presented Ambrose to the General, claiming he had moved heaven and earth to free the heroic young Irish freedom fighter.

Nope, I couldn't do it. I had to burn Col. Norwood to the ground tonight. I couldn't tar Bill Donovan's good name by parading him around the den of a double-dealing traitor. And I sure as shit couldn't justify myself to Ambrose.

You telling me I was starved, beat and deprived of strong drink for several days so's you could do a backroom deal with a bleedin' Limey Communist homosexual?!

I was going to have to spring Ambrose the hard way, that's all there was to it. I patted the 8x10's in my coat pocket and waited for the Colonel to wind down and the sherry-sipping dignitaries to grow bored. It would take a while, now that Sedgewick had placed my jeroboam of champagne in an ice bucket and was working the hand-spun grinder in the kitchen.

The whir and crunch stilled all speech. Coffee beans. Sedgewick was about to brew a pot of real coffee. No one in their right mind would leave until that rich river mud got poured.

It was going to be a long night.

Chapter Forty-one

The coffee and champagne kept the dignitaries sprightly for the better part of an hour. I dragged a table chair to the hearth and tended the fire, kept it crisp and crackling for future use. The partygoers fizzed out at about...aw, hell, I had no idea what time it was. Like me the Colonel kept no clocks, but my eyelids told me it was late.

The dignitaries took their leave in ones and twos, some clutching each other as Sedgewick led them down the rear hall and the back stairs to their waiting cars. The elderly cleric shuffled along behind, then stood on the landing, his papery hand clutching the railing, looking down the steep wooden staircase as if it were the last thing he would ever see. I sidled up.

"Let's wait for the crowd to clear."

"That seems prudent," he said in a warbly voice.

People found their cars. The staircase cleared.

"Forgive me for getting fresh," I said and scooped up his frail frame in my arms and walked him very carefully down the creaky stairs. The parson didn't object, seemed in fact to enjoy the ride. He looked up at me was we made our way down the steps, his gray eyes watery.

"Is that a dog bite on your nose?"

"Yes sir."

"Curious" was all he said.

I set the old gent on his feet when we reached solid ground and looked around for his transport. All the cars were gone. Great. An elderly parson was my date for the rest of the evening.

Then a black sedan crunched up the gravel drive and a driver jumped out and opened the back door, apologizing for his tardiness. This was a bigwig parson apparently. I helped him to the rear compartment. He thanked me for my kindness, took my hand and said, "Keep that nose out of places it doesn't belong."

I laughed. If only I could.

The clergyman settled into the back seat and the car spat gravel as it backed down the drive. I watched them go, thinking of the ancient elevator operator in the Standard Building in Cleveland. The one who saw my scuffed up mush and said, 'You'd best go home.' This was much the same. Was God trying to tell me something?

I climbed back up the stairs. If a huge thunderbolt rent the night sky before I reached the back door I would reconsider my course of action. I stopped on the landing and scanned the heavens. God did not co-operate.

I tried the door handle. Locked, but a tin can I could pop with a hard stare.

I listened at the door. Hearty guffaws from Norwood and Sedgewick, mocking their guests, decompressing after a hard night at the salon. The laughter and conversation died down shortly. I had better do this now.

The strike plate in the door frame was loose. I pushed against the door and stuck my broken-tipped knife blade inside the plate and pulled the door back towards me. With a little jiggling I got the blade pinned against the end of the latch bolt. I jacked the knife to the right, eased open the door and entered Col. Norwood's chalet on *Ernststraße* for the last time.

I looked down the short entry hall. The Colonel had his back to me, seated on the couch, packing his pipe. I crept forward, scouting Sedgewick. He figured to be in the kitchen, cleaning up. I listened for the clank of dishes, heard none.

Okay, so he was in the servant's quarters off the kitchen, changing out of his monkey suit. Where I didn't want him was the master bedroom on the right, behind the hydraulic door. Neither Norwood nor Sedgewick would be pleased to see me again so soon. But only Sedgewick was likely to do anything about it.

I crept down the hall secure in the knowledge that, if the burly manservant burst out of the bedroom and put a slug in the back of the intruder he'd heard jimmying the back door, everyone from Bill Donovan on down would deny any knowledge of my existence. It was a good feeling. It was! It meant I could do as I damn well pleased.

I crept closer. The Colonel struck a kitchen match, ignited his great craggy pipe, took a hungry draw and didn't exhale for the longest time. When he did the smoke came out graygreen and pungent as camel dung.

I tiptoed up behind him, glanced over my shoulder, glanced right to the kitchen. No Sedgewick. And the door to the servant's quarters was closed. I bent down.

"Don't burn all those matches Colonel," I said to his left ear.

He didn't jerk, didn't turn, simply froze in place.

I walked around the couch to face him. "You might want to save one for later."

Col. Norwood struggled to make sense of all this but exhaustion, gin and whatever was in that pipe fought him all the way. He shook his purple cheeks pale, reclaimed himself quickly and, setting his pipe in its gnarled wood holder, said, "I thought we had reached an understanding."

He said it hot but low so that Sedgewick wouldn't overhear. I appreciated the courtesy. Unlikely I would conclude my business before Sedgewick made an appearance but, like I say, I appreciated the courtesy.

"I have something that belongs to you." I presented the scandalous photo of Norwood and Sedgewick.

Norwood's reaction - a fit of giggles and "Sedgie, come look!" - was not what I had hoped for.

Sedgie came rumbling out of his bedroom in stocking feet, cinching up a bathrobe.

"I haven't seen that photograph in ages," said the Colonel. "We're so damnably young!"

Sedgewick, half asleep, muttered agreement and gave me a what are you doing here look.

I stood there like a stooge, holding my lethal weapon, a scandalous photo that my intended victims found both nostalgic and amusing. Could be I'd miscalculated. MI6 knew all about Norwood's secret life but turned a blind eye given his talents and suitability for the cesspool that was Berlin.

Could be, probably was. But Col. Norwood was married to a royal niece or somesuch. In Great Britain, where the daily newspapers loved scandal, and scandalous photographs above all.

I pointed this out to the gentlemen. Their mood darkened.

Colonel Norwood picked up his pipe. "It may interest you to know, dear boy, that my man Sedgewick is quite an accomplished pugilist, won a Royal Navy middleweight title once upon a time. As I know you to be a civilized young man who would not stoop to the use of weaponry in the salon, may I suggest a round of fisticuffs to settle this matter."

"Marquis of Queensberry rules of course."

"Of course."

I stuck the photo back in my pocket and set about moving chairs to make space in the parlor. Sedgewick, who looked as if he wanted nothing more than to go to bed and pull the covers up over his head, looked to his employer for confirmation.

"Well, go on. Give the young upstart what for!"

Sedgewick plodded forward to meet me. A dart gun. When I returned to the States I would tell my spy school instructor to add a dart gun to the list of essential espionage equipment so that, in the future, field agents would be spared the embarrassment of pugilistic encounters with ageing manservant's in woolen socks.

Sedgewick advanced slowly, dukes straight up, guarding his mug. He bobbed and weaved a bit though I kept my hands at my knees and threw no punches. I'm not much of a pugilist. I didn't need to be. The upright, straight ahead style of Western boxing is tailor made for ju jitsu.

When Sedgie got close enough to throw a haymaker I ducked, and danced around behind him. I could have put him down with a rabbit punch to the back of the neck but I figured I would do a buck and wing for a few minutes till the old gent got tired of chasing me around and gave up.

But Sedgewick pivoted, took one big stride and drilled me a good one, a straight overhand shot right above the belt buckle.

Col. Norwood hooted his approval. I windmilled backward, fighting for breath. Sedgewick closed in quick, peppering me with left jabs, then loaded up a lights-out right cross.

And therein lies the problem with Western boxing – Western war-making too. An alert opponent can see what's coming. It's why spies were invented and taught ju jitsu.

I juked left and threw out my right arm just as Sedgewick unloaded, catching the crook of his elbow in mine, using his momentum to dosey-do him around in a full 360.

The Colonel found this very entertaining, Sedgewick less so. He set his jaw and rocked his head side to side. He was seriously cheesed.

Norwood piped up about then. "Leslie," he said crossly, "you've come all undone."

Sedgewick looked down. His bathrobe hung open, exposing his boxer shorts. They didn't have little pink hearts on them or anything so I didn't understand why Sedgewick blushed and gathered his bathrobe and tied it up tight. But mine was not to reason why.

I shot forward and did what I had been trained to do to subdue an opponent quickly. A sidewinding heel kick to the shin, followed by a quick fist to the temple as the opponent bends forward in pain, followed by an acrobatic over-the-shoulder throw that requires hoisting the subject directly overhead.

Sedgewick declined to co-operate with this last maneuver. He wrapped his arms around me and bulled me backwards, his big head in my gut. I cinched him under his belly, flopped backwards and used his momentum to flip him up and over.

Sedgewick's a big boy, this last move took every ounce of strength I could muster. He landed on his back like a ton of bricks. I rolled away. He struggled to rise then fell back, his head bouncing off a ceramic pot. A clean KO.

I climbed to my feet and dusted myself off. I looked over at the Colonel. He had a .45 caliber derringer pointed in my direction. Damnedest gun you've ever seen.

"Why Colonel," I sniffed, "weaponry in the salon?"

He chuckled. And continued in a pleasant tone. "We are on a quiet street here, Harold. No houses nearby."

It was true. He could grease me with his two shot derringer and no one the wiser. Norwood fought to keep his eyes in focus and his gun hand still.

"You don't want to shoot me, Colonel. It wouldn't..."

Norwood closed his eyes and fired his hand cannon, shattering a front window.

I hit the deck and spun away, digging out my Walther.

I hunkered down behind a wing chair. The second bullet didn't come. The Colonel dropped the gun to the coffee table, busting a china cup. I poked my head up to see him open a tiny drawer at the base of his pipe holder and remove something twixt thumb and forefinger. He popped it in his mouth before I could reach my feet.

He turned to me, said, "'Tis been a distinct pleasure, dear boy," then bit down, groaned and slumped over.

Christ Almighty! I scrambled forward and sniffed the air. Bitter almonds. Cyanide!

I wondered should I flee the scene, then moved closer to Norwood and sniffed again. What I didn't smell gave me hope. Shit. I didn't smell shit. Death causes the bowels to unclench. I looked closer. Norwood's wispy nose hairs quivered.

Well, well, quite a dramatic charade the Colonel had engineered, a fake suicide with a phony L pill. Or he'd used sleight of hand. Broken a real capsule to release the odor then pretended to swallow it. Well done and executed in any case. I'd had a little charade in mind myself. Offering to toss the scandalous photo into the fireplace if Norwood told me what I wanted to know, then substituting the other 8x10 at the last moment – the one I had snatched from Norwood's photo album - damning it to the flames while I slid the original in my coat pocket.

A clever gambit. But it was very late and I was tired of playing games. I removed my Walther eight shot and took aim at the Colonel's leaded glass display cabinet, the one that held the precious keepsakes from his long career. I targeted the bullet-riddled cavalry canteen. What was one more?

I squeezed off a round.

The leaded glass sustained a crystalline puncture wound, the canteen jumped off the shelf. Col. Norwood's eyelids flapped open like yanked pull blinds. He sat up.

"Are you quite insane?"

I sat down next to him on the couch. "I must be, I'm talking to a corpse."

I took aim at the display cabinet again and put one smack in the middle of Col. Norwood's Citation of Merit for Honorable Service to His Majesty's Something or Other.

Norwood cringed, he fumed. He reached for the two shot derringer but I snagged his wrist. "Not tonight, Colonel. Tonight's my night."

The Colonel sat back and examined me intently, as if seeing me for the first time. "What the devil do you want?"

I took aim at the Colonel's cut glass crystal bowl, the one that sat on the purple pillow, the one inscribed with the royal seal. "I'm a spy. I want to know stuff."

"Yes, of course. *What*?"

"Two things. The photo I've got tucked away doesn't prove anything. It's not evidence of treason."

Norwood winced at my choice of words. Disgrace was one thing, treason quite another. The penalty under British law was death by hanging. The Colonel wasn't going to admit treason unless I offered him a back door. I shattered his crystal bowl with two 9 mm. slugs to get his attention.

"Think of it this way," I said, off his horrified look. "It's one less thing to pack."

Norwood liked the sound of that. Leastwise he didn't try to strangle me.

"You're a smart guy Colonel. You'd have a place to go and a way to get there if and when this day came. Some sun-drenched former colony where they speak the King's English and have good tea."

I glanced at Sedgewick's supine figure. Out like a light. I continued.

"I will drive home and sleep it off and not sound the general alarm till tomorrow afternoon if you answer two questions. I'll even keep that photo in my coat pocket if what you tell me proves out."

Col. Norwood's scorched patches came together as his face turned bright purple and he erupted, volcano-like. "So ask your two bloody fucking questions already and be done with it!"

I enjoyed that.

"Okay. First question. What is the name and address of your Soviet Case Officer?"

Norwood seemed almost relieved to tell me. I committed it to memory. I let the tension build for a moment. And trained my Walther on the Colonel's prized possession. Winston Leonard Spencer Churchill's gold-plated cedar humidor.

"And what is the second question?" said Norwood, a nervous eye on his prize.

I shrugged. "Why did you betray your country?"

Col. Norwood laughed heartily and picked up his pipe. He laughed some more as he fired it up and sucked smoke. It was my turn to wait. The Colonel grinned. With his purple skin and the graygreen smoke leaking from his teeth he looked scary. He looked like a tribal war mask.

"I will tell you, dear boy, why I betrayed my country," he said, enunciating crisply. "Their checks bounced."

"That's it?"

"Precisely. I do not believe in Communism. I meant what I said about Great Britain needing you cheeky Yanks. But I am sixty-four years old and very tired."

I felt a pang for the old guy, though I never would have pegged him for 64.

The Colonel surveyed the ruins of his display cabinet. "Go ahead. Put a round through Winnie's humidor. I won't need it where I'm going," he said, eyes dark, nostrils flaring. "And I hate the pompous bastard."

I couldn't bring myself to do it. I got up from the silk dragon couch and back walked to the rear door. The Colonel sat motionless.

I grabbed some contraband from the kitchen, stuffed it in a paper bag, slipped out the back door and waited at the top of the stairs.

When I heard the loud report of the .45 derringer and the sound of breaking glass I clomped down the stairs.

Chapter Forty-two

I felt pretty frothy at the top of the stairs. I had achieved results. I had the goods on Colonel Norwood and blackmail material to keep him in line. But I was all fizzed out by the time I reached the bottom landing. The anti-Communist members of the Committee to Free Berlin were a couple hours closer to being mowed down. And Ambrose was still in stir.

I had put aside my personal concerns, my desire to free Ambrose, in order to collect intelligence on a traitor. And yet I knew I was in Dutch, knew that the CO and Wild Bill would not be happy to hear my report. I had been a bull in the china shop of international diplomacy and achieved results without prior approval. And they never like that.

Yeah, it was trickier now. We didn't need a spat with the Brits over their Berlin Bureau Chief, what with the Red Army gunning their engines. I shun't have chased Norwood out of town maybe. He wasn't some Bolshie true believer, just an old sot with a drawer full of rubber paychecks.

And the best network in town. Why hadn't he come to the US with his hand out? Because he knew we wouldn't pay and the Soviets would. Which made the Union of Soviet Socialist Republics the true capitalists.

Lewis Carroll would have loved this town.

I wasn't going to march back up the stairs to re-negotiate. I just wasn't. So now what? Could be Eva was working late next door and knew someone who worked at the Armory. Why not? I'd been lucky so far this evening.

I walked back to the two-story brothel. The wind had died down and the night was still and fine. The lacy curtains downstairs were dimly lit as I approached the side door. I had my knuckles poised to knock when I realized I was flat broke. I had burned through my stash of Lucky Strikes and gold doubloons and hadn't replenished my wallet from my payday roll of twenties.

It was after hours, Madam Sofie would exact a heavy toll. Ah, but I hadn't left Col. Norwood's empty handed. I carried a paper bag containing two tins of liberated duck pate, a bottle of Porto Fino and something more precious than gold.

Easy come, easy go. I knocked. A little tin peekhole door swung open and an eyeball appeared.

"We're closed," said a deep voice.

"I understand. But do me a favor. Tell Sofie that Mr. Hal is here. With a special treat."

"What's so special?" said the eyeball.

I reached into my bag, secured a scoop of coffee beans and held them up to the peekhole. "Take a whiff."

A nose appeared and did as instructed. The door swung open. The joint was mine.

I ankled in. Sofie was in a mellow mood. Stewed to the gills. She gave me a big hug and made a grab for the paper bag.

"Not so fast, Sofie my sweet," I said, holding the bag up high, like a drug dealer making his late night rounds. "I have whole bean coffee from distant lands, which is yours for the taking if I can..."

Eva skittered down the stairs about then. She looked as awful as it was possible for a beautiful woman to look. Washed out, exhausted, her long blond hair wet and stringy.

"You promised me. You say, said, I will call tomorrow!"

I surrendered my bag of contraband to Madam Sofie and met Eva at the foot of the stairs. "You don't look so good."

"What I do is a hard job. Some nights."

"Did someone hurt you?"

Eva shook her head. It wasn't a no exactly, more of a I don't want to talk about it.

I didn't pry. Nothing I could do about it. I led her to a table to the right of the stairs, next to the piano. The keys were dusted with cigarette ashes. The one-armed piano player had gone home.

"I know where Ambrose is being held," I said and looked to see if Eva cared. She seemed distracted, darting her eyes about, tugging at her soggy hair. "Ambrose is being held at the Armory in the Soviet Sector. I was hoping you might know someone who works there. In the Soviet Armory. Eva? Hello?"

She turned to me with an astonished grin, new color in her cheeks. "Is that what I am smelling? *Kaffee*?"

I nodded. She jumped up, planted a kiss on my noggin and went off to get a cup. I understood. News of Ambrose's grim imprisonment could wait. What couldn't wait in post-war Berlin was a cup of real coffee.

My luck held. Eva knew Fritz, a trash hauler who worked the part of the Soviet Sector where the Armory was located, would come in after shift on paydays, stinking to high heaven.

I told Eva I wanted to talk to Fritz. That's when I crapped out. Eva said she didn't know where Fritz lived, had no way to contact him and that he wasn't due to visit for several days. I needed solid intel on Ambrose by this afternoon.

I thanked Eva, drank a cup of coffee and drove to the Soviet Sector, smiling at something Eva had said.

I had asked her, with a mind to securing Fritz's co-operation, what he liked, what his weakness was. I repeated the question because Eva had looked confused. But it was the stupidity of my question that baffled her.

She answered by putting her hands to her luscious breasts and saying, simply, "Me."

She was a survivor, that one. She'd outlive us all.

There was no one on duty when I drove past the Soviet checkpoint. No sign of life in the city at all. My Teutonic clock told me that dawn was near but the moonless sky was black. Leonid had said 'the Soviet Armory on *Blummenstraße*.' Wherever that was. You'd think a highly-trained espionage agent would keep a street map in his vehicle but you'd be wrong.

I drove the empty streets to the first flush of day before I found *Blummenstraße* off a four lane boulevard. It was a side street with an unkempt grassy median down the middle. The Armory was one block south and impossible to miss. A grim concrete quadrangle around an inner courtyard, with slits for windows on the lower floor and barred windows above. It looked new. A building that said, in Russian, we are here to stay.

Trees and bushes in the median made it difficult to get a clear glim of the entry gate. I drove past and banged a U at the intersection with *Krautstraße*. That was the name of the tiny street, I swear. *Krautstraße*.

I drove north, thinking this fortress was going to be one tough nut to crack. I slowed the delivery truck, crawled past the sentry booth and took a mental snapshot. Guard sleeping it off in the booth, big windows to the north inside the quad, upstairs. Shadowy figures stirring behind the glass, reveille at first light.

A one-story windowless bunker to the east.

Barred windows on the interior south side of the quad, upstairs.

A door to the immediate right of the sentry booth, set back from the courtyard. A sheltered entry point.

I drove around for a while after that, looking for a garbage truck making the rounds. I didn't see one. I circled back to *Blummenstraße* and parked the delivery truck down the block from the Armory, in a spot where I could watch the comings and goings from my side view mirror.

I did that for a good thirty seconds before I fell asleep.

Chapter Forty-three

A knocking on the truck window roused me. I sat up and waved at the Soviet MP who was tapping his nightstick on the glass and shaking his head. No sleeping behind the wheel in the Soviet Sector. I smiled and nodded till he drove off with his partner in a Lend-Lease jeep. Dumb place for a catnap, Schroeder.

I coaxed the delivery truck to life. There was one more stop I needed to make. The home address that Norwood gave for his Case Officer, NKVD Colonel Petrov Voynivich. I knew where the street was, had seen it when Ambrose and I first ventured into the Soviet Sector.

I found the address in short order. An imposing villa set back from the street, two miles from the Armory. The rest of the block was in bad shape but the brick turrets and ribbon windows of this turn of the century beauty were intact, as if the Red Army had spared it on purpose.

I drove by slowly, an eye peeled for sentries. When I was squared up with the villa I geared into neutral, depressed the accelerator halfway for a few seconds, then punched it to the floor as I threw the truck in first and jammed the brakes down hard.

It worked. The lurching and bucking and explosion of black smoke from the tailpipe brought a Red Army soldier out the front door and down the steps.

I got the truck rolling again and headed home. It looked like Col. Norwood had told the truth.

I took the three flights of stairs to my apartment one step at a time, bag of contraband in hand. I was beat down to the ankles, looking forward to a couple hours of shuteye before my big meeting with General Donovan. I had my key out when the door stopped me.

It didn't look right. The door was a warped old board that needed a shoulder from inside to get the latch bolt and strike plate lined up. The door wasn't open, but I could tell it wasn't latched.

I hoisted my Walther and checked the magazine. My sharp-shooting display at Col. Norwood's had left me with only three rounds. I got my breathing slowed down and reminded myself that the CO had a key to the place. It wouldn't do to storm in and lay waste to Victor Jacobson and General William Donovan.

But that was stupid. The CO wouldn't bring Donovan to my crummy digs. And he wouldn't come himself with Donovan due in. There was someone else inside my apartment.

I listened at the door jamb, heard a familiar sound and knew instantly who that someone was. I pushed the door open and saw Sean and Patrick Mooney, both sporting scraggly beards.

Sean looked up from the book he was reading and said, "You can put up the gun."

Patrick continued his signature snore on the musty couch, two quick snorts followed by a long ragged inhale, like a chainsaw biting through a knothole. I put up my gun.

"Well now, where have I seen this happy scene before?" I said, referring to the time the Mooney Brothers lock-picked their way into my room at Mrs. Brennan's rooming house.

"Where's Ambrose?" said Sean, tartly.

His brother awoke with a snort, hearing his cue. They were a regular Abbott and Costello, these two. I turned away, put my shoulder to the door and latched it, then turned back to face the music.

"Our mum had her fiftieth birthday last week," said Sean. He was the middle brother, compact, dark-haired.

"Ambey didn't send a card or a telegram," yawned Patrick, the baby brother, freckled and gangly.

"He wouldn't do that," said Sean.

"Not at tall," said Patrick.

"Which is why we're here."

"'Tis."

A wave of exhaustion washed over me, exhaustion so complete that Sean and Patrick seemed to blur around the edges. But I couldn't very well excuse myself and hit the hay, anymore than I could explain to the Mooney boys what had happened to their big brother. Not yet anyway. I needed a minute.

"You hungry? Thirsty? Want to wash up?"

"We'll take a drink of whiskey," said young Patrick amiably.

"And an explanation," said Sean, less so.

"I don't have any whiskey," I said while removing the bottle that I had filched from Col. Norwood. "But I do have a jug of vintage Port. It's thick as blood."

"We're wantin' a drink," said Patrick.

"Not Holy Communion," said Sean.

I went to the kitchen and uncorked the bottle anyway, grabbed three glasses. The sudden appearance of the Mooney boys was perfect. I would have a backup and a lookout going in. We could get right to work on a plan to rescue Ambrose. Everything was jake. Just as soon as I told the boys that their beloved brother had been snatched by the Soviet secret police and imprisoned in a reinforced concrete dungeon.

I returned with the bottle of Port and three plastic juice glasses, set them down on the low lacquered coffee table and made a joke which the young hooligans found amusing.

"How did you get in?"

I poured myself a full glass and crooked an eyebrow. Patrick looked to Sean, who nodded. I poured two more. "How'd you know where to find me?"

"You and Ambrose, you mean," said Sean.

"Ambrose sent us a letter," said Patrick.

I offered a toast. "Welcome to Berlin. Your timing is impeccable."

We drank, kept silent and drank some more.

Then I told them all that had happened. I told them where their brother was being held and didn't mince words about how tough it would be to bust him loose. They took it stoically, bless 'em.

"The good news is we've got some help. General William Donovan arrives today."

"Himself? The Fightin' Harp?" said Patrick, eyes wide.

I nodded.

"Bloody hell," said Sean.

Wild Bill was a Hibernian legend from way back. He won the Medal of Honor commanding New York's heavily-Irish 69th Regiment in World War I.

I didn't mention that I might be on the legend's shit list after he learned about Col. Norwood, or that Ambrose Mooney would be last on Donovan's list of concerns if he made the list at all. I couldn't give them the big picture. But I did tell them I would free Ambrose or die trying.

"With your help."

They drained their glasses of red wine and made the sign of the cross. I smiled at their youthful courage. And thought about their mother.

I had spoken to her once in Cleveland, when I telephoned for Ambrose. She hadn't been pleased to hear from me. And now here I was again, about to kill off her own three sons. I had to do what I had to do but I didn't need both Sean and Patrick to do it. I needed a lookout, but a backup was...well, it would be nice to have as I prowled the corridors of the Armory but I was a seasoned espionage agent with eyes in the back of my head.

I could spare one of them, Sean or Patrick. I could do Mrs. Mooney that small miserable favor.

The boys wouldn't part easily, and calling to mind their sainted mother praying for their safe return would only tick 'em off. So I tried another approach.

"We'll need to get some more L pills before we mount this operation. I've only got one."

"What's that?" said Sean.

"An L pill?" said Patrick.

"Cyanide. L for lethal. We spies keep them handy in case we're captured. And tortured. The Russians have a guy named Beria who's pretty good at it."

I poured more wine and waited to see how this went over.

"An operation is it?" said Sean.

"Bloody impressive," said Patrick.

"And I don't see where any L pills are necessary," said Sean. "If Patrick's captured I'll shoot him dead."

"And if Sean's caught I'll do the same."

I said a silent apology to Mrs. Mooney. There would be no separating Sean and Patrick. I shoved onto the couch next to Patrick, planted my feet on the lacquered table, put my chin to my chest and dozed.

I woke up a minute later. Beards. Sean and Patrick had scruffy beards that made them look like anarchists.

"If you gentlemen expect an audience with Wild Bill Donovan you will have to go to the sink and make yourselves presentable."

Sean sat up with some alarm. "You mean shave?"

"I do."

Sean and Patrick groaned as one.

Chapter Forty-four

"Bill Donovan is a military man, first and foremost," I said to the Mooney boys the following morning after we were all showered and shorn and dressed to kill.

I was surprised to see that they came equipped with brass buttoned Navy blue blazers and silk ties till I remembered that they were wealthy young gentlemen now, courtesy of the Federal Reserve Bank of Cleveland. Well turned out they were, save for the plugs of toilet paper pasted to their shaving cuts. I understood why they had grown the chin spinach. Without it they looked fourteen years old.

"Military bearing in his presence at all times. Shoulders back, chin down."

I demonstrated. The Mooney boys mirrored me.

"Do not speak unless spoken to, and always use sir. Got it?"

"Yes sir!"

We drove south to Dahlem, the traffic light, the weather mild, almost warm. Sean and Patrick were keyed up, chattering like schoolgirls. I was glad to have them on board. My free lancing days were over. I would have to tell General Donovan of my hare-brained scheme to rescue Ambrose from the Armory, somehow convince him to give his blessing. Having two proud sons of the Old Sod arrayed behind me couldn't hurt.

When we arrived at the white brick mansion in Dahlem the redheaded receptionist told me General Donovan had issued 'a change of plans.' The meet was now taking place twenty kilometers south in the town of Babelsberg, just east of Potsdam. She gave me a bright smile and typewritten directions.

"Is this a snub?" I asked. "To the CO?"

She answered by way of gazing at the elderly bartender and the *frau* in a peasant blouse standing around the parlor with no one to serve. The boys and I washed down some finger sandwiches with a glass of champagne and returned to the delivery truck.

I drove southwest as instructed, wondering how I was going to brief the CO about Col. Norwood while in the presence of Bill Donovan.

Victor Jacobson would be on thin ice. He had presided over the brutal destruction of our White Russian network at the hand of his trusted new hire, Leonid Vitinov. I owed Jacobson the courtesy of a private heads up so he could determine what to tell Donovan about Norwood, and when.

We jounced southwest to Babelsberg on cratered roads. The countryside was thickly wooded and lushly green. I turned due west at *Grossbeerenstraße*, Big Berry Road. We passed an enormous bomb-damaged complex of buildings big as airplane hangars, though no airstrip was visible. The road swung north.

I turned right at the park as instructed, drove quiet streets lined with Hansel and Gretel cottages until I found what I was looking for. An 18th Century peak-roofed stucco villa with a circular drive and a four-pillared portico that looked out on a very wide river or a very narrow lake. An MP wearing button-up white leggings stood guard on the front steps.

Sean and Patrick fell silent as I pulled up the drive and parked the truck at the base of the stone steps. The MP saluted. We were expected.

I was anyway. The MP got jinky when he saw the Mooney boys spill out of the truck. He checked his clipboard. They weren't on it. I told the MP that the gentlemen were with me.

Didn't matter. They weren't on his list. "Back in the truck, gentlemen," I said, climbing the steps. "I'll be back in no time."

Sean and Patrick climbed back in the truck like kids sent to their rooms on Christmas morn. I crossed under the pillared portico and pushed the doorbell. It chimed a dolorous tune, I felt a chill. There was something creepy about this old place. I saw a dark shadow behind the opaque glass panels of the double doors. Who was this now, Boris Karloff?

Just a stooped housekeeper with a toucan beak and angry black eyes. She bustled off before I could say a word.

I stepped inside, saw a very formal living room directly off the entry hall, and a big dining room to the right. To the left, a long wide carpeted corridor that ran along the outer wall of the house. All the rooms off the corridor faced the back of the property. Security precaution maybe.

I found the CO down that corridor, sitting outside the door to an office, lost in thought. The door to the office was closed. I told him the Mooney brothers had arrived unexpectedly.

"What do they want?"

"Their brother."

"Shit."

"It's okay sir. They're capable, they'll do as they're told."

"You're sure?"

"One hundred percent."

I told him they were awaiting permission to enter the premises. We went outside. I introduced Sean and Patrick. Jacobson shook their hands. "Welcome to The Little White House."

He explained that this creepy old manse was President Truman's place of residence during the Big Three Potsdam Conference two months after VE Day. We were suitably impressed. He rambled on about Babelsberg, the German Hollywood, site of the Ufa Film Studios where Marlene Dietrich and Fritz Lang got their start. Had we noticed the cavernous sound stages on the drive in?!

He was wound up, the CO.

Jacobson had a chat with the MP, signed something on the clipboard and waved us in. We trooped down the wide corridor to the office with the closed door. Jacobson told Sean and

Patrick that the facilities were two doors down. They took the hint.

"How'd it go with Colonel Norwood?" said the CO when they were gone.

"One question first. Do we know a Petrov Voynivich?"

"He's an NKVD Colonel operating in the Soviet sector."

That was the answer I was looking for. "Voynivich is Col. Norwood's boss."

No visible reaction from Jacobson. "How?"

How did you determine that is what he meant. I wasn't supposed to tell Norwood about Leonid's confession so I couldn't tell the CO that I had done that in order to accuse Norwood of Commie collusion and force a reply. But I had to tell him something.

"The more I chewed on it the more I suspected that Norwood had been turned. Too much coincidence, he was always a step ahead. I wandered off during one of Norwood's long-winded speeches, did a quick search. And found this."

I showed the CO the scandalous photo. I had promised the Colonel I'd keep the photo in my pocket, but we spies lie all the time.

Jacobson shook his head at the stupidity of it, and at the endless bad tidings I brought him. I told another lie. "Norwood thinks I threw it in the fireplace."

"Which was why he gave you Voynivich."

"More or less."

"You could have used it to spring Ambrose."

"Yes sir."

The CO nodded his appreciation. No riot act, no ass chewing. I was home free.

"How did you leave it?"

Maybe not. "I told the Colonel to go to some tropical paradise and stay there."

"You did what?"

Sean and Patrick returned about then. Jacobson, not wanting to dress me down in their presence, lit a cigarette and fumed.

I returned the photo to my coat pocket and wondered who Bill Donovan was talking to behind that closed door. Had to be Klaus Hilde. What a thumb in the eye to the CO. Made to cool his heels in the hallway while General Donovan consulted with a Nazi fugitive. That's the military for you. Hilde was a Nazi, sure, but he was also a general. And generals stick together.

The door opened a minute later. Herr Hilde emerged, spit and polish in a pin stripe suit, beard shorn, sentried by Jug Ears. He turned to Victor Jacobson, bowed and clicked his heels.

Of course, I should have known. Hilde was a *Junker*, a member of the landed Prussian aristocracy who dismissed Hitler as a bumbling corporal until it was too late and who more or less invented modern warfare. The Whiskey Colonels would worship at his feet.

The CO did not return Hilde's Prussian nod. I did, when my turn came.

"I owe you a debt of gratitude, Herr Schroeder," he said, "for your successful mission to free me from captivity."

"You are most welcome, Herr Hilde," I replied. "Sleep well tonight."

Hilde paused before he nodded, uneasily. When I intoned a well-loved lullaby the Brigadeführer turned on his heel and stalked down the hall, Jug Ears scrambling to keep pace.

"Schlaf, Kindchen, schlaf / Ich gebe Dir ein Schaf / Und es soll eine Glocke aus Gold haben / Für Dich zum Spielen und zu halten / Schlaf, Kindchen, schlaf."

The CO didn't ask. He stood up as Wild Bill Donovan stepped out of the office to greet us a short time later. Sean and Patrick stood to attention.

"In here," said Donovan, hand on the door knob.

I gave the Mooney boys a stay-patient palms-down and followed the CO into the dark office, closing the door behind me.

The office had striped gold and brown wallpaper, a white marble fireplace and a massive intricately-carved desk suitable for treaty signing ceremonies. The only light came from late afternoon sun bleaching through the muslin drapes and a two bulb desk lamp capped by a black metal shade.

General Donovan took his place in a high-backed upholstered chair behind the deck. There were no other chairs in the room, no stenographers or adjutants. Wild Bill was flying low to the ground this trip.

"Good work on Hilde," said the General to Jacobson. "He's very knowledgeable."

"That was Hal's doing General."

I got a brief nod. This wasn't the back-slapping Wild Bill I had met in New York. This was a Major General in a foul temper.

"And this Committee that Hilde tells me about. Why wasn't I kept abreast?"

"I cabled you sir," said Jacobson.

"Never saw it. Is it true?"

"We believe so sir."

"Explain."

"I sent Mr. Schroeder to one of their meetings. He determined that the Committee to Free Berlin was a front bent on mayhem."

"On what evidence?"

Donovan said it to me. I think. The downward lamplight cast his face in shadow. I wrangled up my tongue, not sure what to say. No mention of Leonid's double dealing had been made as yet. I wasn't going to be the one to reveal my CO's major career embarrassment to Bill Donovan. But how to explain it elsewise?

Tell the truth. The best of it anyway.

"I went as a Stars'n'Stripes reporter, General, got a very cool reception, as if they were hiding something. When I went to leave I was greeted warmly by a founding member who assured me that the Committee was on the up and up."

"Make your point."

How to say this? I wasn't going to flat out lie to the Great Man.

"Our counterintelligence officer Leonid Vitinov informed me in advance that I would be so approached. And that the approacher would be an NKVD agent."

Well he did. Inform me. Leonid just didn't know he did.

Donovan filed this away this without comment. "What else do you have?"

I looked to Jacobson. He answered for me.

"Mr. Schroeder reports that Col. Norwood of MI6 has been compromised by the Soviets and is in the process of fleeing to a distant country."

"*John* Norwood? Who knows about this?"

"Just the people in this room General."

Donovan looked to me for further explanation.

"The Colonel admitted this to me personally sir. He's been reporting to Col. Petrov Voynivich, Soviet Sector."

Donovan didn't ask why Norwood made this stunning admission to me. Didn't want to know the sordid details maybe. I could keep my scandalous photo in my pocket.

Wild Bill looked me over. And smiled. "You have been keeping your eyes open, haven't you?"

"Trying my best sir."

"Where is Norwood now?"

"I'm not sure General, but as of about 0300 hours he was still in his chalet on *Spirchenstraße*."

Donovan gave me a long and complicated look. I came clean.

"I didn't say anything till now because I promised the Colonel I would give him a chance to flee in exchange for the identity and location of his Soviet Case Officer. It seemed a good bargain at the time, perhaps not so good now in the cold light of day. Col. Norwood has a way of confusing a person."

I braced myself for a tongue lashing that didn't come.

"Did Colonel Norwood indicate why he turned against the Directorate?"

"The who, sir?"

"The Directorate of Military Intelligence, Section Six," said Donovan impatiently.

I'd always wondered what MI6 stood for. "Yes sir. The Colonel said their checks bounced."

Donovan exchanged a knowing look with Victor Jacobson, and said, "Let's move to the Club Room."

Wild Bill jumped up from behind the massive desk as if he couldn't wait to get out of there. We followed him out into the hall. The CO introduced Donovan to the Mooney brothers. The Fighting Harp invited them to join us, to their infinite delight.

I too was glad to be out of that dark office. There was something sinister about it. Walking down the hall I realized what it was. That dark room would have been President Truman's office during the Potsdam Conference, which had adjourned in early August. About the time Truman made the decision to drop the A bomb on Hiroshima, incinerating more than 100,000 Japanese.

Truman gave the order in that room. I knew he did, I could feel it. It was a momentous decision, a horrific decision, and the correct decision in this man's opinion. But not one you wanted to cozy up to.

There were ghosts in that dark office. Thousands of them.

Chapter Forty-five

The club room had a piano, a checkerboard table with checkers lined up and, by the rear window, two of those low slung leather wing chairs you need a winch to climb out of. An orderly took our drink orders. We followed Donovan's lead. Pabst Blue Ribbon beer.

Bill Donovan seemed back to his old self in the new setting. He asked the Mooney brothers their names, and what county they hailed from.

"County Cork sir," said Sean, shoulders back, chin down.

"By way of Cuyahoga County, Ohio," said Patrick, likewise. The boys did a quick take to one another and concluded, in tandem, "USA!"

This brought a twinkle to Wild Bill's baby blues. We stood around and shot the shit and waited for beer and generally had a fine time until the General asked Sean and Patrick why they were here.

The boys froze. Me too. The CO intervened on our behalf. "It's something we need to discuss General."

Shiny cold bottles of Pabst were served. Also bowls of mixed nuts, pretzels and a plate of rollmops. The others ignored these pungent rolls of marinated herring so I appropriated them for myself. They came with wedges of rye toast. Perfect.

Our roles were reversed in the club room. We took chairs to enjoy our snacks while Bill Donovan remained standing, and held forth.

"The auction houses of France are suddenly flooded with valuable oil paintings. Also sterling silver, cut glass crystal, gems, gold jewelry and the like." He shook his head. "This is what we are reduced to. Intelligence from French art house auctioneers."

I sought to fill in the blanks. "What is the significance General? Of the flood of contraband?"

"The ruble's almost as worthless as the reichmark. The Reds would need hard currency in order to mount an invasion."

"Which is why they're selling all their captured German loot in France?"

Donovan nipped at his beer. Obviously.

The CO and Donovan moved to the wing chairs by the window for a huddled conversation. I overheard the occasional heated contraction - *don't, won't, can't* - and decided this wasn't a conversation I wanted to overhear.

I looked to the Mooney brothers, seeking distraction. Sean was eyeing the piano. "You know how to play?"

"Sure. We both do."

They did at that. Sean took the high keys, Patrick the low. They were halfway decent, plunking out an Irish ditty on a piano that Truman had likely set a spell at. Wild Bill hoisted his beer in salute. The boys liked that.

Donovan's information had been sliced thin and served sparingly. He knew much more than art house auction proceeds. He would have access to Army Intel cable intercepts and Air Force flight surveillance reports, State Department briefs and scuttlebutt too. 'In order to mount an invasion' he had said. That tin map in the Comm Center, the one with all the red magnets crowding the Elbe, was becoming very real.

No wonder Donovan hadn't gigged me for letting Col. Norwood scamper off. Good riddance to bad rubbish was his thinking. It was time for serious men to take charge.

I was ginned up and ready to roll, half drunk on half a beer, eager to make my case for the rescue of Ambrose and all that would follow. But Jacobson and Wild Bill were still deep in conversation, Jacobson doing most of the talking, Donovan sipping beer from the bottle, answering with brief remarks. It went on like that for two beers.

At last Donovan stood up and shook hands with Jacobson and walked over to the piano. My CO gave me a quick thumbs up.

He had made the case for me, had, apparently, convinced Wild Bill to approve my hare-brained scheme to rescue Ambrose. I nodded my profound thanks.

All I had to do now was work out the operational details. Figure out precisely how to infiltrate the Soviet Armory, locate, liberate and exfiltrate a heavily guarded prisoner while pausing to snap photos of the machine gun emplacements set up to mow down the Committee to Free Berlin. That's it. That's all I had to do.

My cranial cavity was a whirlygig of pressing questions and concerns so I'm not really sure if Major General William J. Donovan spent the better part of an hour singing Irish ditties with the Mooney Brothers at the piano.

But that's the way I remember it.

Chapter Forty-six

A thought occurred when I climbed behind the wheel of the delivery truck after our session with Wild Bill.

We had agreed that the operation to free Ambrose would launch tonight. The CO informed the boys and me that we wouldn't be permitted any heavy weapons or explosives, if we were captured no one had ever heard of us and so on and so forth. Then he went to the trunk of his Horch and presented the boys with two clean Colt .38 Specials and a box of ammo. He gave me a set of handcuffs and his Kine Exakta camera with the flash attachment. Then he shook hands all around and wished us Godspeed.

The thought that occurred was this. Sean, Patrick and myself were about to get our necks wrung doing something that Colonel Norwood said he could do with a phone call. Was it too late to bring the Colonel back in? Norwood and Sedgewick weren't going to drive to the South Seas. They were likely at Templehof right now, waiting on a flight. We could be there in an hour. I would give Norwood his scandalous photo back as payment for the favor, tell him that General Donovan wished him a happy retirement.

I opened the truck door and put my foot on the running board. I kept it there.

"Are we coming?" said Sean.

"Or going?" said Patrick.

"I'll let you know in a minute."

It wasn't that I didn't want the Colonel to have the last laugh at my expense. I didn't but it wasn't that. I would don a big red nose and inflatable shoes to free Ambrose from captivity.

But it wouldn't work. Sean, Patrick and I were going to have to do it ourselves, for a little reason and a big one. The little reason was that I had to gain entrance to the Armory in order to take snaps of the machine gun emplacements, thereby alerting the Committee to the trap and averting World War III.

The big reason was that I owed it to Ambrose to do it myself. If the Soviets said no to Norwood, which was likely given what they had brewing, they would then know we were zeroed in on Ambrose and would redouble his guard. Or ship him off to the Lubyanka. We had one shot to rescue Ambrose and it was ours alone.

"We're going," I said and fired up the truck.

I talked the Mooney boys through the layout of the Armory as I drove east through Babelsberg at dusk, the delivery truck thrumming happily. Sean sat in the passenger's seat, Patrick took the transmission hump.

"It's a quadrangle. Barracks on the north side, detention cells upstairs on the south, best I can figure. Entry gate's on the west."

"What's on the east side? said Sean

"That's the armory part."

"How do you know?" said Patrick.

"It's a one-story vault with no windows and a ribbed steel door."

"How do you know the detention cells are on the south side?" said Sean.

"Upstairs," said Patrick.

"Barred windows on both sides. There's a guard at the entry gate. He's the key. We get hold of him and we've got a key ring and a hostage going in."

"How do we plan to?" "Get hold of him?" said Sean and Patrick.

"He sits in a glass booth with an alarm button or a klaxon horn. We can't risk swarming him, and the old hey pal, got a match routine's not gonna fly. We need something unexpected to lure him out of that booth."

"A damsel in distress," said Sean.

"Beat up, clothes ripped," said Patrick.

"Yeah."

"Says she's been raped by a Russian soldier."

"Unexpected gentlemen. That probably happens twice a week. But I like the damsel in distress angle. How else can we work that?"

Pursed lips and head scratching from the Mooney's. But I had a ridiculous idea.

"Howzabout a tearful woman with a babe in arms, presenting the Russian love child she can't care for?"

"I like it, I do," said Sean.

"Where we gonna get a babbie?" said Patrick.

I shrugged. "Who says it's real?"

"Doll wrapped in a blanket?" said Sean.

"Mummy sobs, lays her bundle down and runs away," said Patrick.

"Luring the sentry out of his booth!"

"What do you think Chief?"

I drove down bomb-pocked *Grossbeerenstraße*, the setting sun showing off, painting the scudding clouds gaudy colors. "I think that I am fortunate to have you devious young hooligans on my side. Now shut up and let me think." They did so. "And stop staring at me."

The boys turned away and pretended to admire the scenery. I considered the babe in arms ploy. It was just ridiculous enough to work. But who played mummy? Eva came to mind, but she had done enough.

It would have to be Anna. Anna had a stake. Me. I was her ticket to New York.

I looked over at Sean in the passenger's seat. He was biting his cuticles. Patrick was in the back, stretched out on an Army blanket. "What you chewing on over there young man?"

"My fingernails"

"I can see that. I meant what's eating you?"

"Well, you've got a gun, right?"

"Of course. Walther P-38."

"So we got three pistols against an armory. Bit of a mismatch, in'it?"

"The number doesn't matter, Sean. If we have to fire a shot inside the Armory we're dead and buried."

Sean nodded and looked out the window. I drove north to Berlin.

Chapter Forty-seven

I stopped at the butcher shop when we got back to town, bribed my way in after closing time again. Life was good in the American sector. Miguel directed my attention to several thick T-bones in the glass case. I bought four, damned if our last supper was going to be beef stew from a can.

We crossed the street to a *Spirituosengeschäft*, which is Kraut for hooch hut. I bought a fifth of Jameson's for the boys and a bottle of fancy French Bordeaux for myself. And Anna. It was time to ride to the rescue. Rescue her from her safe house in Kopenick, embrace her warmly, then inform her that she had been drafted to join us in a suicide mission.

I dropped Sean and Patrick off at the apartment, gave them the key, the hooch and the beef and said I'd be back in an hour or so.

The boys wanted to know where I was headed. "Off to get mummy and her bundle of joy."

I wound my way southeast on Berlin's meandering thoroughfares. The neighborhood took a turn for the worse when I entered the Soviet Sector, the shops and apartment buildings beat to hell during the Red Army's ferocious siege of the city. A siege that on *Dorpheldstraße* in Kopenick looked as if it had just finished up last week. I drove past a blackened Wehrmacht Tiger tank sitting in an empty lot, a Soviet flag stuffed in its gun turret.

I turned left and hunted the address Eva had given me. The tidy bungalows on the cobbled side streets were largely intact. And to look at 178 *Gloriastraße* with its striped awnings and white and purple lilacs was to conclude that World War II had never taken place.

I dragged Anna's two ton suitcase out of the truck and knocked at the front door. And again. I walked around and knocked at the back door. I peered in a window hung with a small square of tatted lace. A kerosene lamp smoked and guttered on a bedroom dresser. Where the hell was she?

I dug out my knife and eyeballed the double-hung window. It was secured with a simple turn clasp but I had to punch a hole in the glass with my knife butt to get at it. I slid the window open and listened. I couldn't identify what I heard but I heard something.

"Hello? Anna?" No answer. What did she say her friend's name was? Tanya? Tattia?

"Tattia? It's Hal Schroeder, Anna's *Freund*."

I sensed movement but didn't see it, heard another faint something, different than the first. A quick skittering sound. I stuck my head inside the window and sneezed. Cat dander. Ivan the Terrible was near.

I hauled myself in through the window and did a room to room, gat in hand. It didn't take long, the house had only five rooms. I found a pot of oatmeal on the stove, still warm. A kitchen drawer sat open. One that held knives. There was someone here, unless they had run out the back.

Dummkopf, you should have identified yourself when you first knocked. I made another circuit and looked harder. "Come out, come out, wherever you are!"

I found someone hiding under the bed. Ivan the cat. I asked him where Anna had got to. He hissed and darted away. He didn't like me anymore and who could blame him? I had promised to ride to the rescue at first light. No telling what dark imaginings Ivan and his mistress had endured in my absence.

I searched the bedroom closet, the coat closet, even the kitchen pantry. I searched the backyard, the tool shed and the detached one-car garage piled high with stacks of yellowed newspapers and political fliers, tinder for the fireplace. There was no one to be found. Yet there had to be. Anna would know better than to leave the premises. She and Tattia might have been dragged off by enemy agents but I didn't think so. The NKVD had bigger fish to fry at the moment.

I went back inside and looked again. The house had no cellar but it had an attic. All tidy bungalows have an attic. I searched the ceiling in all five rooms, found no entry point. This was now, officially, ridiculous.

I heard the first sound again, the one I'd heard outside the window. Closer now, but muffled. A long low sound, a moan maybe. Where the hell was it coming from?

I checked the closets again, found a ceiling panel in the bedroom closet. It was just big enough to squeeze through. I grabbed a table chair from the kitchen, carried it to the closet, climbed up on it, removed the ceiling panel, lit my penlight and decided to announce myself before I thrust my head into the dark hole.

"Anna? It's Hal Schroeder."

Smart move on my part. Anna's face came into view. She looked half mad, eyes wide, pupils dilated, cheeks smudged with soot. She held a carving knife the size of a wheat scythe.

"Sorry I'm late," I said. Stupidly.

Anna dropped the carving knife to the floor and burst into tears. I helped her down from the attic. She wept convulsively as I held her up, salting my shirt with her tears.

"I knew...I knew...I knew you were dead...I knew."

"And yet here I am. Big as life and twice as ugly."

Anna hiccupped snot from her nose. I got out my hankie and cleaned her up. I told her not to worry, that Leonid would not hurt her anymore.

"You do not know."

"What don't I know Anna?"

"What they do, how they are."

"How are they?"

Anna didn't answer my question, just hugged me like a tree trunk in a hurricane. I picked her up and carried her to the kitchen. It was my turn to make tea.

But Anna didn't want any tea. I tried. I set her down on her own two feet and grabbed for the kettle but Anna wouldn't let go.

So we held each other. For a long time. I had forgotten how it felt. To hold a woman I cared about in a crushing hug, hearts thudding against one another until our pulse and our breathing became one. Then we let go and stepped back.

Anna wrapped her glorious mitts around the nape of my neck, feathered my hair with her fingertips and kissed me lightly on the cheek.

I returned the favor. Her skin was sticky with tears, taut and soft as the whisper she dropped in my ear. "I am want you now."

We started slowly, tenderly, bending back over the sink, sliding our clothes off. Then we gave in to the hunger, let our bodies tear into one another, mouths sucking, hips thrusting. Minds racing. Anna wrapped her skinny legs around me and climaxed with a feral scream. I gave out with a knee-buckling groan a moment later. Anna tightened her legs to hold me up.

We disengaged and pulled our clothes back on.

I did anyway. Anna pulled up her skirt and panties but kept her pale blue sweater hiked up behind her. Her breasts were beautiful, girlish and innocent. Upturned, blue-veined. A bead of sweat clung to an erect nipple. Anna followed my look and pulled my head down. I caught the quivering drop on the tip of my tongue before it fell. Anna moaned, and pulled her sweater back into place.

We backed up a step, flushed and a little embarrassed. I asked what became of her friend.

"She was in fear, when I came. I had to...How to say?"

"Beg? Plead?"

"Yes. Beg to stay."

"Where is she now?" Anna shook her head. "She left you, she went away?" Anna nodded. "When? When did she go away?"

"After I came. *Gestern*."

Yesterday, that was good. If Tattia was a plant installed by Leonid to keep watch on his wife Anna would have been snatched by now. But Tattia wasn't working for Leonid. Of course she wasn't. It would never have occurred to the arrogant little shit that his wife needed watching.

"Anna I have friend, *gut* friend, from America. He was kidnapped." Anna shook her head at the word. "Taken, *nehmen*, by Leonid. He is being held in the Soviet Armory." Anna didn't understand.

"He is in jail." I held imaginary bars. "His brothers, *zwei Bruders*, have come here to help me free him." I swung open the cell door. "And we need your help."

"How I can? Help."

I explained our plan and the part that she would play. This took a while. When Anna understood she said, "This is not joke?"

"No. I wish that it were."

"It seems to me...*dumm*."

"It is *dumm*. It's a *dumm* job I have, dressing up and playing pretend, playing make believe." I did a bit of flouncing around to illustrate.

Anna laughed at me. "I know this, what you say. I know how to do this...make believe."

I'll bet she did at that. "So you will help us?"

Anna gave me a sideways look. "You haf brought to me my *Handkoffer*?"

"Yes Anna, I haf brought your suitcase."

She grinned, and said the American word everyone in the world loves best. "Okay."

"Go find Ivan," I said and went off to ransack the house for props. Tattia didn't have any dolls or stuffed animals to hand so

I grabbed a crocheted comforter off the sofa and looked around for something to stuff inside. A cracked flower vase on the sideboard filled out the blanket nicely, but our precious bundle needed a head.

Anna stood at the front door, overcoat buttoned and cat hauling basket at her side. She followed me to the kitchen.

A basket on the counter by the ice box held a cabbage and two onions. Too big and too small. I looked behind the basket, found a fat turnip that had rolled off the pile. I wedged it into the neck of the flower vase and handed the bundle to Anna. She cradled it in her arms. We had another odd domestic moment just then as she rocked the bundle ever-so-gently.

"What can we call him?" she said, looking up at me, eyes bright.

I thought about it. How to properly name a cracked flower vase with a turnip for a head?

"We'll call him Hal Jr."

Chapter Forty-eight

I carried Anna's two ton suitcase up the three flights of stairs to the apartment, stopping to gasp for air on each landing. Anna carried Ivan in his wicker basket. When we reached the door I used our top secret knock to announce my presence. Shave and a haircut, two bits.

Patrick answered, his eyes shiny with whisky. Sean looked up from the couch where he was reading. Anna and I entered the parlor, set down our grips and shrugged off our coats. The room was cold. Patrick closed the door behind us.

"Sean, Patrick, this is my friend Anna."

They mumbled greetings. Anna and I stood there as the Mooney brothers appraised us like cattle at auction. They sensed that funny business was afoot, could smell it maybe. I had compromised my authority.

"I'll open that bottle of wine," I said with a nod to the guttering fifth of Jameson's on the low lacquered table. "We've got some catching up to do."

I looked to Anna and hiked my head toward the kitchen. Her cool gray eyes said she would stay put. I hung our coats on the coat rack. She took a seat on the wobbly chair opposite Sean and Patrick on the couch.

By the time I returned with two juice glasses of Bordeaux Anna had Ivan curled up in her lap and Sean and Patrick sitting on the lip of the couch, leaning forward. I stopped behind the boys to listen.

"Your Mister Schroeder, he is *gut* at this job. *Sehr gut*. I was keep like a bird, a bird in a..."

"Cage," offered Sean.

"Yes so. A bird in a cage. Your Mister Schroeder, he have open this cage to..."

"Set you free," said Patrick.

Anna smiled. "Yes so. Your Mister Schroeder knows about what he is doing."

This heartfelt endorsement got the boys to nodding. I hoped it was true. I hoped I knew about what I was doing.

I handed Anna a glass of wine, turned to Sean and Patrick and asked how they liked their steaks.

"Medium," said Sean.

"Bloody," said Patrick.

I returned to the kitchen and chopped the onions I had liberated from Tattia's kitchen and fried them up in the stick of margarine I had likewise liberated. I put the steaks on the broiler tray and slid them in. If there's a more mouthwatering combination of aromas than broiling steak and frying onions I would like to know about it.

Pepper and A-1 were the only missing ingredients. I wasn't going to round up any steak sauce around here but we were not going to sit down to our last supper without pepper on our steaks. I searched the kitchen cupboards and drawers. I considered trolling the halls with a dollar bill but shouted out a stupid question before I did.

"Anyone have any pepper?" Anna wrinkled her brow. "*Pfeffer.*"

I followed Anna into the parlor. She opened her two ton suitcase and rummaged in her pile of silver cutlery and fine china wrapped in sweaters and underwear. She came up with a crystal shaker and handed it over. It held just enough black pepper to season the T-bones blistering in the broiler.

"*Vielen Dank, gnädige Frau.*" Thank you, dear lady.

"*Sehr gerne geschehen, mein Herr.*" You are most welcome, kind sir.

The steaks were great. Conversation around the small table just off the kitchen consisted primarily of groans of pleasure not normally associated with the dinner hour. Bone skinny Anna beat us all to the finish line, with an assist from a furry creature at her feet.

When Anna cleared the plates I ran down the operational details. I wasn't a lone wolf anymore. I was a goddamn miserable commanding officer responsible for the lives of my subordinates. How in the hell had that happened?

"We launch at 0300 hours, which is 3 a.m. to you raw-assed rookies." The Mooney's half-lamped eyelids snapped to. "If the entry booth guard is snoozing we cuff and gag him. If he's on alert Anna will lure him from the booth before we pounce. Once he's cuffed and gagged we search him and the booth for passkeys. Failing that I'll jimmy the door to his left and walk him up the stairs. We threaten to cut his goozle if the jailer doesn't open the cell. If the jailer's somewhere sleeping it off I pick the cell lock. Patrick you're lookout, Sean's my backup. Any questions?"

Sean and Patrick, bellies full of steak and whisky, could only manage one.

"Should we disguise ourselves?"

"Like we did at the...you know."

"No masks, no kerchiefs. We're not crooks. Now go, take the bedroom, sleep it off."

The boys shuffled off. Anna settled onto the musty couch with a fresh glass of wine. She kicked off her shoes and put one leg up on the low slung table and flexed her toes. Prettiest foot you ever saw.

I got my Walther from my topcoat, sat down next to Anna and ejected the spent clip. I examined the mag chamber, the breech, the bore and the muzzle and dry fired a couple times. The gun was in working order.

I jacked in another clip. I had one more in reserve. I should have cleaned the bore with powder solvent and lubricated the action with oil but I hadn't thought to grab my gun cleaning kit when I packed up to travel to New York-Antwerp-Berlin and it was too late to return to Mrs. B's rooming house in Cleveland to retrieve it and anyhow it didn't matter. We weren't going to win this night with guns.

I went down my tick list. Gas in the truck. Knife. Lock picks. Camera and flashbulbs. Penlight. Handcuffs. Gags.

I didn't have any gags. I went to the kitchen, grabbed a dirty dish rag and tore it in two. Done. Now what?

L pill. I had one cyanide capsule, wrapped in tinfoil and tucked in my billfold. Anna should have it just in case. I removed, unwrapped and offered it to her. She pushed my hand away. She knew what it was. She wasn't interested.

I took a sip of fine French wine and relaxed. This was something I knew well. War. War is every vile horrid thing they say it is and then some but it has one redeeming feature. Clarity. We would win the battle to free Ambrose or we would lose. Planning and preparation were important, worry and speculation were pointless. We would know soon enough.

Soon enough, soon enough. Too bad I had no earthly idea what time it was. My Teutonic clock was rusty. Co-ordinated timing would be crucial. I knew I should borrow a wristwatch but I had a superstition about 'em ever since The Schooler got croaked and I didn't want to jinx the operation by changing up now.

Anna wore a dainty wristwatch, face turned to the underside of her wrist. I asked her what time it was. She showed me. 8:50. I took her exquisite hand in mine, squeezed it and drifted off, setting my mental alarm clock for 0230 hours.

"*Süße Träume*," murmured Anna.

Sweet dreams.

Chapter Forty-nine

I dreamt of sweet-smelling wheat fields and far off mountains crowded with black firs and leafy green *Buchen*, veils of steam nestled in the ravines. I was high above, soaring like an eagle. Then I woke up. Anna was snoring softly besides me on the couch. I borrowed her wrist. 0228 hours. My Teutonic clock was back in working order.

I went to the kitchen sink and splashed cold water on my face and had a crazy thought. I didn't need to rouse these good people from their peaceful slumber and send them off to die. I could do this myself. The guard in the entry booth was the only two-man pinch point and I could wangle my way past...

Anna bucked me aside with a bony hip and dunked her head under the freezing water and kept it there. My crazy thought went away. I went to the bedroom to wake the Mooney boys. Protruding feet and mops of hair were the only sign of them, so burrowed into the rutted beds were they.

"Time to rise and shine gentlemen." They slept on. "Up and at 'em ladies!"

Still nothing. I positioned myself between the two cots, grabbed the steel frames of each and yanked. Sean and Patrick tumbled to the floor. Sean awoke and jumped to his feet. Patrick laid on his back and snored. He had a rosary clutched in one hand.

"Throw him in the shower. We go in ten."

I went back to the parlor to inventory my equipment, laid everything out on the low lacquered table. The pipes groaned, Patrick howled. I picked up the German-made 35 millimeter single lens reflex Kine Exakta the CO had given me and looked it over. It was a thing of beauty, with a synchronized flash attachment and shutter speed that went all the way up to 1/1000 of a second. How the guys who designed it managed to lose World War II I couldn't tell you.

Anna was down on one knee in the kitchen, searching drawers for a dish towel, her wet hair piled atop her head. She held it in place with a pot holder. An ideal moment to test the camera.

"Say *Käse*," I said and pushed the shutter button. The flash bulb popped as Anna looked up. She cursed me in Russian and pushed me out of the kitchen.

I burned my fingers replacing the flash bulb, gathered up my gun, knife, penlight, pick set and handcuffs and stuffed them into the pockets of my topcoat. I ducked into the bathroom to check on the boys. Patrick stood naked and shivering, trying to dry off with a threadbare towel, his teeth chattering like castanets. Sean was combing his hair in the mirror, cool as a cuke.

"Use the toilet," I said.

I went to the bedroom and changed into a clean shirt from the dresser drawer, tied up a necktie while I was at it. I smelled like a late shift stevedore but I looked like one of Wild Bill Donovan's Ivy Leaguers.

Not quite. The knot was too tight. The Ivy Leaguers let you know they were top drawer by observing the rules with a smirk. Ten dollar Brooks Brother's ties? Of course. Cinched up into a proper Windsor knot? Never.

I loosened my tie and set forth to achieve what I had been charged by General William J. Donovan to do. Rescue Ambrose. Keep the Committee to Free Berlin from attacking the Soviet Armory. And stop the Red Army from rolling across the Elbe.

Okay, I could do that. But not with a full bladder. The Mooney boys were still using the bathroom. Anna was bent over in the parlor, wringing water from her hair. I went to the kitchen and relieved myself in the sink.

There. I was now ready to make Western Europe safe for democracy.

We clomped down the stairs at 0250 hours. All the stuff in my coat pockets made me clank like the Tin Man. We reached the street. The night was clear and cold, no moon. Just right. We hurried down the block toward the delivery truck I couldn't yet see.

I was new to command, unused to dealing with the big picture. Which in this case meant posting a sentry to guard the proud steed that would carry us to victory. Scavengers were everywhere, that the truck still had a battery and four tires was a minor miracle. Did we still have the truck? I could've sworn that I....ah, there it was, parked behind a flowering tree, tires still in place. I noticed a problem as we got closer however. The windshield was fogged.

I flagged out my arms and halted the procession. "Heads up. We have company."

I surveyed the truck. No busted windows. Whoever was inside knew how to pick a lock.

So what? Not a post-war Berliner didn't know how to pick a lock, filch a car battery or make supper from rainwater and tree bark. There were refugees inside the truck. Displaced persons escaping the cold. That's what they were. That the delivery truck was known to the NKVD by now was beside the point. They were smart, the NKVD. Too smart to hide in a truck and fog the windows. If they wanted to ambush us they...

"We going to do something here Chief?" said Sean.

"Yes we are. I'll jump in. If gunfire erupts, run like hell."

Sean looked worried.

"Probably just some vagabonds."

"You sure?" said Sean.

"Let me do it," said Patrick.

"Nah," I said, "this is my job."

I stepped forward and keyed open the driver's side door before they could argue. "*Wachen Sie auf. Zeit, zu gehen.*" Wake up. Time to go.

No answer.

"*Ich weiß, dass Sie dort hinter sind.*" I know you're back there.

No response, nothing stirring. I stepped into the cab with my gun and penlight, aimed both at the back of the truck and said, "What the fuck?"

A skeletal old man in a ragged coat sat in the far corner, arms hanging limp, eyes glassy. Dead as a mackerel. I clambered back to make sure. His skin was still warm.

Shit. Was this an omen? Or just another night in Berlin? I closed the old man's eyes and searched his pockets, found a well-used ice pick suitable for lock picking. No wallet, just half a pack of Chesterfields, the sum total of his wealth.

Take a breath Schroeder. Don't hyperventilate yourself into a brain spasm. The old man just wanted a sheltered space to breathe his last. It doesn't mean anything. It's not a curse, a warning or an omen.

When Sean said "What's up?" I almost shot him. He was standing in the cab, one foot up on the transmission hump, a ghostly silhouette.

"We've got a situation." I shined my penlight on the corpse.

"Jesus, Mary and Joseph." Sean crossed himself. "You know this man?"

"No."

"What do we do about him?"

"We roll him in a blanket and set him on the sidewalk."

"Patrick is terrible superstitious. It would be better if he doesn't see this."

I squeezed a sigh, groan and curse into one long breath. "All right, I'll duck out and stall him. You haul our friend out the back. There's a blanket back there somewhere."

I crawled back to the cab just as Patrick was climbing in. "False alarm, nobody there." I nudged him back out to the pavement. "Sean's just tidying up back there. You know how he is."

"Sure. Just like Mum." The truck's ribbed gate rattled open. "I'll give him a hand." I snagged Patrick's wrist. "He can handle it. We need to talk."

Patrick, who didn't care to be separated from his older brother for longer than ten seconds, stood down for a moment. "What about?"

What about? Good question. I lowered my voice. "I think you know."

Patrick thunk himself cross-eyed. "I do?"

Anna was standing on the sidewalk, watching Sean deposit a rolled-up corpse at the curb with one eye and looking a question to me with the other. I stifled a yawn. Not to worry.

"You're the key to this operation, Patrick. When Sean and I go upstairs to spring Ambrose you, Patrick Mooney, are the last line of defense. It's a big job. Can you handle it?"

Patrick grinned, jauntily. "Damn straight."

I squeezed his arm. "Good. I knew I could count on you. The Mooney brothers are stand up guys. Each and every one of you."

What the hell was Sean doing, saying a Requiem Mass? I was running out of bullshit.

"Have you got your .38?"

"Yes sir," said Patrick, craning his neck, itching to go see what his brother was up to.

"You know your duties and responsibilities?"

"Yes sir."

I was about to ask if he had donned clean socks and underwear when I heard the blessed rattle of the truck gate closing. "Okay, time to go."

I pulled Patrick into the cab. He jumped into the back to join his brother. I leaned over and opened the door for Anna. She climbed in and sat erect in the passenger's seat, her hands folded primly in her lap.

I lit the truck, let the pistons and motor oil get reacquainted and said, as I geared into reverse, "We're off. Off to show Joe Stalin and the Communist Party what a group of can-do Yanks can do!"

The Mooney's war whoops covered the sound I felt through the soles of my feet. A sickening crunch, a snap. I pictured clearly what I had backed over. The old man's ankles dangling from the curb. Had I severed his feet from his legs? Or were they still connected by mangled tendons and shattered bones? If so they wouldn't be for long. I had to pull forward to get this adventure underway.

"What was that?" said Patrick as I pulled away from the curb with another crunching thud. No one had the heart to tell him.

My old man was a melancholy German, the polar opposite of his jolly brother Jorg. But he could surprise you. He gave me a book for my fourteenth birthday. "The Power of Positive Thinking" by Norman Vincent Peale. It was hokey but I read it cover to cover. And was glad I did.

"That was just a bump in the road Patrick. Look to the future, think happy thoughts. That's my philosophy boys and girls. Accentuate the positive, e-liminate the negative, and don't mess with Mister In-between!"

Chapter Fifty

We had smooth sailing as we drove north on *Bundesallee*. The streets were empty at the late hour, electric power stations shut down for the night. The only sign of life the occasional candle flickering in a dirty window, three floors up. I kept thinking about the old man with the crushed ankles despite myself. A happy portent for the night ahead.

We drove in silence, Anna next to me in the passenger's seat, the boys standing in the back, hanging onto angle-iron brackets where the delivery truck's shelf racks used to be.

I turned east on a side street, no sense parading down the Ku-damm. Shadowy figures who were stripping a panel truck melted into the darkness as we rumbled by. I rolled down my window to make sure I was hearing what I heard. The far off *hoo hah, hoo hah* of a siren. An ambulance or a fire truck, no cause for alarm.

I said so aloud and plowed east toward the Soviet Sector, dodging rubble and bucking through bomb craters, looking for a way back to the Ku-damm, not wanting to blow a tire on this ill-advised detour. I am, it must be acknowledged, one hellaciously bad commanding officer. I hadn't determined if we had a functional spare.

I found my way north to *der Kurfürstendamm* and stopped. Something was up. Two sirens were sounding now, in counter-point, one near, one far. I looked out the windshield for signs of a fiery glow on the horizon. Sean and Patrick were clustered behind me now. Anna leaned forward. The Berlin sky was black.

I drove east on the Ku-damm, nervous as a tick. Not good. A strong leader radiates confidence at all times. Say something, Schroeder. Lighten the mood.

"Good news, gentlemen, Anna and I made a baby. And not the way you're thinking. Show the boys our bundle of joy dearheart."

Anna put her hand to her mouth. "Oh!"

"You don't have him? You forgot Hal Jr.?"

Anna tittered at my wide-eyed panic. She hooked her thumb. "Hal is in back." She put her cheek to her palm. "Sleeping."

Oh, *ha*. A hook and ladder truck, siren blaring, sped past. I relaxed my death grip on the steering wheel.

"Okay, listen up."

I checked the side view mirror, caught a pair of headlights a block or two back. Now what?

"We're listening Chief," said Sean.

"Hard," said Patrick.

I curbed the truck and turned to face them and waited for the wash of headlights and the whoosh of tires. The trailing car passed without slowing.

"Okay, once we have the booth guard in hand Patrick hides himself in a setback to the right of the booth, by the staircase door."

"What am I looking for?"

"Ignore any routine comings and goings, which should be few at this hour. But if a buncha Russian soldiers come running, give us a shout."

"And what's my assignment?" said Sean.

"Keep your mouth shut and follow me around. Any questions?"

None. I shoved the truck in gear and headed east. The Ku-damm took us south of the Zoo Garten then swung southeast to Potsdammer Platz, where we crossed the Soviet checkpoint without incident. Nobody home. I noticed something different in the Soviet Sector. Streetlights. The Reds had round-the-clock juice.

I turned northeast and down a hill, toward the narrow Muhlendamm Bridge over the Spree. The truck's fuel gauge dropped from half a tank to almost empty somewhere along in there. Great.

We crossed the bridge, drove north for a dozen blocks and turned left on a two-lane boulevard that had been recently renamed. I knew that because the street sign read *Karl Marx Allee*. We were north of the Armory now.

I drove west till I found *Blummenstraße* and nudged the truck southward down the side street with the grassy median overgrown with shrubs. The Soviet Armory was on the other side of the block. I chugged fifty yards past the entry gate, parked the truck and killed the engine.

"Patrick, front and center."

He stuck his head in the cab.

"Go hide behind that clump of bushes back there, on the median. Watch the sentry booth. If the guard's sleeping it off report back immediately. If he's awake observe him for one minute to determine how alert he is. Watch for any signs of activity in the quadrangle. Repeat what I just told you."

Patrick did so. "Good. Now go."

I opened the door and stood on the running board. Patrick climbed past me and scampered to his observation point with shoulders hunched and head swiveling, just as I had done a thousand times behind enemy lines.

I got back in and ran details with Sean. He was to snap the pictures of whatever machine gun emplacements had been put in place to welcome the Committee to Free Berlin. He wasn't to fire his weapon unless I was dead. I showed him how to work the camera.

A breathless Patrick appeared at my elbow. "There's no one there."

"At the booth?"

"Yes. Nobody!"

"Probably in the can. Resume your post and report back in five."

"Yes sir."

He took orders well, the tall redhead, tripping back to his clump of shrubs like a kid at scout camp. Would his brother do likewise? Patrick was dumb and reckless, which was fine. Big brother Ambrose was smart and reckless. Even better. But middle brother Sean, he was thoughtful. Not what you look for in a soldier.

Patrick appeared at my elbow in five minutes time. "The booth's empty, the quadrangle's empty. Not a bleedin' soul."

This wasn't good news. The guard was more asset than liability. I wanted his key ring, I wanted him as a hostage going in.

"Return to your post. Give it another three, give me a wave if he shows."

"Yes sir."

"What's it mean Chief?" said Sean, crouched behind my shoulder.

"Damned if I know."

"You smell a trap?"

"I don't see how."

"Then shouldn't we, you know, go now?"

"I'll do the thinking Sean."

Smart people are such a pain in the ass. He was right of course. I could jimmy the door while the boys kept watch, get the drop on the jailer and use his cell door key. It was better than sitting here waiting for Russian MPs to jeep by and give us a cold once over.

Dammit all to hell, why does it never, under any circumstances, work out as planned!? I watched Patrick watching the sentry booth as two minutes ticked into three. The booth guard didn't show.

"Anna," I said, wagging the steering wheel to and fro, "can you drive a truck?"

"I can drive tractor."

"Close enough. What time do you have?" I pointed to her wristwatch. She showed me. 0355. I pointed to the six on her watch face.

"If we have not returned by this time, four-thirty, drive to Dahlem and tell Victor Jacobson what has happened. Do you understand?"

"Four-thirty, Dahlem" said Anna coolly, just the slightest flicker of fear in her eyes. "Victor Jacobson."

"That's right, that's good."

Patrick appeared at my elbow again, his face sheathed in sweat. "No one, nobody."

"Anna, lock the doors and hide in back. And crack open your window so the windshield doesn't fog."

I demonstrated on the driver's side window. She did the same on her side, and mustered a smile both brave and sad. It was a moment I would remember. Anna didn't know what the hell was going on, yet she was game for what came and hang the consequence. I leaned over and kissed her on the lips. Hard.

My kiss was welcomed. But when I puckered up to say something she put her fine fingers to my lips. She knew the rules better than I did. Tender sentiment before combat is bad luck.

I jacked open the truck door and stepped out. "Guns in your pockets gentlemen. Walk don't run."

We stopped at the clump of bushes and took a look. No sign of life. I fished out my pick set. "Make yourselves small, wait for my signal. If you spot someone coming toss a rock at me."

I crossed the street and checked the glass booth. A half drunk mug of tea sat on a small desk next to a spread-eagled newspaper. I surveyed the quadrangle. No one in the courtyard but all the upstairs windows were lit. The ones on the north side, the barracks windows. What the hell? Not even Marines rolled out at 0400.

I moved to the setback and attacked the door to the staircase and the detention cells upstairs. It had a key knob lockset that surrendered without a fight. Also a rim lock, a deadbolt separate from the doorknob. The rim lock was not engaged. The door opened.

I waved the Mooney brothers over. Patrick crossed in a hurry, Sean paused to dust himself off. I showed Patrick his spot in front of the set back door.

"On your mush, bo." Patrick got down on his belly to peer around the corner at the courtyard. "Sean, follow me."

He did so, dragging a raggedy trail of unasked questions up the dark concrete staircase. Why was the guard booth empty? Why are the barrack's windows lit? Why wasn't the door bolted shut? I had no answers for him.

I stopped two steps shy of the second floor corridor. It was dimly lit. I leaned forward, put my left cheek to the gritty floor, saw no one. The jailer's station stood at the far end of the hall – a high desk with a crook neck reading lamp, still lit. I turned my head the other direction. We were alone and unsupervised. Things were going far too well.

I got my Walther in hand and stood up. Sean and I scuttled right, down the corridor, past the machine gun emplacements in the south-facing windows, mounts and sand bags in place, guns absent. Sean stopped to snap pictures.

I checked the detention cells on the north side of the corridor. They wouldn't keep Ambrose in a cell that faced the street. The first two were empty. The third held a sleeping heavyset man who stank of vomit.

I approached the fourth and last cell on the balls of my feet, barely breathing, sick to death. I had scarcely given Ambrose a passing thought in the mad run-up to this moment. No time, didn't want to. There would be time enough for guilt. A lifetime of guilt and mortification of the flesh if Ambrose wasn't alive and kicking in the next cell.

He wasn't.

Or was he? I shone my penlight again. It must be a talent peculiar to the Mooney brothers, the ability to burrow into a cot and disappear. I saw only the back of a coppery head of hair.

"Ambrose," I hissed, my pulse thudding against my temples. "Ambrose!"

He didn't stir. I dug out my pick set and set to work on the cell door, which was something like trying to pry open a drawbridge with a toothpick. My folding knife didn't work any better. Damn lock was medieval.

"This might help," said Sean.

He was standing behind me, the smartass, holding the ring of keys I should have looked for at the jailer's station.

"Good thinking." I took the ring of keys and got lucky on the third try.

I pushed in, eager to rouse Ambrose and get him down the stairs. But Sean put a finger to his lips and crept closer to his brother, who was snugged down into the mattress like a hot dog in a bun. Sean sat a haunch on the cot's thin railing and smiled down at the sleeping figure.

"Get your lazy arse down to the sacristy!" he said in a lilting high-pitched voice. "Father Macahey can't celebrate Mass all by himself, now can he?"

No response. Sean shook his shoulder. "Ambey? You okay?"

Ambrose didn't move. Sean turned to me, his face ashen. I played along, looked stricken. When Sean turned back his brother was sitting up. He was pale and hollow-cheeked but his eyes were bright.

"You say something, mama's boy?"

Sean buried his head in his brother's chest. Ambrose ruffled his hair. I spoiled the moment. "Time to go gentlemen."

Ambrose shuffled his feet into a pair of cardboard slippers. He was wearing filthy drawstring pants and a baggy gray workshirt that smelled like old cheese. Sean doffed his coat and draped it over his brother's shoulders. I rumpled the blanket and wadded up the pillow to make it look like the bed was still occupied.

I locked the cell. We made our way down the corridor, Ambrose limping along gamely, leaning on his brother. The bastards had worked him over good. Sean had to pick Ambrose up and carry him down the dark concrete stairs. I replaced the ring of keys at the jailer's station.

We found Patrick right where we left him, on his belly, keeping lookout.

"What's the report?"

Patrick did not look up. "No activity in the quadrangle, no traffic in or out."

"Any sign of movement in the barracks?"

"No sir."

"Well done. Now stand up and hug your brother."

My eyes swept the quadrangle as the Mooney brothers threw their arms around one another. Patrick was correct, there were no silhouettes in the barrack windows, no figures moving about. So where were they, the Red Army troops rousted out before the crack of dawn?

We had done everything we had come to do, in twenty minutes time. I should take yes for an answer maybe and get the hell out. But my neck itched.

"Go to the truck. Wait five minutes. If I don't show drive to Dahlem and get Victor Jacobson out of bed."

"And tell him what?" said Ambrose, all business in a blink.

Should I say this? I had nothing to go on, less than nothing. Which was precisely the point. We didn't have zero guards in an armory that was expecting an armed assault. We had a negative number. Minus two.

"Tell Victor Jacobson that Hal Schroeder thinks Operation LUNA is underway."

Ambrose nodded his understanding and extended his hand. I kept mine in my gun pocket. "We'll do that later. Beat it."

The Mooney Brothers ran across the street. I crouched down in the setback, doing what I do best.

The absence of the booth guard and the jailer might simply mean they knew the assault wasn't coming tonight. I'd estimated it would take 72 hours to get the go ahead from Moscow. We were only at hour 36. So why were the barracks lit up? With no one moving around?

My gaze drifted downward. The first floor of the north wing had doors but no windows. A muster room where the troops assembled to receive orders. That's where they figured to be.

I waited three long minutes and saw nothing. Time to go. I checked the street before I crossed, saw fast-approaching high beams two blocks south. I got down on all fours and rolled myself across the street, hid behind the clump of bushes on the median.

The high beams belonged to a big car, a limousine, a brand new Soviet Zil right off the assembly line. It pulled into the Armory's entryway and sounded its horn. A man in a black leather coat climbed out of the back seat and stalked angrily to the guard booth. He reached in and pushed something. The gate opened and the Zil entered the quadrangle.

I recognized the man in the leather coat. It was Gerhard, the blond-haired apple-cheeked founding member of the Committee to Free Berlin. The tumblers clicked.

The White Russian freedom fighters had seen their ranks decimated during their collaboration with us bumbling Yanks. My visit to the Committee had spooked them, prompting an emergency meeting where, rather than voting to cancel or postpone their attack on the Armory, they voted to advance the date. Advance it more than Gerhard and his Soviet bosses had in mind. Gerhard would have argued strenuously, saying it was premature. He would have been shouted down. Democracy is messy that way.

Gerhard would have phoned the Armory Commander and instructed him to call an assembly of all personnel for an urgent briefing with a big announcement.

The Committee to Free Berlin is on the march!

It didn't make sense for the booth guard and the jailer to abandon their posts to join the briefing. but it didn't have to. Not in the military.

I briefly considered sneaking back upstairs to lay in wait for the machine gunners. But that was plain suicide and I wasn't in the mood.

My Teutonic clock struck midnight. Five minutes had elapsed. I had missed my own deadline.

I ran for all I was worth, down the block, waving my arm frantically as the delivery truck pulled away from the curb and rumbled south down *Blummenstraße*. The truck found a higher gear and I slowed to a walk, lungs burning. I had no one to blame but myself. Anna and Ambrose had followed my instructions to the letter.

The delivery truck swung a clumsy left turn at a cross street two blocks away, stopped in the intersection, backed up, turned left, stopped, backed up, turned some more. They were coming back for me!

I crossed the grassy median to intercept them. Ambrose was at the wheel. Guess his brothers didn't know how to drive. Or big brother wouldn't let them.

Big brother skidded to a stop when he saw me standing in the street. I jumped into the cab and flopped in the passenger's seat.

"You disobeyed a direct order."

"Yeah," said Ambrose, "I'm like that."

I stuck my head out the window. No headlights behind. Ahead was an Armory on full alert. "How are you at backing up?"

"Watch me."

I tried not to. The parked cars along the curb bore the brunt as Ambrose gouged his way rearward in a trail of sparks and snapped off sideview mirrors. But he got it done, swinging the truck's rear end into the cross street and lurching south down *Blummenstraße*, grinding the clutch like a butcher making ham salad.

I ran it down. "Some of our White Russian friends, members of the Committee to Free Berlin, plan to attack the Soviet Armory sometime before dawn. Which gives us about thirty minutes to intercept them and prevent a massacre that might start a new world war."

I paused to let that sink in. And catch my breath.

"I figure the Russian limousine that just pulled into the Armory came north across the Spree, ahead of the freedom fighters. That's our pinch point."

"What is?" said Ambrose, gamely, weakly.

I squinted at him. "You okay to drive?"

He grinned. "Never better."

"The Muhlendamm Bridge, just south of here. It's narrow. We park sideways near the northbound exit and roll out to block the lane if we see a truck coming. Anyone got a better idea I'm all ears."

Anyone didn't. Ambrose asked a rude question.

"How do we convince them to turn around?"

"I don't know."

"Ah, you'll think of something."

I had better. They would be coming hard, the members of the Committee, the smell of blood in their nostrils. They would need some convincing. More than that. What they would need was an immediate reason not to cut us to ribbons.

I thought about it. Well, they weren't likely to open fire on a woman. I could put Anna out front and let her try to calm the wild-eyed freedom fighters. She spoke Russian. She stood a better chance of success than the rest of us.

Like I say it's a despicable profession.

"Remind you of anything?" said Ambrose.

"What's that?"

"Driving to a big showdown at a narrow bridge, a good lookin' Mick at the wheel."

"I might remember something about it."

"Seems a long time ago, don't it?"

"Yes it do."

I guided Ambrose to the bridge, keeping my eyes peeled front and back. We hadn't approached the Armory by this route but I'm a Kraut, I have a good sense of direction and a keen sense of time. The direction we needed to go was south-southwest and the time we had to get there was somewhere between now and never. The Armory jailer would discover the empty cell any time now. Gerhard and heavily-armed NKVD would come hunting. We had to find the members of the Committee before Gerhard found us.

"This heap's on empty, Boss."

"Then speed up before we run out."

"Sure ting."

I found the bridge right where I left it. A two lane road with scant cover ran alongside the river's northern bank. Nowhere to hide.

Gerhard and his thugs would make a beeline for this spot. There were other bridges across the Spree, I could instruct Ambrose to drive down the road to the next one. He had been starved and tortured on my watch, he didn't deserve to die thirty minutes after gaining his freedom.

Tough shit.

"Park in that warehouse driveway, to the left, north of the road," I said. "Back it in, shut it down. We'll kill the lights and try to look like we belong there."

Ambrose backed the truck in without hitting anything. The spot provided a head on view of the bridge and the feeder road that sloped down from the south.

Anna climbed forward and perched on the transmission hump as if she knew what I was about to ask. "Are you willing to speak to them?"

"The Byelorussians which are coming?"

"Yes."

Anna shrugged her bony shoulders. *Who else can do it?*

"I want you to tell them that we work for General William Donovan. Wild Bill Donovan."

I tried to remember if Donovan and the OSS had collaborated with the White Russians toward war's end. Wasn't sure, didn't matter. Anti-Communist freedom fighters who spied for us now got their eyes gouged out and their bodies bound to fence posts with barb wire.

Our photos of the Armory machine gun emplacements were supposed to make our case, convince the freedom fighters to stand down. But our photos were still in the camera.

"Never mind, Anna. There is nothing we can *sprechen* that they will *glauben*."

Anna nodded. "What then?"

A thought occurred. I squeezed her hand.

"Sean! Patrick!" They scrambled forward. "Go to that corner and look north. If you see a big car with vertical high beams coming south give me the high sign. We want to ram them broadside, time your signal according to their speed of approach. Got it?"

They nodded.

"Go!"

Sean and Patrick piled out and took their positions, peering around a building at the northeast corner of the intersection, Sean standing, Patrick below him, on his belly. I told Anna to take cover in the back of the truck. "Wedge yourself behind the wheel well."

She didn't understand. I jumped up to show her where to brace herself then returned to the cab. Ambrose, at the wheel, wanted to know the plan.

"The White Russians will want hard evidence. One of their members is...oh screw, I'll explain later."

I hoped to present the Committee members with a crumpled Soviet Zil containing their founding member Gerhard and assorted Blue Caps. That was the plan anyway.

A large truck crested the feeder road and sped north, downhill toward the bridge. It looked like a rubble hauler. A quick pass under a flickering streetlamp confirmed that.

So what? They could squeeze two dozen troops into one of those long dump trucks. And what better way to cross Berlin without attracting attention?

Didn't scan. The Soviets had coddled their duped recruits to this point, held meetings in the swank *Admiralspalast*. They wouldn't send the members of the Committee to Free Berlin off to battle in a dump truck.

We watched the truck gear down and approach the bridge at a stately pace. The back end rattled like cup on saucer as it crossed the span paved with iron planks against the bomb damage. The rubble hauler was empty.

I looked to the corner. Sean had wandered off but Patrick was doing jumping jacks trying to catch my eye. Apparently the Zil was southbound, and our timing was shot to hell.

The rubble hauler proceeded slowly across the intersection, blocking our view. When the intersection cleared I saw only the brassy red tail lights of the Zil blurring across the bridge in the opposite direction.

Shit.

I clutched at straws. Gerhard wouldn't interfere with the Committee members if they passed in the night, now that the Armory was poised and ready for their attack. We might still intercept and blockade the freedom fighters. They would probably mow us down and go on about their business but we might get lucky and convince them to stop and reconsider, to turn tail and retreat. It was possible. Also the moon might fall out of the sky and smash the bridge to smithereens.

I called out the window to Patrick. "Where's your brother?"

"Other side of the street."

"Get his ass over here!"

Sean strode up a few moments later, in no particular hurry.

"Where'd you go?"

"I saw the dump truck rolling down the hill, then I saw the big car coming the other direction, fast. You said to time our signal according to their speed of approach but we had an intervening vehicle. So I did a Patrick after a pub crawl."

"A what?"

"I staggered across the street, singin' songs. The limo slowed down some when they saw me. I waved at them, friendly like, stood in their way."

"And?"

"They drove by me and crossed the bridge."

"How many in the car?"

"Couldn't tell, headlamps blinded me."

"Okay, nice try. Return to your post and fetch Patrick."

This was my small favor to Mrs. Mooney, posting Sean at the corner where he would look north for further pursuit vehicles that wouldn't come. Patrick would throw himself into the fray no matter what. But if we intercepted the troop truck and things got ugly Sean could flee on foot. He was too smart to sacrifice himself in a hopeless cause.

Good for him. Someone needed to live to tell the tale.

I looked up the hill to see high beams bearing down at a furious pace. Vertically stacked high beams.

"Crank it Ambrose."

The engine turned over nicely. Patrick reported to my window.

"You're wantin' to see me?"

I reached out and hauled him in through the window by the back of his belt. Could be that Gerhard had got to thinking about that drunk stumbling across the street with no open *Bierstubes* nearby and had decided to bang a U and take another look.

I told Ambrose to put the truck in gear but he had already done so. Patrick sat himself on the transmission hump and braced his arms against the dash. The Zil slowed some as it approached the bridge, slowed some more as it rattled over the iron planks. The limo came to a stop. Best I could tell they hadn't spied us. But they saw Sean.

I had misjudged the thoughtful middle brother. Sean took off running, sure, but only to lure the limousine into pursuit, into making the slight left turn necessary to continue north, which exposed their flank to our front bumper. I'm pretty sure I told Ambrose to ram those Commie bastards at that point but could be he floored it before I got the words out.

I do know we smacked the right rear of the Zil very hard, causing it to spin around and slam up against us, head to tail.

I looked down at the back end of the limo. It sat flush on the pavement, the rear axle snapped in two. Two dark clad men in the back seat were shaking off the cobwebs. I couldn't see the driver.

Ambrose backed up the truck and swung around while the men in the back seat tumbled out the far side door. We rammed the limo amidships just before the dark clad men sprang to their feet and opened fire with what looked like MP-43 automatic assault rifles. God help us.

I bit my shoes as the windshield dissolved. Patrick dived in back. Ambrose ducked below the dash while keeping the steering wheel to the left and the gas pedal down, bulldozing the Zil west toward the river.

The gunners must have fanned out, the better to rake the delivery truck with eight millimeter rounds that didn't penetrate the truck's double-walled hull, God love this old bucket o' bolts. But in the absence of return fire the gunners would jump up on the running boards and fill the cab with molten lead. They would do this very soon.

I got my Walther in hand and popped my head up to peek a look.

A burst from the gunner to my right was high. Best he did was part my hair, shatter the window frame and spray my cheek with hot metal shavings. I slumped back and played dead.

Every shooter takes a moment after he fires, whether it's a single shot from a hunting rifle or a burst from a machine gun, to see what he's done. This guy was no different. I took his moment of appraisal to empty my Walther eight shot in his direction.

I'm pretty sure I greased him on round three but I had another clip in my pocket so I kept at it to make sure. He was reeling backward by round five, shooting skyward as if celebrating New Years. And he was splayed out on the pavement by round eight, staring up at nothing.

The gunner to the left was wasting ammo on the hood of the truck, trying to kill the engine that was bulldozing the black limo sideways. The Zil yawed over on its side as the truck plowed forward.

That's when we ran out of gas.

The gunner got a wide grin and stepped forward to finish us off, hesitated when Gerhard jack-in-the-boxed out of the limo's side window with a bloody face and a dazed expression. And me with an empty gun. Gerhard shouted something at the gunner.

"Patrick!"

"Right here Chief."

"Target your weapon, ten o'clock!"

He didn't know the lingo maybe. I elaborated as I searched my pockets for the spare clip. "Shoot the asshole with the machine gun."

Patrick tried. He sent a hail of bullets out the blown up windshield, over the crouched down body of his eldest brother. Sean, back at his post on the corner, joined in.

They were terrible shots. So bad they were good. The machine gunner cranked his head around furiously, searching for the source of all the ricochets. I found my spare clip and jacked it in.

That's about the time it all opened up, like a widescreen shot in a Hollywood epic. Gerhard struggling to squirm out of his tipped over limo, the machine gunner taking cover behind the Zil, and the big tarp-covered troop truck cresting the rise and bearing down on the bridge with its headlamps blaring.

The troop truck slowed at the improbable sight before it, slowed down and crept forward across the bridge in fits and starts, like a great hulking beast sniffing the ground for prey.

I squinted my eyeballs for all they were worth, glimmed two men in the cab. They held a brief animated conversation and stopped the truck. On the bridge, about fifty yards distant. They killed the headlights.

I told Patrick to reload, give his .38 to Ambrose and take cover in the back of the truck. He obeyed without protest. Ambrose sat up behind the wheel. I wiped blood from my face with my coat sleeve and tried to think it through. The back of my head hurt.

The two men in the truck cab figured to be NKVD. The remaining members of the Committee to Free Berlin, the White Russian cannon fodder, would be in back. The men in the cab would know who was in that overturned Zil, wouldn't want the troops to see their founding member squirming out of a Soviet limo. That's why they killed the headlights. They would have to wait for Gerhard to squeeze his frame through the jagged window and make his escape. It was my job to make sure that didn't happen.

"Cover the machine gunner," I said to Ambrose and took aim at Gerhard with scorched eyeballs and a wobbly arm. He was a stationary target not ten feet away and I missed him. Four times. Gerhard wrangled himself out of the busted window and ran off to my right, almost stumbling over the dead gunner on the pavement. I missed him some more.

The machine gunner to our left popped up from behind the Zil. Ambrose squeezed off two before the gunner shredded the roof of the cab with a wild burst. Ambrose and I ducked down amid a shower of rust.

When we resurfaced the machine gunner was sprinting east along the river, in the opposite direction. I grabbed Ambrose's wrist. "Save your ammo."

Someone rang up the tarpaulin of the troop truck, revealing a full company clad in battle fatigues.

I took a closer look. I couldn't see much in the pre-dawn dim washed by a sputtering street lamp but it looked like the poor dumb White Russian freedom fighters had been issued American M-1 carbines. There was no mistaking those big-notched muzzles. Christ. *Izvestia* would have a field day.

The NKVD man in the passenger's seat of the troop truck jumped out. He shouted orders. The troops deployed behind him, M-1s at present arms. The driver turned on the high beams. The war party started towards us.

"Try the headlights."

"Fat chance," said Ambrose.

But they blinked on, freezing the advancing party for the moment. I wanted to see who I was dealing with.

I didn't recognize the man who gave the orders. He had not been on the stage of *der Admiralspalast*, I would have remembered. He was tall and reedy, had thin hair pasted down in greasy strands, wore little round spectacles with black rims and made my skin crawl at fifty paces.

Three pistol shots rang out. At a distance, to my right. From the direction that Gerhard had fled. Where the hell was Sean?

Spectacles barked another order. The troops fanned out in a semi-circle behind him and brought their American-made carbines to bear. Gerhard was long gone, their way to the Armory was cleared, save for an unknown number of individuals in a bullet-riddled delivery truck. Time to speak up. I stuck my head out the passenger's window.

"Gentlemen such rude behavior! I am your American friend Hal Schroeder, from Stars and Stripes!"

Spectacles understood every word but he wasn't the one I was trying to reach. I raised my voice. That always helps when people don't speak your language.

"We met at *der Admiralspalast!*"

Spectacles led his war party closer. Big-notched muzzles zeroed in on my forehead but didn't fire. Spectacles was unsure about something. Could be he knew we'd been passing ourselves off as gunrunners. Could be we were sitting on crates of American-made pineapples. Concentrated M1 fire risked an explosion that would crater the bridge.

Anna appeared at my side. "I will talk for you now."

I ducked back inside the cab. "Please. Tell the troops that their mission has been sabotaged by the NKVD."

Anna squinted. She didn't understand. I pointed to the overturned Zil. "Tell them that Gerhard Dunkel was in that car. Gerhard Dunkel."

Spectacles and his war party were twenty paces away now. Anna poked her head out the blown up windshield. If Spectacles recognized her as Leonid's wife he gave no sign. Anna gave out with a torrent of Russian that went on for a longer time than a literal translation of my remarks would require. I didn't mind. She seemed to be putting her point across.

But the troops didn't lower their weapons.

Spectacles stepped forward, ahead of his troops. He leaned an arm on the side of the tipped over limo, glared fiercely and spat something vile in Russian.

Anna laughed at this remark, and got louder. She said the name of her husband, Leonid Vitinov! She said it more than once. This made me nervous. We were supposed to be friendlies. Then Anna called the reedy man by name. Fyodor.

Ah ha, that would do it. Fyodor. Why would the wife of a Blue Cap know the head freedom fighter? This would make it clear to the troops that their anti-Communist operation was being run by a stinking son of Stalin.

But the troops did not waver. Fyodor had trained them well. Or I'd gone poozle stoopid.

Anna clambered over Ambrose, jacked open the door and stepped out of the truck before I could grab her.

Sonofabitch!

I had been the beneficiary of entirely too much good fortune in this screwy town. I'd eluded Blue Cap sentries after setting a fire in Anna's apartment, survived a suicide assault on a Soviet armory without a shot fired, and the wife of an NKVD Major had admitted me to her boudoir. Twice.

But it looked like my luck had just run out.

Anna marched around the overturned Zil and continued to hector Fyodor but that no longer mattered. She addressed herself to the troops, and that didn't matter either. Not now. What mattered was her stepping out. War is simple. You're on one side of the barricades or the other.

Could be the CO was right. *The Russians, with their dark history, are best of all.*

Fyodor and Anna jawboned away in Russian on the other side of the limo. Maybe Anna didn't understand what her stepping out of the truck would signify, maybe she was simply doing her damndest to keep us alive. Which didn't explain why Fyodor was playing along, wasting precious time.

It seemed to me that Anna and Fyodor were staging a distraction for our amusement as their troops crept closer for a quick clean kill.

The three far off pistol shots meant that Sean was likely dead. Anna's stepping out of the truck meant that we were about to join him.

But not quietly. We would do our bit to stop the assault on the Armory and prevent World War III.

I told Ambrose to shoot Fyodor in the head.

Ambrose didn't do as instructed. He was looking out my window with a twisty grin. "Well feck me all to hell."

I followed his look. Everyone did. What we saw was most unexpected. Gerhard Dunkel, hobbling toward the bridge, a bloody stain down one leg. Sean Mooney walking behind, prodding the founding member of the Committee to Free Berlin with his .38.

"Oh Jayz," said Ambrose happily, "I won't never hear the end of this."

I eyeballed Fyodor. He wore an expression of acid contempt as he watched Gerhard approach, and who could blame him? No spy worth his salt gets captured alive.

I eyeballed the White Russians as Sean marched Gerhard back to his Soviet Zil. The troops turned to one another in shock and confusion. And lowered their M-1s. The jig, as they say, was up.

I blew out a breath and relaxed for half a second.

Half a second.

That's all it took for Fyodor to slip the grenade from his coat pocket, pull the pin and pitch it through the blown up windshield.

I made a two-handed grab for it in midair. Had it for a split second, then dropped it to the floorboard at my feet. I groped around feverishly.

"By your right foot, in the corner," said Ambrose calmly.

I grabbed it, felt the deep grooves in the cast iron shell. A pineapple. A gift from Leonid no doubt.

They were smart, the NKVD. Smart about subversion, counterintelligence and false flag recruitment. Not so swift about weaponry.

The Red Army grenade they call the *limonka* has a quick fuse. You pull the pin, you toss the lemon.

The US Army pineapple has a considerably longer fuse time. The head Commie in Charge should've watched a few Hollywood war flicks maybe, noticed how the plucky dogface always counts to three after he pulls the pin.

Fyodor had tossed this pineapple way too soon.

I could have chucked it out the passenger's side window, but Sean was in frag range. I could have chucked it out the driver's side window but Ambrose was still sitting upright for some reason and I didn't want to risk having it bounce back off his noggin.

So I heaved the grenade back the way it came, through the blown up windshield. And shouted "Incoming!" as loud as I could

The White Russians scattered and dove for cover. They knew what *incoming* meant. Anna did not.

The pineapple bounced off the side of the Zil and fell to the pavement on the other side.

Anna looked down, at the tumbling grenade. She looked up. At me, over her shoulder as she ran away with short quick steps. I couldn't see well enough to read her expression.

Ambrose and I took cover one last time. The explosion slammed the limo up against our front bumper.

Then everything got real quiet.

"You okay?"

"Never better," coughed Ambrose.

I called to the back of the truck. "Patrick?"

"Present and accounted for!"

I tried to laugh. I combed debris from my hair and looked down at my hand in surprise. It was covered in blood.

I don't remember anything after that.

Epilogue

And that's how I became the Little Deutsch Boy.

I'm back on my barstool at the Harbor Inn, Wally at my side. He's as full of fermented carbonation as ever. Keeps me humble, Wally does. He listens to my stories, nods in the right places and then goes on for twenty minutes about how I think my life is so godblamed difficult I should try hauling four bags of groceries up three flights of stairs on a shriveled leg, slaving over a hot stove for hours, chopping boiled turnips and fried chops into weensy bits because Mama's store-bought choppers don't fit right and keep falling out on her plate!

I laugh, and order another round of Carlings from sweet Rita behind the bar.

I spent two weeks in a U.S. military hospital in Heidelberg where they specialize in head trauma. Seems there was an eight mil machine gun round that I hadn't accounted for. One that carved a quarter inch groove in the back of my skull.

Funny what you don't notice in the heat of battle.

They took good care of me in the hospital, dressed my wound twice a day, drained a lot of pus. Ugh.

I didn't sustain any permanent brain damage. Not so's you'd notice anyway. I was in and out of consciousness the first week, mostly out. The CO stopped by for a brief visit somewhere in there.

He said that Bill Donovan had broken precedent and leaked an edited version of our story to the international press in hopes it would open some eyes to the serious nature of the Soviet threat. This blew what little cover we had left so Global Commerce, Berlin, was shut down. Victor Jacobson didn't seem too busted up about it.

I asked about the Mooney brothers. The CO said they were safe at home in County Cork. Saints be praised.

Jacobson said he had squeezed everything he could from Leonid Vitinov before releasing him to his Soviet case officer. What he'd done was dispose of his major career embarrassment and left it to Laventia Beria to take proper care of the dapper little shit.

I had thought that well done and executed at the time. I'm not so sure now. We ad hoc operatives were a group without adult supervision. We were on the honor system, we had to enforce the rules ourselves. What the rules were with regard to a midlevel officer repatriating a blown Soviet double agent without informing his superiors I couldn't tell you.

Victor Jacobson shook my hand and thanked me for my service before he ankled off. I wasn't expecting a tickertape parade you understand but I was a bit cheesed at the perfunctory pat on the head. Until Becky my day nurse handed me a sealed envelope the CO had left behind. It contained twenty crisp cecils and a stateroom ticket on the R.M.S Queen Mary, Antwerp to London to New York City. I recuperated in a hurry after that.

But on to more important matters.

I lied when I said I couldn't see Anna well enough to read her expression. I saw her face quite clearly. I see it every ten seconds, waking and sleeping.

What I saw -what I still see - are three expressions.

Blank-faced shock as Anna hears me yell *incoming.*

Wide-eyed fear as she looks down at the tumbling grenade.

Furrowed confusion as she turns to flee and looks at me over her shoulder, through the blown up windshield.

That's the part that keeps coming back, that last look, Anna's lips half open as if to ask *why would you do this*?

When I came to in the hospital I asked Nurse Becky a woozy question. Would you happen to know the kill zone of a pineapple?

She humored me, said she didn't know right off the top but would find out. Not two hours later Nurse Becky gave me the grim report.

The effective kill radius of an Mk 2 pineapple is five yards.

Anna was dead, she had to be. The reason I didn't ask Jacobson about her when he came to call is that I didn't want to know it for a fact.

Anna didn't betray us, I understand that now. Her long winded harangue of Fyodor was sincere. She wasn't staging a distraction so the troops could close in for a clean shot. That is she was, but she didn't know it.

Fyodor needed only one brief answer from Anna before giving the order to open fire. *Are there any explosives in the truck?*

I should have doped that out at the time but I was otherwise occupied and assuming the worst and working backward and...*Goddamn it all to fucking hell.*

Anna had survived World War II. She was married to an NKVD agent. She should have known better than to leave the truck!!

I have one keepsake. It came in the envelope Victor Jacobson left for me. He had developed the film in the Kine Exakta, the camera Sean used to photograph gun emplacements in the Armory. I had forgotten about the first pic on the roll. Anna in the kitchen before dawn, holding her wet hair in place with a pot holder as she searched for a towel to dry off.

I had intended a lighthearted snapshot. But Anna's pinched expression was an echo of her over-the-shoulder look as she fled the grenade. *Why would you do this to me?*

I hated the damn thing.

Wally clears his throat and offers me a shelled peanut for my thoughts. I hoist my beer mug and offer a bottoms up toast to the Red Army and World Communism. Wally says I should lower my voice. I do that, and offer my explanation.

The thing that saved us was a little man.

All armed forces have a top down command structure, but the Reds are ridiculous about it. When Gerhard made his frantic phone call to the Armory Commander and ordered him to assemble all personnel for an important briefing he didn't mean it literally He didn't mean the booth guard and the upstairs jailer should abandon their posts.

But the little man - Gerhard's subordinate - took him at his word. Which is what you do to survive in a system that permits no individual initiative. His blind obedience allowed us to get in and out of the Armory undetected, foil the plot and tell the tale.

You see? A little man changed the course of history!

Wally says his shoulder hurts from holding the mug up and could we please drain our beers now.

We do. I'm out of practice. Wally beats me by a good two seconds.

And that's the full report.

Yes, Mrs. Brennan kept my room vacant at her boarding house and, no, I didn't forget my promise. I sent a one pound sampler of Godiva chocolates to the unwitting neighbor who buzzed me in to Anna's building. Frau G. Unkel, Apt. H, 1832 *Spirchenstraße*, Berlin, Germany.

I had to call Godiva's New York office to place the order, then wire them the money. I included a message to be sent with the package.

Hier sind Ihre versprochenen Schokoladen, gnädige Frau. Ich bedauere die Verspätung.

Here are your promised chocolates, dear lady. Sorry for the delay.

Could be I am brain damaged but that note put a smile on my mug all day.

Book One is available online and at bookstores.
Visit our website at bluesteelpress.com